Across the Faebridge

Across the Faebridge

by

Shiloh Darke

Gypsy Shadow Publishing

Across the Faebridge

by

Shiloh Darke

Gypsy Shadow Publishing, LLC.
Lockhart, TX
www.gypsyshadow.com

Library of Congress Control Number: 2021940702

eBook ISBN: 978-1-61950-643-5
Print ISBN: 978-1-61950-645-9

Published in the United States of America

First eBook Edition: March 22, 2021
First Print Edition: June 14, 2021

Dedication

To every mother who has lost a child. For every moment you wish there were some fairytale story which could simply come carry you away from the pain. For the strength you find to pull yourself out of the hurt and keep surviving day to day.

To every girlfriend or wife who has lost the one she believed she would spend the rest of her life with, be it from illness, or accident. The pain can be all consuming. It can leave you feeling as if life isn't even worth living anymore.

Reality is a harsh pill. But we all know we would never trade the beautiful moments just not to have the sorrow.

***

My prayers.
My love.
My respect.

***

This story is for you.

Prologue

Long before our story takes place. About one hundred and fifty years earlier...

The Mage cradled the baby in her arms. Casting a worried glance over her shoulder, she waited impatiently on the Bakru. The little menace had promised to be at the bridge hours ago. She was tired of waiting. If she were discovered, kidnapping a Fae child, and smuggling it across the bridge to the mortal realm, she would be put to death. Fae children rarely survived in the mortal realm.

She looked down at the baby girl, gazing up at her with a silent intelligence. After a moment, the Mage whispered softly, "I'm sorry. I don't want to do this. But at my Master's behest, I have no choice. To fail means many others will die. Not just from our Clans, but from all of the Clans. I must do this. Forgive me."

She smiled sadly at the baby in her arms. "I've made arrangements for you. The family who is taking you will raise you as their own and you shall thrive there. I don't wish you harm, little one. But my Master's plans have the sacrifice of seeing to it the young Prince never finds his Soulmate. He must not bond with her, otherwise his rule will be solid."

She had no idea what made her speak so honestly to the child, other than the knowledge the babe was too young to make heads or tails of what was being said anyway, and it calmed her nerves. "It isn't even you who will be the Princes' Soulmate. But the fates have foreseen his mate is descended from your bloodline."

She sighed, shaking her head. "We are pretending he ordered me to kill you, but we both know we can't. We decided it would be as well to remove you from the Fae Realm. Your bloodline cannot produce a possible soulmate to the Prince of the Elves if your blood is no longer here." She cooed at the baby. "Isn't that as good as dead? I think surely it must be. But you will be safe. You will have a chance at a happy, mortal life."

No sooner had she finished speaking to the baby, than the Bakru appeared. The Mage turned up her nose while glancing at the disgusting creature. Bakru were gnome-like creatures, who were able to do magical and sometimes despicable favors for those willing to pay a price. The Mage had weighed all her options while planning what she could do which would do no lasting harm to the baby. Unfortunately, this was the only plan she could come up with. And the price had already been discussed and after she knew the baby was safe and sound, would be paid.

By taking her to the mortal realm, she was cursing her to a mortal life. But at least it was a life. Silently, she asked the powers that be to forgive her betrayal to her people. The Prince was closer to her than she cared to admit. In fact, her sister was the young Elf's mother, so, in essence, she was not only betraying him, but her own sister, as well.

She reluctantly, let the little gnome-like man take the baby from her. She cringed inwardly as he cooed in a toothless show for the child, who began to cry in earnest in his arms.

The Mage watched with a sad expression. "You promise me this child will be given to a good family. They'll take care of her?"

The Bakru turned beady eyes in her direction. "I may be evil by your kind's standards, Mage. But I assure you, the family this child is going to will love her as their own. She will have a good life. I dare say, much better than she would have here with the likes of *those things* hunting her like an animal, trying to assure she does not live to grow to womanhood. It is a shame though. She deserves her heritage. To be chosen to give a sacrifice without even being old enough to know what that sacrifice is. *For shame...*"

Considering his words, the Mage nodded. "Thank you." She said softly as the little man turned and made his way across the bridge without even a backwards glance in her direction. She watched as he disappeared within seconds, taking with him any opportunity she could have had to change her mind.

The Bakru had told her when he delivered the baby to her new parents, she would feel her magic drain. He had said she'd never be powerful again. Now, all she would have would be an ability to see people's memories and feel their destinies. Basically, in a matter of seconds, she would go from being a strong magical being, to a simple medium with a way to see things, but no power to stop anything she saw beginning to come to pass, as she once had.

As she turned to walk away from the bridge, the pain hit. Crying out, she fell to her knees and curled in on herself as the magic she had been born with was stripped from her, much like the top layer of skin might be taken from a livestock animal about to be slaughtered. The pain was excruciating and robbed her of all coherent thought while it drained away her not only her magical essence, but her happy true memories of the man she loved. As she and he had both agreed, she had to have her memories of the kind and loving man she cared for replaced by a hateful, cruel monster.

She lost all track of time as wave after wave of the pain crested over her, stripping her of the most natural parts of who she was. Tears slipped down her cheeks as she accepted the price she paid, reminding herself silently; it was worth it, as now the baby was safe. With the Shades locked away with the sleeping Drowmonger, the residents of the Fae Realm would be safe...

One

"Seriously, Kinsley, I'm fine. I thought long and hard about it before making my decision to come here." The woman paused as she turned in a slow circle, taking in the humble, yet charming cottage she now called home. "I promise, when you come to visit, you'll fall in love with it too." She chuckled softly. "I dare say, you might decide to take up residence in my guest bedroom." Another pause, "Oh, hush! You of all people know me better than that. This is exactly the kind of place I thrive in. I can feel the urge to get my paints out again already building. I need that."

The last words she spoke were a little hushed as a wave of emotion hit her. The silence in the cottage was palpable as the woman listened to her friend speak. When at last her voice broke the quiet, it was sad. "I don't mind the loneliness. Not here. Here, there are no memories of the family I had, save the ones I brought." A sob escaped her, but she covered her mouth with a shaking hand, forcing it away and taking a deep breath. "I have to move on. This is how I'm doing it."

The woman on the other end of the connection said something that made the sad lady laugh. "Yes! And even though I am in the country, now that I'm here, I'm actually closer to you. Less than an hour and a half away, if I'm correct. You will have to come for dinner soon. Maybe we will stay up all night, drinking wine and watching old movies. Just like old times."

She smiled and said, "I love you too, Kins. I promise we will get together soon. I only need to finish getting all these boxes unpacked." She nodded in response to the woman who could not see her, "Yes, soon. I promise. I love you too. Have a good evening."

Leanna hung up the call and dropped her cell phone down on the end table, then wiped the sweat from her brow. The movers had delivered the furniture to the house on time earlier that week. But they had been in such a rush to leave once they finished unloading, she had held her tongue about asking them to help arrange it into any semblance of order.

Truth be told, she was grateful they had put the furniture in the right rooms without too much of a fight. Once they had taken their leave, she merely rolled up her sleeves and got to work. She used any and every ounce of energy she would have expelled fighting with them about what went where, just to do it herself. The only breaks she had taken had been to eat or sleep. As a result, five days after she had opened the door to her new home, it was finally beginning to feel like hers. The living room, kitchen, and master bedroom were done. A small smile crossed her lips. The first real smile she had put on her face in years. For so long, she had felt like it was too much of a fight to paste on a fake one.

She didn't feel like fighting. Lord knows, she had gone through enough of that for the past seven years. It was a memory forever etched in her brain as the worst time of her life; a nightmare she couldn't wake up from. Yet, it was laced with some of the strongest love and hope she had ever felt.

Squaring her shoulders, she looked at the two boxes that sat unopened at the far side of the room. Seven years of a precious little life, but this was all she had been able to keep. The therapist had told her when she had given her suggestions for a fresh start, to get rid of everything except for the most important. "Keep the things that give you the best memories." That had been her suggestion.

She had tried. She had gone through every single thing in Daniel's room, and donated all the big things; clothes, toys, bed, study desk... all to Goodwill. When all those things were gone, she had gone through the last things. The baby book she and Max had made together during the first years of their son's life. Those were the good years. They held the promise of a lifetime of memories to come; not just what had ended up being fleeting moments that would be gone in the blink of an eye.

This had not been the first time she had to do this, but the second. The beginning of it had been when the phone call had come in the middle of the night when Daniel was four. Max had been on his way back from a business trip when his plane crashed. There were no survivors. Leanna remembered standing outside Daniel's room that night, watching him sleep and wondering how in the hell she was supposed to tell their son the person he loved above all else was gone.

It had been a hard road; one she was not sure she could travel. She hadn't signed on to be a single parent. That took balls. It took far more energy than she was capable of. She had known she was doomed to fail.

But she had survived. Daniel did too. He had been her little trouper. Always told her he was the man of the house and he'd never leave her. Somehow, they survived. Life was good. The love they had for each other helped them through those first couple of years without him.

Then Daniel got sick. A mere two years after his father had died, he was horribly ill. Two and a half years of constant tests had never revealed what was wrong. Still, the sweet boy was brave and reassuring, all the way to the end. Test after test. Procedure after procedure. The pain was so bad, she knew he really wanted to quit... but he tried his hardest for her. He never wanted her to worry.

Even in the end, he held her hand and tried his hardest to comfort her. "I won't leave you, Mom. I promise you aren't losing me."

Leanna had known then that her son was alive simply because he was so worried about leaving her alone. If he weren't worried over whether she could handle being alone, he would probably have already given up his fight against his illness and gone to be with his father.

Knowing she had to release him, she climbed into the hospital bed with her brave seven-year-old, held him to her, and tried her best to give him a brave face. "Daniel, I know you don't want to leave me. I know you are worried about me being alone, baby. But I am not the one who is important right now." She took a deep breath, to stifle the sob which had threatened at that moment and tried to smile. "I think... I think, maybe Daddy needs you." She squeezed him a little tighter before adding, "And maybe I'm being selfish trying to keep you when he needs you so much."

Daniel smiled at her and reached up to wipe a tear from her cheek. "I love you, Mommy."

When he closed his eyes, Leanna had to fight the urge to shake him back awake. Part of her felt like her lungs were shutting down and she'd never breathe again. But instead, she continued to hold him as he drifted off to sleep. She listened to his frail breathing and said a silent prayer to the powers that be to end his suffering and give his soul safe journey to his father's side. After her prayer, it had only taken his little body thirty-four minutes to let go of its fight and move on. She gave in to the tears then and cried for all she was worth.

When she finally left the hospital and went home, the empty house that greeted her was too painful to be in. She had left that night and stayed with her parents for the past year, while she had been trying to find out who she was again, without the two people who had meant the most to her.

When she was finally able to go through everything, she did what the therapist had suggested. She had put aside the things that gave her the dearest memories and dedicated a single box to each of them. One box held the possessions of her husband which included his wedding ring, his watch. His favorite football jersey and the old baseball cap he was wearing when he proposed. The other box was dedicated to her son.

When she finally felt ready, she began looking for a new home, one that didn't leave her feeling so alone and miserable. Funny thing was the house she fell in love with wasn't exactly close to civilization. In a strange way, it made her feel as if it were as alone and miserable as she was.

The home was a decent size: two bedrooms, two baths, made of old cobblestone. Originally, it was a guest house to a much bigger manor house. The realtor had told her it, the family cemetery, and the ruins were all that remained on the land after the manor house had burned down at the turn of the nineteenth century. No one had ever wanted to restore it. The family of the caretakers had lived and cared for the smaller home for years; even after the manor had burned. Eventually, the owners had given it all to the caretakers.

They had lived there for a few generations. But eventually, their descendants had tired of caring for the place and decided to leave. Renters had come and gone, but no one even looked twice at buying the property in all these years; a fact which intrigued her, not only as the price was dirt cheap, but also because she found the place to be extremely beautiful.

The land was breathtaking, with old oak and willow trees, and there was a creek that ran the length of the property. It was complete with a cobblestone bridge which was perfect for crossing the river from one part of the land to the other. The Cobblestone was also a mainstay for both the cottage and the ruins of the manor, because to go between the two places one had to cross it.

Looking out the window from the guest house, Leanna could see the remains of the old home in the fading sunlight. She wondered what the people who had lived there were like. What stories must their lives have had to tell? Had any of the women who had lived here lost their husbands or children? What must their lives have been like?

Of course, the logical side of her knew there was no part of this place that empathized with her loss. But the dreamer and wishful thinker in her had a small wish that this place knew how she felt and would perhaps help her to heal. Taking a deep breath, she grabbed her sweater and putting it on, stepped outside and slowly began making her way to the ruins. She knew there was nothing there but rubble, but suddenly the need to see it up close and personal was overwhelming. The urge to hold one of the stones in her hand and feel its weight was almost dire. She would only stay for a few moments. She patted the pocket of her sweater, assuring herself her small flashlight was still there.

As she began to cross the cobblestone bridge, intent on inspecting the long since destroyed home, Leanna wondered at her sense of urgency. Why did she care? She had not even really given it a passing glance when she had viewed the property but for some reason, she just needed to see it closer now.

No sooner had she stepped off the bridge than everything changed. The fading light of day was gone; replaced by the almost blinding light of morning sun. Her steps faltered as she looked around, perplexed. Gone were the ruins of the manor. The fading light of day was no more. Not a single cloud littered the sky. The air was crisp and clean, and the breeze filtering through the trees had the unmistakable scent of lilac.

Turning in a slow circle, Leanna took in her surroundings in baffled amazement. The only thing she saw which still looked familiar was the bridge. Everything else was different. Tempted to pinch herself, she faced away from the bridge and found herself face to nose with a Dragon. Huge, with black, green, and gold scales, and eyes the color of bluebonnets; it stared at her with what she could only hope was simple curiosity.

Not even trying to discover if the beast was friendly, Leanna turned and ran as fast as she could back over the bridge, the scream in her throat lost in transit. As she ran, she silently begged any deity listening that the Dragon wasn't following her.

As her feet hit the ground on the other side of the bridge, it was near dusk again. Sliding to a halt, she stared at the little cottage she had happily thought would be her new home. Panting for breath, she turned back and looked the way she had come. Everything appeared completely as it had before she ventured onto the bridge.

"What the hell?" she whispered softly. "I've gone completely nuts!" She looked again at the bridge before backing slowly away and shaking her head. "Nope... no. Not me. I am not even going to try to rationalize this." She chided herself softly as she turned, and half stumbled, as she ran back to the cottage. Opening the door, she slammed it and pressed her back against it. Then looked up at the ceiling even as she felt for the latch on the door, locking it.

When she heard the lock echoing in the bolt, she breathed a sigh of relief. "I'm just tired, right?" She rationalized aloud. "I've been unpacking all damn day. I'm exhausted. I need sleep."

She nodded her head, as if affirming what she had said. "Just as soon as I have a glass of wine." As she spoke, she headed into the kitchen. Yes, a glass of wine was exactly what she needed...

...Vlameir Jareth sat atop his Dragon companion, Torlek, a look akin to shock in his ice blue eyes. The dark-haired woman had skin that looked to be kissed by the sun itself, yet he had still almost believed her to be a specter. For a moment, he was not even sure she had just been there. But she was. Yet, almost as fast as he had spotted her, she was gone. He wouldn't have believed her real if it hadn't been for the lingering scent of lilac and lavender.

How did she stumble upon this place? The bridge on the other side had not allowed anyone from the human realm to cross into the Fae lands since right after he had been crowned. That was nearly seventy cycles ago.

Children stumbled into their world quite often. They were still open and could easily believe and accept the existence of a Magical world existing parallel to their own. Most times, their visits were brief and weren't often repeated.

Sometimes, they would return frequently. Some became so used to the Fae world that in time, they would make the decision to stay. King Vlameir trusted his people. Every human who had chosen to move to his Realm had long before shown their hearts to be pure and open to the magic of it. He knew they would be a welcome addition. But they had all journeyed here first when they were children...

For this adult mortal woman to travel through the gateway into his world, there were three truths that would have to vibrate within her soul... First, she would have had to endure tremendous sorrow. Second, she would have to been at a point where she was desperate to make a change in her life. And third; She would have to be someone who believed in magic still, even with all her heartbreak. The third was an incredibly difficult feat. mortal hearts were famous for only enduring so much pain before they lost faith in any and all magic.

As he sat astride Torlek, pondering the condition of her heart, the Dragon took that moment to speak. "Well, that was an interesting development. It's been quite some time since I've seen such a pretty little thing waltz across that bridge." There was a soft hint of humor in Torlek's tone.

Shaken from his thoughts, Vlameir huffed, "Was she pretty? I think I had *no* opportunity to notice, you startled her so." He chuckled softly. "Indeed, she was so startled to see you, I'm afraid she might have been running to try to catch up with her heart."

Torlek recognized his friend's playful banter and joined in light heartedly. "So, I startled her? Well then, perhaps I should cross over into her realm and apologize. At the very least, I should introduce myself, so she knows I meant her no harm."

Vlameir scowled as he nearly barked, "You'll do no such thing! Dragons have not crossed over into the human lands wearing their true forms in near three thousand years. The last time was near disastrous!"

Torlek inclined his head in agreement. "Well, then, what would you have us do? The fact she crossed into our world means she has need of us. At the very least you should send someone over, if only to be assured she is okay, and not still in hysterics."

Vlameir opened his mouth to argue, but instead found himself remembering the stricken look in her eyes. Torlek was right, but he had no intention of sending anyone to check on her. He was fully capable of checking on the mortal on his own. No one in the kingdom had an inkling of his powers of stealth. "Very well. I shall go and see how she fares."

As he spoke, he slid off Torlek's back and was rewarded by the Dragon turning to look him in the eyes, questioning, "You? But you are the king. It's unheard of for you to cross over into the mortal world without so much as a guard."

Vlameir held his hand up to stop Torlek's complaint. "It is nighttime right now in her world. I will use my powers to go to her invisibly. No one will see me. Not even her."

The Dragon shook himself, letting his wings spread for a moment. The stretching showed off a metallic luster of a green and gold sheen on his black scales. Purple eyes took in the Elf Lord. Torlek had a feeling, things would not go quite as Vlameir planned, but he knew better than to voice his concerns. Lowering himself down to rest on the ground, he watched warily as his friend turned and made his way to the bridge between the two worlds. Muttering softly to himself, "We shall see."

The cobblestone cottage looked so dark and quiet, for a moment Vlameir wondered if he had been wrong in his assumption this was her home. But as he drew closer, he could hear her inside. Pausing for a moment, he checked to be certain he could enter her home without alerting her.

When he tried the door, he found it locked and smiled. Smart girl. She was alone on a piece of property that was far from other mortals. It would be foolhardy not to bolt the door appropriately. Many humans suffered with minds endlessly clouded with malice and greediness. As a rule, Vlameir had little to do with them. He rarely traveled into their world and up until now, he had not given much thought to whether one of them needed to be allowed into his Realm. He was used to being petitioned when one of his people believed a human was worthy; he never minded testing their hearts to see if they were earnest in their desire to join the Fae Realm.

Over the years, there had indeed been a few who were deemed worthy and given a place among the Fae. But not all who petitioned for asylum were accepted. Many had their memories wiped and were sent back to their existence in the realm of mortals.

Vlameir took a deep breath, summoning his magic, and drawing it from his core to his fingers. With a simple flick of his forefinger, he slid the lock open, affording him access to her home. Closing the door behind him and relocking it, he moved silently through the house, barely taking notice of his surroundings as he followed the strange sounds the woman was making. It sounded to him as if she were crying. He wondered what could make her cry like that.

As he neared the room she was in, he paused when he heard her voice. "I don't know about all this. I had thought moving someplace new would help. I mean, I left our home; I walked away from most of the things that remind me of the two of you. I mean, it's not like I really need the house to still have the memories."

Stepping through the doorway, he saw her sitting on the floor, leaning against the wall and going through a box. The sadness he felt radiating from her made his own chest ache.

He watched her wipe a tear from her cheek as she sniffed. "I simply feel like this wound will never shut. How long will it take for me to quit feeling so empty?" Her voice broke on a sob, and Vlameir watched as she buried her face in the stuffed toy and cried harder. Looking away from her, his eyes quickly fell upon the obvious happy family photo and he easily understood the source of her devastation. She had lost them both.

It took every ounce of discipline he had not to move to the sad woman's side and scoop her up in his arms. He ached to sooth her and try to ease her pain. Instead, he stood back, clenching his fists, and simply watching with his invisibility enchantment surrounding him. Reaching into her mind, he looked through some of her flitting memories as she visited them.

The desire to try to erase her pain was overwhelming, but he knew to do so would expose her to a world he could not be certain she deserved to know. He was the king. As such, he had an obligation to his own people, who depended on him and trusted in his decisions to be true and fair for all—not merely to a human who his heart went out to because of her pain.

He watched as she lay on the floor, clasping the precious toy to her like a lifeline. Soon, it was apparent she was asleep, and he faced yet another decision; leave her on the floor or take her to her room. For the fraction of a moment, he paused, before muttering under his breath and turning to search out the other bedroom.

It was just down the hall. The room was simple. A full-size bed stood in the far corner. Next to it was a nightstand with a lamp sitting on top. The bed hadn't been made. Light blue sheets with a warm patchwork blanket adorned the bed, along with two fluffy pillows.

As he approached the bed, he caught scent of an almost intoxicating fragrance. It filled him, reminding him of a garden of honeysuckle on a warm springtime morning. His heart pounded as he considered the implication of what had just transpired before he shook his head. It couldn't be her. Her fragrance would only affect him in such a way if she were his intended.

Stepping back from the bed, he shook his head to clear his senses. It couldn't be. Such things between Fae and mortal were simply not possible. In all his centuries... In all the studies he'd done... Through every story he'd ever been told... Never had a soul connection been spoken of between their two worlds. It was unheard of. The mere short lifespan of mortals was telltale enough as to how doomed such a relationship would be. The Elf would either have to give up his immortality and cross into the mortal realm to accept a mortal life, or the human would have to accept the elixir of life, and from that moment on, never return to the mortal realm again for any extended amount of time.

While it was a decision sometimes chosen, it was not one to be done lightly, and not usually a decision born from a love connection. Most often, it was tied to health or such... Sometimes, the elder Elves, ready to leave life behind, had chosen to cross into the mortal realm and in essence, become mortal. Although such decisions were occasionally made, it was seldom done, and even more seldom spoken of.

Gritting his teeth, he dismissed the thought and returned to the room where she lay sleeping on the floor. Stepping close to her, he dropped his invisibility and bent to pick her up, grabbing the small stuffed toy as he did, so he could keep it with her. She nestled immediately into his arms and whispered, "I miss you so much, Max." Her head rested on Vlameir's shoulder, and the fragrance of her hair assailed his senses, stirring his loins and giving him a fierce desire to protect her.

Unable to stop himself, he stared at her. Her beauty captivated him, and the scent he inhaled from her very nearly intoxicated him. He knew she spoke of her deceased husband. Just a few minutes in her mind had alerted him to the extent of her losses. However, unable to stop himself, he kissed her forehead and whispered back, "I've missed you too." *Even though I never realized it until now.* He added silently. This sudden influx of emotions baffled him. In all his time as king, he had never desired a mate.

He had taken an occasional lover, of course. He was a man, after all. But the desire to keep a woman at his side indefinitely had never happened to him before. He was stunned at the level of emotion that consumed him. She was mortal. Until today, she had been completely unknown to him. Yet suddenly, here he was, wanting to carry her out of this house and away from all these memories which caused her such pain.

Channeling his self-discipline, he forced himself to ignore his desire to simply carry her away, instead taking her into her bedroom. Gently, he laid her down on the bed, and covered her slowly with the blanket. As he reached to place her toy beside her, she opened her eyes, and he waited, holding his breath, expecting her to scream.

Instead, he found himself smiling and fighting back a chuckle when she sighed and nestled farther into the bed, saying in her sleep, "What a nice dream." As she drifted back off.

Gently, he smoothed back her hair from her face, then impulsively, leaned down to kiss her lips lightly. "Would that I could share in your dream, beloved." He paused, observing her for a moment longer, before deciding to give her the gift he considered.

Placing his hand on her cheek, he spoke softly, "From this day forward, you will be able to release the pain and sorrow you feel for the loss of your loved ones. Instead, you will start to feel blessed for the time you had with them and the love you all shared as the regrets and pain slowly start to fade into the background. Their memories may be bittersweet, but it will become a sweet joy to remember instead of such a bitter pill." Silently, he added, *you will remember me on a subconscious level. We will be together soon.*

Swiftly, he turned and quit the room. He paused long enough to turn off the light in the room she had allocated as a vigil for her son and husband. Then continued, out of the house, locking her door again behind himself. As he moved swiftly down the stairs, he felt, rather than saw Torlek. He chuckled when his eyes rested on his Dragon friend, sitting beside the porch, in the form of a feline.

"A cat, Torlek? I'm a bit surprised you'd venture into the mortal realm in such a way."

The black cat turned its purple eyes in his direction. "You said I could not come to the mortal realm in my true form." The cat seemed to smirk, "You said nothing about assuming the form of a creature that already existed openly here. Besides, what would you have me do? I will not leave you unprotected in this place." He sent his thoughts to Vlameir in an exasperated voice. "It was either this, or an owl. And I figured I could get closer as a cat."

Vlameir chuckled at his friend's response. "What would you do if danger had come, Torlek? Purr them to death?"

The cat fairly growled at Vlameir's teasing. "You know full well although I assume a different form while I am here, I do not forfeit my abilities to do so. I am capable of protecting you quite proficiently, I might add."

The Elf inclined his head with a small smile. "I do know, Torlek. I am grateful to have such a powerful friend and chaperone watching out for me."

The cat rose from the steps of the porch and stretched before moving to Vlameir's side, asking, "So the woman? What do you make of her situation? Do you believe she will be visiting the Fae Realm again?"

The Elf King nodded, "Yes. I am quite certain she will visit again." He hesitated for a moment before adding, "If she is who my senses tell me she is, I am of the mind she will eventually stay; as my Queen."

Torlek stumbled in the taller grass and caught himself short, staring after Vlameir with as stunned an expression as a cat could have. "But she's human. Her very lifespan makes being your queen an almost certain impossibility."

Vlameir turned back to Torlek and nodded. "I'm not saying anything at this point, Torlek. There are ways around this issue. You know that as well as I. But this woman... There's something about her; about her fragrance... I cannot explain it, but I feel it is quite possible she is my intended." Facing the bridge, he continued walking even as he added, "Why else would I have her scent imprinted on my soul already? Even now, it is here, surrounding me, engulfing me as if it is part of the very air I need to survive." He gave an intense shake of his head. "It is the very reason I am literally running from this place. If I do not leave here now, I will not leave without her."

Torlek said nothing, but instead contemplated Vlameir's retreating backside with a speechless gaze. As he followed behind him, he mused to himself, *Well, this is an interesting turn of events...*

Two

Leanna woke feeling refreshed. Yawning, she stretched and rolled onto her back from her side. As she came more fully awake, she realized she was in her bed. Sitting up, she looked around, confused. She remembered running back to the house after the whole incident at the bridge.

She remembered fixing herself a large glass of wine and sitting down in her favorite chair for several moments as she worked to calm down. Then, she hadn't forgotten... going to the room with her husband and son's things and sitting on the floor going through that damn memento box, with the glass of wine in her hand, and tears streaming down her face. But she had no idea how she had gotten to her room. Surely, she hadn't blacked out. She'd only had the one glass of wine. That wasn't enough to make anyone black out.

As if in answer to her silent pondering, the scent of an unknown man's cologne filled her senses. A moan escaped her as she breathed it deep. It was a musky woodland scent with what she could only describe as morning rain. Where the hell did it come from? And why did eyes the color of arctic ice pop into her head when she remembered the smell?

Her hand rested on the stuffed toy. Looking down at it, a small smile flitted across her lips. She remembered this teddy bear. She had bought it when she was still pregnant with Daniel. It was one of those bears deemed safe for babies. It was now a faded pastel blue. The eyes were a green cross stitch, as was the nose, which was black, as well as the mouth. Nothing on the toy could cause a baby to choke. That was the whole reason she had gotten it.

Never had she imagined that this would be his favorite toy. He had never slept without it. It had gone with him on every trip. It had been the thing he had held so tightly to when he lost his first tooth and was brave for Daddy to pull it.

The night he had died, the bear had been right by his side. She had started to bury the bear with him, but something had held her back. Holding it to her, she buried her nose in it and inhaled deeply. It reminded her of the way his hair had always smelled after his baths. Closing her eyes, she waited for the gut-wrenching pain that always assailed her heart.

Instead, she remembered his laughter. The way he had always come to her with his arms wide open, demanding hugs and kisses. *"I love you, Mommy. I'll love you forever."* It was what he always told her.

Instead of finding herself overcome with tears, Leanna found herself smiling, and answering his imaginary voice with the same answer she'd always given him. "I'll love you beyond forever. Nothing will ever change my love for you." She started to take the bear back to put with Daniel's things, but stopped.

Turning back to her bed, she put the toy on her pillow. Somehow, it seemed to be where it belonged now. "How about you just stay in *my* room now?" she asked the bear quietly. She stood staring down at it for a moment, almost expecting the toy to reply. Instead, his cross-stitch eyes seemed to stare back at her as if to ask what took her so long to realize his rightful place.

With a shake of her head, she chuckled as she turned and left the bedroom. For the first time since she had moved into the home, she passed up the extra bedroom and went straight to the living room.

In the corner, almost as if it had been pushed in the corner to punish it, sat a large wooden crate, with a treasure chest lid. Inside were her sketch pads and paints and brushes. She hadn't opened it since her son had died. Truth be told, she had not had any desire to try to be artistic at all. She had felt as if that part of her was dead.

Strangely, today she was inspired. She wanted to go out to the bridge. She had no plans to attempt crossing it. Honestly, after what had transpired the night before, she wasn't sure she would ever cross the bridge again. She wouldn't try to guess what had happened, but she knew she didn't want to meet that purple-eyed monster again, lest it decide to eat her.

But she wanted to sketch the bridge. And the trees that lay beyond. It was quite beautiful. She doubted she could do it justice, but it felt like a relief to focus on something else besides her sadness for once. Maybe the doctor had been right. Maybe the pain would lesson by the change of venue.

When the aroma of fresh coffee reached her, she inhaled deeply before speaking. "At least I didn't forget to prep the coffeepot yesterday!" With a spring in her step, she approached the chest and opened it with a smile. There, tucked away safely on top, was her sketchpad, and some drawing pencils, as well as her shader and eraser. Grabbing them, she made her way to the kitchen and made herself a cup of coffee in one of her insulated mugs.

Then, in a few zip-lock bags, she threw together some crackers, cheese, grapes, and some diced turkey meat. Putting them all into her lunchbox, along with a cold bottle of water, she adjusted the strap before putting it on her shoulder. On her way out, she grabbed a blanket off the back of her couch and bundled it under the other arm with her sketchpad. Walking with purpose, she intentionally left her cell phone behind. She didn't need or want any distractions from the outside world today. The cottage was in clear view from the bridge, so she left the door unlocked, only pulling it to as she stepped outside.

A soft breeze blew, carrying the scent of the honeysuckle that was growing nearby. Breathing deeply, Leanna sighed and smiled. Today felt good. She had no idea why today felt different, but for the first time in such a long while, she felt as if everything was going to be okay; *she* would be okay.

When she reached the place where she felt was the best view of the bridge, she spread out the blanket. Once she had it all organized, she sat down, and picked up the sketchbook. Opening it to the first blank page, she paused to look at the scene before her.

Within moments, she was using her pencil in strokes, beginning to define the outline of what appealed so much to her about the land. Her eyes barely even looked at what she was drawing. She didn't need to. She could feel the distance between the trees and the clouds. She could feel in her heart, the way the breeze affected those things. The bridge came into it beautifully. It was at the forefront of the picture, with the huge old oak to the left of the scene, and two cypresses throughout, peeking past the bridge, almost as if saying hello. A few stones from the main house that had burned down were in the distance, standing at attention, as if guarding the property, all while protecting the history of the place.

Then there was the cat. A rather large, black feline, sitting on the rail of the bridge, watching her with open curiosity. She paused for the first time in her work to pay special attention to him. He was looking back at her with an expression of interest, as if he might be willing to make friends.

"Well, hello there," she said in a friendly voice as she set the sketchpad and pencil down, then reached for her morning sustenance. "I was about to take a break and have a snack. Would you like some?"

She reached into the bags of turkey and cheese, pulling out a few pieces for him, and set them on the corner of the blanket, just in case, before turning to her own food. She took a few bites, before washing it down with some water.

Glancing back toward the bridge, she saw the cat had left that spot. She spied him out of the corner of her eye, edging closer to the blanket, to investigate the morsels she had left him. She continued her snack, paying him little mind, hoping not to frighten him away, in case he was a feral.

She knew when he had settled into his snack and seemed to have either accepted that she was there or had simply forgotten her all together. She finished her grapes, then washed it all down with some of her water. After a moment, she poured some into the small cup that came with the lunchbox and set it by the kitty.

He raised his head from the food and regarded her silently before dipping it down to investigate the water, taking a small sip before looking back up at her. She offered him a smile. "Want another piece of cheese?" she held out the offering in the palm of her hand.

The cat regarded her without any disdain, then moved closer and began eating the treat from her with satisfaction.

Gently, she reached out with her other hand and stroked him one time, beginning at his ears and traveling down his back, to see if he was accepting of her attentions.

When he finished, he looked back at her with an expression full of intelligence and curiosity. "Do you belong out here?" she asked softly. "There aren't any neighbors for about three or four miles. That's an awfully long wal—" her voice broke off as she really looked into the cat's eyes.

For a moment, she was almost frozen solid. Her heart rate tripled, and she bit her bottom lip with what she was sure most people would think was an irrational fear. Then, as her hand dropped, she said in a shaky voice, "You have purple eyes."

The cat sat back on its haunches, observing her for a few moments. Then she felt him touch her mind, *"Well shucks... You noticed that, did you?"*

When she simply sat there, her back ramrod stiff and didn't respond, he crouched down, as if to look at her closely and said, "I'm really harmless. I would never hurt you. I promise. But you were so startled last night, I felt it only right to come and be certain you were okay today."

Leanna stared at him as if he had grown two heads, still silent as death at the prospect of actually being spoken to by a cat. She was still trying to wrap her mind around it when he spoke to her again.

"I really had no intention of startling you. I swear it." He paused for a moment, before adding, "I would ask if the cat had your tongue, but under the circumstances, I fear that would be incredibly bad form."

At his words, she sputtered and nearly choked for a moment, before beginning to laugh. Shaking her head, she covered her eyes with her hands, muttering to herself, "Have I lost my mind? Yes! Of course, I have!" She whined and rocked back and forth before looking through her fingers at him. "I'm having a conversation... With a cat... And apparently, not only can he talk, but he has a *fantastic* sense of humor." She hummed to herself for a moment, before sighing. "This is why everyone watched you so closely after Daniel died. They were all afraid you would lose your mind to the grief." She shook her head, answering herself almost immediately. "But you were feeling better. You didn't cry first thing when you woke up. You even came outside to paint. Is this the first sign of a nervous breakdown; talking to purple eyed cats?"

Torlek watched her with an expression akin to pity for a few moments before answering, *"Well, actually, I'm trying to have a conversation. You, on the other hand, are jabbering to yourself and trying to convince yourself you've lost your mind."* Did he just smirk? Then he continued, *"I know you most likely do not want to believe me, but you most certainly have not lost your mind. I am the Dragon you stumbled upon. But for obvious reasons, I cannot show my true form to you here. However, I did want to check on you while his Majesty slept."*

"His *Majesty?*" Leanna asked, acknowledging the truth of their conversation. "His Majesty who?"

The cat answered, *"King Vlameir Jareth. He is the rightful King of Light Elves in the Realm of Fae."* There was such honesty in his voice, Leanna almost believed he wasn't a fantasy contrived by her mind. *"He came to check on you last night to be certain you were well after the fright I had obviously given you."* The cat continued, trying to explain. *"But of course, you have no memory of that, do you?"* He shook his furry little head, before beginning to pace from one side of the blanket to the other. *"Of course, she has no memory of that, you tweedled-headed dolt. Vlameir protected her mind from it. She probably only thought he was some fantastic dream."*

At his words, the vision of the beautiful blond man with startling ice blue eyes came to the forefront of her mind, pulling a gasp from her lips. "He carried me to bed." She expelled in a huff. "He smelled like fresh woods and clover in the rain. He scooped me up in his arms and carried me to my bed."

As she spoke, the vision went from a faint, almost discernable dream, to a vivid honest memory, full of color and sound as well as his scent. The pounding of her heart echoed in her ears as loud as the thoughts in her head. Suddenly, she not only remembered him, but found herself hearing his ponderings as he had moved through her home. His fears at her being alone in the countryside as well as his wishes to take her pain away from her as he had stood by and watched her cry.

Then she remembered his spoken words, in his deep melodious voice. She remembered his stating, as a matter of fact that her pain would no longer be unbearable. Instead of feeling such loss at the memories of Max and Daniel, she would feel the blessing of what time she'd had with them.

Then she felt something shift inside herself. All at once, she knew she would know this man and know him well if he came to her. She knew his heart. He would never be able to hide his emotions from her. She also knew the same was true for her. There would never be a time when she could lie to this man. He would know her as well as she knew herself.

The sudden knowledge was foreign and overwhelming. She felt confused and frightened, as well as amazed at how deeply her heart responded to him from only the new memory she now had. What would it be like when he were there with her? How would she act? Part of her wanted to hug him and thank him for trying to rid her of her pain. Another, more private part of herself wanted him to keep her with him and refuse to let her stay here. A fervent, desperate desire filled her for him to insist she follow him back to his Realm.

Stunned by these rampant emotions running through her, she felt the blush filling her face. Her hands went to her cheeks, humiliated at the knowledge the cat could see. Instead of trying to hide it, though, she instead faced him. "What's happening to me? Why do I feel all these things? I feel as if I'm flooded with not only my own emotions, but his as well." Panic made her hold her breath for a moment before continuing, "Is this even possible?"

The cat seemed to stare at her in wide eyed shock. *"It's called the Coalescence Soul-bond, and until now, I have never actually seen it. But yes, it is possible. I believe you're in the middle of it."*

Looking from the cat down to herself, she asked in a trembling voice, "The middle—" she paused, moaning uncomfortably. "What exactly is it and when will it stop?"

Torlek moved closer to the beautiful woman, concerned for her as well as elated for his friend. *"When an Elf finds someone who is not from his or her own race, whose soul they believe could be that of their intended, they ask the Creator for validation."* He tilted his head, *"Vlameir voiced to me last night his suspicions of your identity. I know he had sent up his prayers to the elders. It seems they didn't waste any time in answering."*

This was all too much. Setting about putting away her art supplies, she made her decision to ignore what was happening. She knew deep down she was not going to be escaping whatever this was, but she wasn't ready to handle what was coming. She'd be lying if she tried to say she was.

Not wanting to be rude to the purple-eyed beast, she inclined her head to him by way of farewell. "Have a good day, Mister... uh... Cat." Not waiting for a response, she wasted no time going back to the cottage without even so much as a backwards glance.

She knew his gaze followed her, but she refused to look back. To do so would be admitting to him, as well as to herself, that she believed the conversation she'd just had was real. That was something she simply couldn't bring herself to do yet.

Reaching the safety of her little home, she slammed the door shut and leaned heavily against it. Closing her eyes, she breathed deeply. Somehow, she knew she didn't have long before the Elf King would be formally introducing himself. Even with every ounce of her common sense telling her this whole situation was insane, she realized it was true. She also recognized the fact she was now tied to this Elf King.

So, her mind reasoned with her, the only other matter to consider was: how was she going to deal with this new development? Would she befriend this Elf man and see what developed from it? Or would she tuck tail and run?

The words left her mouth, answering her thoughts out loud. "And where the Hell would you go, Leanna?" she scoffed angrily. "You have nowhere else to go. You have no one else to go to. And you love this place! Why would you leave?"

So, putting away her art supplies, she busied herself with setting a simple stew simmering in the crock pot for dinner and preparing for the guest who would come as soon as the sun went down. She didn't have much, but she would be as gracious a hostess as she could.

She tidied up her home, assuring herself it was clean and welcoming. By evening, a slight chill was in the house, so she built a fire in the fireplace to help warm the living room/dining room combination. He might not be hungry or even cold when he arrived, but she would be certain she was prepared if he were either.

Three

Vlameir stood, staring at the bridge. Torlek sat a few feet from him, waiting to see what his friend was going to do. Minutes passed, yet the Elf made no move toward the entrance to the mortal's world. The Dragon's shiny gaze slid in his friend's direction. "I'm sure she's expecting you, Vlameir."

The Elf King nodded. "Yes, you said as much." His expression was brooding and undecided. "I am not sure it is a good sign that she expects me." He added after a moment.

Torlek raised an eyebrow in Vlameir's direction, "Why is that? I would think you'd be excited at the prospect of not having to hide from her." Irritation crept into the Dragon's voice. "If you continue to drag your feet in this situation, I may just decide to take your place. Leanna is quite lovely. I might shift into human form and go reintroduce myself and see if I can't make her forget about you and all your procrastinating nonsense."

Vlameir rounded on Torlek, his eyes flashing like blue flame. "You'll do no such thing! She belongs to me!"

The anger in his voice did not even give the Dragon the slightest discomfort. Instead, he simply looked bored. "Yes, I know. Which is why I am having difficulty believing you haven't moved to begin this romance yet. It will take more than simply seeing you to win her over." He smiled, albeit sadly. "She has already loved once, and if the emotions I sense from her are correct, you have some big shoes to fill. It will take some time to win her heart. For now, I would suggest working on earning her trust. For the moment, that'll be hard enough."

Concern replaced Vlameir's agitation. "Do you think it will be so hard? I feel as if our souls have already begun to bond." Worry filled his eyes. "I've never wanted the bond. But now that I feel its beginning, I find I'm somewhat impatient to see it completed. The urgency I feel to bring her home is near impossible to resist."

"Yet you have no choice." Torlek answered. "Her soul is already feeling the bond between you beginning, but her heart feels it is betraying him. I am sorry, my friend. But you are forced to compete with a memory; and from what I sense, it is a good one."

Vlameir half scowled as he turned from his friend and regarded the bridge with a sense of unease. "Very well. I shall force myself to move slowly. Even though I want nothing more than to take her away from there."

Without waiting for Torlek's response, Vlameir used his magic to call a bouquet of moonrise roses to him. They were roses, exactly like the ones in Leanna's world. But they were an iridescent color of moonlight. They could only be found in the Fae Realm. However, they could live forever, as long as the vase they were put in was filled with cool fresh water every day. At his summons, they instantly appeared in his hand, tied with a silver ribbon. With a nod of approval, he turned and crossed the bridge, vanishing from his Realm and the Dragon's view.

Leanna sat in front of the fire, staring at the amber liquid of the wine in her glass. It had been perfectly chilled an hour ago, but her nervous apprehension had made it almost impossible to do more than take a few sips of the drink as she had waited. It was almost an hour after dusk, she thought, looking at the clock. Perhaps he wouldn't be coming after all.

As she began to rise from the chair to dispose of her drink, a knock echoed through the cottage, making her nearly drop her glass. Quickly, she recovered, moving to put the glass in the kitchen sink. Then, turning to face the door, she took a deep breath and blew it out slowly. "Nothing to be nervous about, Leanna," she said softly. "You're only making a new friend and making sure he understands that's all it can be."

Opening the door, she opened her mouth to greet him, but instead, stood mute, staring at the beautiful man before her. His eyes were exactly as her vision had remembered them to be. His white/blonde hair was worn loose and flowing. Its length easily reaching his waist.

What did surprise her was his attire. Aside from his hair and eyes looking completely ethereal, his clothes were simple enough, and easily confused for normal, if not a little fancy, in her world. Black pants that were surely leather with boots that were just as elegant. His shirt was a dark blue tunic style that buttoned down and tucked into the pants.

Stunned at both his attire and beauty, Leanna mentally chastised herself. "Oh, good grief. I am so sorry. I shouldn't stare," she said softly, blushing as she looked back to meet his gaze, only to find herself even more entranced with his sudden smile.

He didn't say anything, but simply held her gaze for a moment longer, before lifting the flowers in his hand to her view. "For you," he said in a silky deep voice and Leanna could feel herself slipping back into thrall of him.

Coming to her senses, she stepped back, opening her door wider to allow him in. "Please come in." she reached to take the flowers from him, her fingers brushing his, sending a shock through her and stealing her breath. Hoping he did not notice her response, she turned her eyes back to his, just in time to see he too was affected by their brief touch.

Somehow, it was comforting to know he was as moved as she was; although she could not even imagine it was anywhere near as deeply. She wondered exactly why she was so starstruck by him. Was it because she knew full well, he wasn't human? Was it the hint of his pointed ears peaking out through his long platinum tresses?

He was so captivating. She could only imagine the things he had seen; the places he had been. By way of comparison, she was quite certain she was probably boring. She had never really been many places, and for sure nowhere near as amazing as the Fae Realm. Hell, she had barely learned how to survive on a horse's back. Here he was, the Elf whose best friend was a Dragon. Nope. It was safe to say she was dull in comparison to him.

He took that moment to come the rest of the way into her house and closed the front door behind him. "I am not one who is too affected by colder weather, but it is a chilly night, and your house is going to lose its warmth if we

28

stand with your entry open to the elements the entire time we are visiting."

Leanna laughed nervously. "You're so right. I'm sorry I just keep staring. You must think me incredibly rude."

The corners of his mouth lifted even as his gaze never left hers. "I would be more surprised if you didn't stare, at least a little." He slid his hand over his face, not quite touching it. "How many Elves have you met?"

His smile was infectious, and she found herself joking back, "Besides the ones who help Santa on picture day?"

His brow lifted, "I'll have you know, Santa always borrows my workers. He owes me a boon." At her shocked look, he laughed a bit louder. "I speak in jest."

She joined in his laughter and gestured at the roses. "Let me put these in some water."

He followed behind her to the kitchen, taking the moment to explain about the roses. "They will live forever, as long as you change their water each day."

Vase in one hand, roses in the other, she turned to stare at him. "Forever? You mean they will outlive me? Really?"

He shrugged, "Or as long as you want them. I can well imagine; you wouldn't have use of them forever."

She looked from him to the roses, truly seeing them for the first time. "On the contrary, I'd like to paint them." She brought them to her nose, inhaling a scent that was rose, but seemed to be kissed by another, more exotic fragrance. "These are exquisite. I've never seen such a rose."

He tilted his head in acknowledgement of her words. "They are special. The scent they radiate is their interpretation of your heart." As she filled the vase with fresh water, and added the flowers to them, he explained. "The roses are empathic. They sense your mood and in response put out a perfume that complements it, and at times, helps to improve it."

She carried the vase to the living room and placed the roses on the coffee table before turning back to face him. "They are amazing. Do they need a specific amount of sunlight?"

He had stayed in the entryway to the kitchen and was simply watching her. When he realized her question, he gave a slight shake of his head, offering softly, "They are a moonrise flower. They do not need the sun. You could put them in a room with no light, and as long as you change their water daily, they will never cease to bloom for you."

Leanna looked at the roses, smiling at his thoughtfulness before turning back to him. "I don't know if you've already eaten, but I made some stew. I thought maybe you would join me?"

He said nothing. For a moment, he simply stared at her. Then, he nodded. "I would be honored. Although, you did not have to cook for me. I was not expecting it."

She waved him off, explaining, "I have always cooked. For a while, I had a family to cook for. Honestly, I still haven't gotten used to only making enough for myself." For a second, the emotion of her confession stole her words and she stopped walking and stood with her head down as she regained her composure. When she turned to face him, Vlameir could still see the emotion in her eyes, even though she had staved off the tears. "Sometimes, I think I never will."

She gestured to the crock pot. "I would actually be incredibly grateful if you would help me eat it. Maybe even take some to your Dragon friend. I'll never be able to finish all the leftovers on my own. It'll just go bad." She looked away from him, biting her lip before adding. "I'm not sure I'll ever relearn how to cook for just myself again."

Vlameir chuckled. "Well, while I wasn't expecting it. I do thank you, and so will Torlek. He loves human food." At her surprised expression, he added, "We usually come once a month, and he wears a human form to eat at Pizza Hut. We usually get a large meat lover. It's his favorite.

Leanna nodded, laughing, and turned to put some in bowls. "Why not?" she mused softly. "A Dragon who loves pizza. Of course." After she served his, she turned to pour him a glass of wine, as well as one for herself.

As they ate, she found Vlameir to be easy to converse with. They discussed the differences between their homes, the almost medieval beauty of his world, as well as the modern aspects of hers. She was somewhat stunned to discover they had no phones in his world. But then, felt somewhat jealous to find that the reason for that was because Elves had the ability to reach those they had a bond with telepathically.

"Wait; hold on... Do you mean to tell me, you can reach anyone you want to, merely by reaching out with your thoughts?" she sat back from the table, stunned."

Vlameir nodded. "Well, of course I can. We would have had the need to come and steal your technology for communications if we had not. Our world is as big as yours. But... it is different." He took a sip of his wine, then continued, "You have many amazing technical things. We have true magic. Where it is weakened to the point of simply being a whisper here, it flows through everything in my Realm. It is as real and true as the blood that courses though your veins. And every Faeborn can call on it." He paused for a moment before adding, "At least, most of them still do. There are places in our Realm where the use of magic is waning.

Leanna watched how his eyes lit up as he spoke of his home. She envied how obviously happy and proud he was of it and his people. "It sounds beautiful." She murmured. "I'm jealous. I wish I could see it."

Vlameir raised his glass in silent salute to her with a gentle smile. "You will, Leanna. I promise you will. Soon."

She found she had a wonderful time with Vlameir. After they finished their glasses of wine, he helped her wash the dishes and watched her put away the food after she fixed a special bowl for him to take to Torlek.

They sat in the living room for a time. She showed him some of her best sketches. They were all of scenery. He appreciated her eye for detail, complimenting her on how vibrant she made it all look.

She shrugged his compliments off. "Scenery is easy. For the most part, it doesn't move."

It was then he looked up above the fireplace and saw the painting of her husband and son. For a moment, he felt a jealousy flare up within him. She was his intended. He felt her soul bonding to his even now. The knowledge that she had found love before he found her made a piece of his heart ache, but he pushed aside the pain and regarded her thoughtfully. "You do portraits?"

She looked from him to the painting he had just been staring at. "It's been a long time, but I used to." She returned his gaze with a small smile.

For several minutes, they were simply silent. Then he asked in a soft voice. "Could I commission a portrait from you?"

Leanna's eyes widened, surprised. "Uhm... Of whom?"

Vlameir put his hand on his chest, "Me, of course. I have always meant to have one commissioned to go in the Generations Parlor. But I've never found an artist I trusted." As he spoke, his eyes went back to the painting. "The parlor has portraits of the kings and queens who have ruled throughout the centuries. Your work seems to almost bring the subjects to life. It has an element every other artist I have met lacks." When he turned back to her, he smiled, "I will reward you, of course. Handsomely, I promise."

She opened her mouth to refuse, but something in his eyes gave her pause. She couldn't tell him no. "I'll have to get some supplies. I don't have everything I would need."

Vlameir stood and moved through the distance between them, until he stood beside her. Offering her his hand, he helped her to her feet when she accepted it. Her breath caught in her throat when he leant down to kiss the inside of her wrist. "Cross the bridge tomorrow evening, at dusk. I shall be waiting on the other side for you. You need not bring anything aside from yourself. I will make sure anything and everything you need is there at the ready."

She could still feel the soft warmth of his lips on her wrist. It made her feel like swooning, which only irritated the hell out of her. But instead of refusing him, she simply nodded, "Okay. I'll be there."

His smile at her acceptance was radiant. His beauty took her breath away, making her feel awkward and foolish. What was wrong with her? She felt like a moronic schoolgirl with a crazy crush!

She didn't have time to ponder her feelings for long. He interrupted her thoughts as he bent to pick up the food she had prepared up from the coffee table. "I shall be waiting for you. As for now, the hour grows late, and I must get back before my guards come looking for me. As it is, I am sure Torlek is already pacing and swearing at me in his native tongue."

She followed him to the door, thanking him for coming. "I'll see you tomorrow, then. Goodnight."

He turned and looked at her for a moment and it was all she could do to not throw herself in his arms. With a slow movement, he reached up with his free hand and brushed her hair out of her face. "You really are breathtaking, Leanna. I will count the hours until I am able to see you again and show you my world." He leaned down and before she even realized what he was doing, his lips grazed her forehead, lingering long enough not to be a simple friendly kiss. When he stepped away, he inhaled deeply, before turning and stepping outside. "Fare thee well until the morrow, sweet lady."

She had to fight the urge to follow him out the door. She stayed put and uttered a soft goodbye before closing and locking the door to keep from making a fool of herself. Expelling the breath she had been holding, she leaned her head against the doorframe. "Good God, what am I thinking? The man is an Elf. No! He's MORE than an Elf! He's an Elf King, no less!"

Turning to go to her room, she glanced at the clock, then stared. It was well after two in the morning. He had arrived at just a little after ten. She knew they had visited for a while, but she never realized he'd been there for over four hours.

She hadn't had such a nice time in so long. It had felt good to have someone to talk to. But she wasn't fooling herself. He was an amazing person. And he was so far out of her league she'd have to spend a decade in charm school just to earn the right to be in the same room with him. "He's royalty, Leanna. Get over it!"

Forcing herself to push the remaining naughty thoughts of him out of her mind, she changed into her nightgown and went to bed. She would do his painting. If she could manage it, she would make a copy for herself which she could look at in the privacy of her home and remember the night he had helped her forget her loneliness.

Four

When Vlameir arrived the next evening at the bridge, he had already taken every measure to ensure Leanna had everything she needed for his portrait. Of course, he fully intended to make sure this was a long project where she had to spend as much time as possible in the Fae Realm, with him. If all went according to his plan, by the time the portrait was done, she wouldn't want to leave.

He smirked when Torlek sat beside him, asking, "Do you think she might bring some more of that stew?" The Dragon smacked his jaws and made a contented yum sound after his question.

Rolling his eyes, the Elf answered, "Honestly, my friend. Should a female ever come seeking advice from me on how to win your heart, I shall endeavor to tell her, simply appeal to his stomach. It is that which rules him."

The Dragon guffawed at Vlameir's words. "That is not entirely untrue. Any female wanting to win me over should have some sort of skill with cooking." He shrugged, "it would be the best way to win an argument with me, at least. I simply can't argue if my mouth is full."

The two regarded each other with lopsided smiles before turning back to the bridge and hearing the portal open. Vlameir smiled broadly when he saw Leanna coming across. She had her sketchbook in hand and a bag thrown over her shoulder.

"Leanna, I was almost afraid you had changed your mind." He offered as he approached her.

She smiled warmly at him, explaining, "I was a little intimidated when I started across. It is a strange experience, to say the least."

He nodded his understanding. "Hopefully, it will not feel so awkward after you've done it a few more times. Once you get used to it, it will be nothing special."

He immediately regretted his words. He had known about the portal his entire life. To him, it was the norm. She had just found out. Of course, it was a special thing to her. It probably made her rethink everything she knew.

To know Elves and Dragons were real meant she would have to re-examine every other thing she had ever doubted to be real. If her world was big enough to host a Fae Realm as well as a mortal one, then that had to mean life probably did very well exist in other parts of the galaxy as well. Funny how when a door to one possibility opened, all the others would too. He hadn't considered that until now.

Vlameir reached for Leanna's bag, "May I carry something for you? I told you I would see to all your needs while you were here."

She allowed him to take it from her, answering, "I have to do sketches first. I only brought my sketchbook and my pencils. For now, I will need to do several different sketches of you, so I may get a feel for the line of your face. I hope you don't mind. It will take a while if I am to do you justice."

He stared at her for a moment before answering, "Take as long as you need. I am in no hurry. The more time you take, the better we will get to know each other." In fact, the idea of her taking her time with his portrait made him happy. Each time he saw her, he could feel his heart slipping deeper into the bond that was forming between them. He wondered if she felt it as well. Was she fighting it? If she knew it was inevitable, would she welcome it?

Reaching out, he took her free hand in his. "Leanna, allow me to show you my home." He led her toward Torlek who stretched his wings before kneeling, making it easier for her to climb up on his back.

Leanna stopped short, staring at the Dragon's back. "Oh, wow. Uhm... I'm not sure I can—"

Sensing her fear, Vlameir squeezed her hand. "I won't let you fall. I promise. Trust me."

Her eyes searched his and after a moment, she nodded. "Okay. I trust you." Willingly, she followed him to Torlek's side and watched as he placed her bag and sketchbook in a pouch that fit snugly against what looked to be some type of saddle.

When he saw her examining it curiously, he said, "Torlek was worried you might be nervous about riding his back without harness. He won't wear one for me, but for your comfort, he even suggested it."

Leanna smiled at Vlameir before turning back to Torlek. "Thank you," she said simply.

The Dragon beamed at her. "You're welcome, dear lady." Vlameir nearly laughed as it occurred to him that his friend was possibly as smitten with Leanna as he was. As he helped her onto the Dragon's back, he followed her up, settling into the seat behind her, and wrapping his arms around her waist. Silently, he vowed to never let her go. She was too precious a treasure and he knew to give her up would break his heart.

As he felt her relax, leaning back against him, he reminded himself to take things slow. He must not frighten her away by revealing his heart too fast. Resting his cheek against hers, he spoke softly, "And away we go."

No sooner than he had spoken, than Torlek stretched out his wings and in one great whoosh, took to the air, flying smoothly up.

Leanna knew a moment of panic, but Vlameir's arms around her waist coupled with the beauty all around them, eased her. As she stared down at the beauty all around her, a feeling of peace she had not felt in a long time made her relax into his arms. The countryside was breathtaking. She felt like she was catching a glimpse of what her own world must have looked like long before all the things men called progress started coming along.

Her heart leapt at the peaceful feeling she got from it all. There was a safety here. It filled her the moment she had felt Vlameir's arms wrap around her. Closing her eyes, she leaned her head back against his shoulder and took a deep breath. As she released it, she opened her eyes.

In the distance, she could see what looked like a village. At its center, was a castle. "Oh my God..." she breathed softly. "I've stepped into the middle of a fantasy, haven't I?" she asked him, but was unsure he'd heard her.

"I suppose it depends on what kind of fantasies you have, and where you want them to take you." His embrace tightened for a moment before he asked her, "Where do your fantasies take you, Leanna?" Is this where you would want to be?'

His soft deep voice, coupled with the touch of his lips against her ear, made a small tremor run through her. She felt his question to her core. A part of her longed to tell him yes. She felt safe here, within his arms and away from all the painful memories. Yet something held her back. Her logical side told her she had only barely met the man and didn't know enough about this place even to consider staying here. Yet, her heart sped up at the thought of leaving the mortal realm behind and moving here instead.

Instead of giving voice to her true feelings, she chose to reply with a truth they both had to accept. "I know nothing of this place. Not its customs, or even how your people view my kind. I don't even know if I would be accepted here. Although I do love the beauty I've seen thus far."

She felt Vlameir's cheek rest against hers. The silence was deafening to her as she waited for his reaction to her words. She was half afraid he would give voice to her fears of not being accepted by his people. Oddly, the idea unsettled her. She already recognized a connection to this man she hoped he truly felt as well. A deeper part of her bore a guilt from the voice in her head that kept screaming her attraction to him was a betrayal to Max. Max was gone. He had been gone for several years now, and this was the first time she had even looked at another man.

Before she could ponder the question too deeply, she heard Vlameir's voice speaking softly to her. "My people are going to love you. There are not many of them who bear humanity any ill will. The ones who do still believe in letting each person prove who they are instead of judging all based on the deeds of a few. They are just slower to trust." He hesitated before adding, "There are those who distrust others, based solely on their backgrounds. I think that is true of every culture, in my Realm, as well as yours. But we strive to keep it at a minimum by teaching tolerance and acceptance." He sighed, then added, "it is the way we are all taught from the time we are children."

Relaxing a little more into his arms, she smiled., "I wish all my people were that way. There's so much hatred in my world these days, life can be somewhat scary."

Before Vlameir could answer, Torlek landed atop the castle. The Elf slid off his back, then turned, reaching up to assist Leanna. She met his eyes and trustingly reached out to meet him. After her feet touched the ground, he didn't immediately release her, but instead, held her close for another few moments, his eyes never leaving hers.

When he spoke, his words were sincere. "I will not lie to you. There are those who will not agree to your being here. Your arrival means their hopes for taking my throne are gone."

Confused, Leanna asked, "What do you mean? How does my presence have anything to do with your throne? I don't understand."

Vlameir sighed, releasing Leanna and stepping back from her. "You feel the connection between us. I know this." When she nodded, confirming the fact, he continued, "That is a connection between soulmates. It does not simply evolve anytime we connect with others. Even in friendships, it can take years, even decades to form." He looked away for a moment, as if searching for the right words. "But the instant I met you, I could feel its tendrils reaching out and wrapping around my heart. I'm connected to you now... in a way I had all but given up on feeling."

"In my world, if a king does not find his intended within the first hundred years of his reign, he must either accept a bride chosen for him by his people, or step down, allowing another ruler to take his place."

Leanna's eyes widened and she repeated the one word that had stuck in her mind from everything he'd said, "Bride? Uhm... Shouldn't that be someone who hasn't already been married and had children?" She stumbled over her words and backed away from him a little. "I mean, I'm used goods. I'm also mortal. Doesn't that make us incompatible?" She began listing the reasons, counting down on her fingers all the while shaking her head.

Vlameir took her hands and squeezed them in his own. "Calm," he breathed. "Be calm." After she had taken a few deep breaths, he continued in a soft voice. "I am not asking you to agree to anything yet. I have time. Time for you to grow to know me, as well as my world. And as for your concerns, your mortal life would end should you chose to stay here. The rate you age has already slowed considerably by our connection. But please rest assured, I would never simply assume you would be ready for this yet." He offered her a beautiful smile that made her heart sputter. "We have time."

Contemplating his words, she looked over her shoulder at Torlek, who was looking in a different direction all together, as if striving *not* to eavesdrop, then back to the Elf who had just as much as announced his plans to court her. "What if I don't ever feel as you do? What if all I feel is friendship? Or if I'm unwilling to uproot my entire world and move here? I've already been married to the person I saw as the love of my life. I lost him." She shivered with a sad expression coming over her features. "If I fell in love with you, there would be the risk of that happening again. There's always the risk. I am not sure I ever want to feel that kind of pain again."

Vlameir moved to her side, once again closing the gap between them. Even now, he felt the bonds between them strengthening. He knew she would come to love him. He felt it in his soul. But he also knew her pain demanded he take time. To allow her that, he said in a low voice, "If you never come to love me, I will accept it. I can be only your friend if that is all you can see me as. Although you would always know I felt much more."

Before he could say more, Torlek cleared his throat. "Can we disperse with all the heartfelt riffraff? I would very much like to see her reactions to the castle, and you still must introduce her to the Court." As the Dragon spoke, he spread his wings and allowed himself to shrink, keeping his form, but becoming the same size as they were.

Leanna stared in baffled fascination as the Dragon continued to change before her eyes. The wings shrank away completely; his head's shape began to change as well. Before she could even blink twice, his entire visage had changed from Dragon to human. Instead, a man with long shiny black hair stood before her, dressed in what appeared to be leather and silk robes. In fact, he looked very much human. The only telltale sign that he was not, was the almost teal hue of his skin and the bright purple eyes that took her in with amusement as she gawked.

He looked from her, down to himself and back again with a slight shrug. "I prefer my Dragon or even my cat form, but the king," he looked pointedly at Vlameir, "Prefers I look this way in his Court."

Vlameir turned to glare at Torlek, whose own gaze was sending daggers in his direction answering, "Only because you're rather clumsy with those wings inside the castle." He knew the biggest reason his friend was baiting him was because of how fast he had revealed his inner desires to Leanna.

He felt a little spark of jealousy at the way she was staring and couldn't stop himself from adding, "Honestly, your inclination to jump up on things with that cat tail of yours isn't much better." He didn't miss the sarcastic lift of Torlek's eyebrow at his words but ignored him all the same as he turned back to Leanna.

He remembered full well how his friend had cautioned him against moving too fast with her. He simply had not been able to help himself. He had felt if she knew how swiftly he was losing his heart, perhaps it would influence her to throw her own caution to the wind.

With a sharp nod of his head, he bowed before Leanna. "Forgive me. I got carried away by having you here. Please, allow me to show you around. I am hoping you feel as I do about my home."

Still fighting her frazzled nerves at his confessions, she forced herself to smile. Pushing her concerns away, she took his offered hand and let him lead her to the tower door. She resigned herself to forget what had just transpired for now and focus on the task at hand; become more familiar with his world and find the spot where she wanted to draw him. As he led her down the stairs, with Torlek trailing them, she wondered if perhaps the Dragon would pose for the pictures as well.

Five

Vlameir led Leanna down to the room below the tower they had landed on. It was a sitting room, of sorts, although no longer used much. It, as well as the connecting bed chamber had belonged to his sister. At the thought of her, Vlameir found himself smiling. The story of his sister could very well have been a tragic one, if he had not been a different man from his father. She had been over a decade older than he when she had left their lands. It had been well before he had even entered adolescence, but he still thought of her fondly.

Hanna had chosen a path frowned on by their family. Vlameir did not judge her, but there had been many in their world who had. His people were the Light Elves. They followed the path of Light. The Fae she had fallen in love with was Dark. While there were many of those who chose a much darker, more sinister path, most of them were not evil by any means, but because of their skin, they were unable to spend extended amounts of time in the daylight.

To become one of them meant to live beneath the ground, coming out only later in the evening and during the dark of night. They also favored the drinking of blood of those who were in daylight as a way of gaining the vitamins they lacked by not spending time in the sun.

It was they who had given first given mortals the inspiration for their stories of vampires, although the amount of blood they took from their donors was no more than a vial at a time. One vial was enough to sustain one of them for as much as a month and was *not* their only source of sustenance.

His sister had fallen in love with a prince of the Dark Fae. They were much like Elves, but where the only difference between Elves and mortals were their longevity and pointed ears, the Dark elves of the Fae also had fangs, as well as wings, and could control their size. They could be as small as a lightning bug, or as big as the Elves were.

Vlameir remembered the night she had professed her love for Roerik, the Fae prince. Their father had been furious. He had demanded she cut all ties with her love and marry the man they had chosen for her at birth. She had refused, and with a final, tearful kiss to Vlameir's forehead, bid him farewell, and left.

It had been their way during the time of his father's reign. The men of their world were free to choose their mates. But the women, especially those of royal birth, were not free to choose their own paths. It was always chosen for them. It was a rule Vlameir had always believed to be unfair. But he had bit his tongue and waited. He could not sway his father from his ways. He knew he would have to wait to enforce the needed changes for his people to progress. And it had been a successful decision. His people had flourished from it.

When the day had come for his rule, it had been the first law he changed. Many of the Elders as well as his father, were mortified, but he had stuck to his instincts and insisted the women of their Courts had the same strength of mind and heart as their male counterparts. He also had gotten in touch with his sister and made sure she knew of the changes he had made to the laws as well as the fact she and her Dark Fae family were welcome in his Court anytime.

They had accepted his invitation and had come to Court for a time. But because of Roerik's inborn aversion to sunlight, they were unable to stay in the towers. He could take indirect sunlight for small amounts of time, but too much could prove painful.

Instead, Vlameir had commissioned a portion of the unused dungeons to be renovated, so their chambers when they came to visit were now found below the ground level. It had not been a hard thing to do. Criminals had not been held in the dungeons since long before his own father had been born.

As they passed through the bed chambers, Vlameir paused, turning to Leanna, "While you are here, please, feel free to use these rooms as your own. If you would like to stay while you are working on the portrait, you may sleep here."

She looked at him with wide eyes, before looking around the room in awe. "I-I don't know what to say. I mean, I wasn't expecting to be staying. I d-didn't pack any clothes."

Nervously she bit her lip and Vlameir stared for a moment before recovering himself. In attempt to make light of the subject, he asked softly, "Leanna, is your only concern for staying a few days here the lack of clothes?"

She opened her mouth to say something about being missed; but stopped and stood in silence as a hard truth hit her, pulling tears to the surface. No one would miss her. She had moved to a place where she didn't really know anyone. Her parents had left on a cruise overseas and would be gone for over a month.

There wasn't even anyone at home. No son, needing help with homework. No husband waiting for a homecooked meal. At the unbidden thoughts, she found herself fighting for air. Gasping, she clutched her chest and fought to regain control of her breathing and her heart.

Alarmed, both Vlameir and Torlek rushed to her. Vlameir, being closer, swept her up into his arms and moved swiftly to the bed by the far wall. The Dragon was not far behind, pulling back covers and fluffing pillows to try to see to her comfort.

The Elf King was the first to speak. "I am sorry, Leanna. I did not mean to upset you. I was only trying to see what we could do to encourage you to stay for a while."

No sooner had he spoken, than she was shaking her head. "It isn't your fault. I'm so silly. I had never considered..." she paused for a moment, as if searching for the right words.

When she looked back into his eyes, a sad expression had crept into hers. "I don't know why it's never occurred to me before now. But I only realized for the first time since Danny's death; there is no one waiting. No one is expecting me home for any reason. I am suddenly realizing I'm actually almost completely alone. I'm one of those people who really has no one." Saying it out loud felt like driving an invisible knife into her gut. "I have a friend who actually lives close by, but we didn't have any plans to get together for a while, yet.

"My parents are still alive. But they are traveling abroad and the only communications I'm getting from them right now are postcards." She smiled sadly. "The latest one was from Italy.

"I have other friends. But after Max, and then Daniel died, they all acted like they were walking through shattered glass barefoot when trying to talk to me... *If they try to talk to me.*" She chuckled mirthlessly, "I've become a pariah, and I didn't even realize it. Not until just now. I guess I can stay for a night or two. It isn't as if anyone will be looking for me."

Vlameir smiled at her gently. "I'll send for the seamstress. I'm certain she'll have some dresses which will fit you in her shop."

Leanna started to sit up, "I don't want to be any trouble."

Vlameir stayed her with his hand on her shoulder. "My precious little mortal. Will you please stop thinking you are a hinderance?" He leaned closer to her, bringing his eyes level to hers. "Understand me. I want you here. Even if I have to have the seamstress make you new dresses from scratch, I will not view it as any trouble. Not at all."

Leanna felt the color rise in her cheeks and looked away from him. "Thank you," she said softly. She felt his hand cup her cheek and couldn't stop herself from looking back at him. When she did, she found herself staring at him. *He's so beautiful,* she thought inwardly before catching herself and awkwardly leaning back against the pillow. What the hell was wrong with her?

She had never been the type to fawn over a man. But she was totally enamored with him. Everything about Vlameir called to her. She was afraid it was making her stupid. But more than that; she expected that whatever they were both experiencing wouldn't last. It was only an infatuation. It would end soon and then where would she be? Alone again.

Torlek spoke up then. "Why not rest for a while? Vlameir can summon the seamstress and when you awaken, she'll get you all fixed up and ready to be presented at Court."

Leanna looked between the two before nodding. "If it would be okay, I wouldn't mind a little nap. I meant to take

44

one earlier today, but time kind of got past me and I didn't get around to it." Truth was, as excited as she was at the prospect of taking in this new world that had just opened up to her, she was also strangely exhausted. She didn't really understand why, but she was. It made her feel a little disappointed after how excited she had been earlier in the day.

Vlameir looked very closely at her, an expression of concern evident on his face, before nodding. "Very well. I will make the arrangements and give you some time to rest." He watched as she nodded her thanks and leaned back against the pillows, closing her eyes.

She kept them closed as the two exited the room, leaving her alone in the peacefully quiet room. When she heard the door close, her eyes opened then, and she looked around the chamber. The bed she lay in was soft and huge. Pink and purple satins adorned it, with sheer lace curtains gathered at all four corners, falling in cascades from the ceiling.

The room was a neutral cream color, but the lavender and rose colors blended in all around, accented from the chairs and echoed by flashes of gold and wrought iron tables and a blonde wood armoire in the corner. Wall sconces hung in various places along the walls, to be used when the light from the sun shining in from the balcony began to fade.

The room was fit for a princess. The kind of place someone would expect for a special member of royalty. And why wouldn't it be? It was like something out of a fairytale.

As soon as the thought came, she giggled. Well, of course it was something out of a fairytale. She was in the Fae Realm. What else did she expect?

With a smile on her lips, she nestled down into the comfort of the beautiful bed, in the beautiful room, and gave up all her cares for the moment as she resigned herself to sleep.

She never saw the eyes watching her. She completely missed the smile that came to the lips of her watcher. He considered speaking to her before she fell asleep; but thought better of it. She was here now. There was time for talking to her later. She looked as if she needed a good rest. He wondered how often she had not slept through the night.

He shrugged it off. It did not matter anymore. All that mattered was she was here now. He knew eventually she would decide to stay. There would be plenty of time. After all, time did not exist in the same way here.

Six

When Leanna awoke, it was to find a seamstress who introduced herself as Mardina and an elderly hairdresser who simply nodded her greeting at her door. Both ladies greeted her in a way she imagined royalty was addressed. She had tried to insist the ladies call her by her first name, without the Lady part in front of it, but both women had completely refused.

"I would never address you in such a way. It isn't seemly." Mardina insisted in a kind but firm voice. "At least, not until we know each other a little better." She smiled and winked, her bright green eyes sparkling with a friendly intensity. She was tall and slender, with strawberry blond hair that even with it pulled back in a ponytail, fell in soft ringlets to her hips. "Now, let's get you bathed and dressed so you can be presented to your people."

Leanna looked at the lady oddly. Surely the woman did not want to tend to her bath, the way one would help a child. "Uhm… I'm sorry. If you could show me where I need to go to bathe, I can do it on my own. You don't have to physically help me," she whispered, knowing full well her cheeks were red as turnips.

The maid looked at her a moment, before laughing whole heartedly. "Oh, good heaven's no. I didn't mean to imply I would bathe you as a child. I only mean to show you where it all is and how it works. Then, I will tend and make sure your clothes are ready and help you into them if you have need."

Turning, Mardina led the way to a section of the room which Leanna had not really noticed yet. It was by the toilet room, but she had not seen it. When Mardina pressed a hand to a certain spot on the wall, a panel slid away, revealing a beautiful bathing chamber, filled with steaming water, resembling a huge hot tub, made to look like a garden oasis. Along the far wall, water flowed like a waterfall, down and into the spa.

Mardina knelt beside the tub and picked up one of the beautiful flowers surrounding the tub. Turning to Leanna, she explained. "They look like flowers, but in truth, all you need do, is pull the petals away and the inside is scented soaps. The White ones are for your hair. They have both washing and conditioning properties. The pink and burgundy ones are for your body. The pink is simply a body soap. The burgundy has exfoliating agents.

"When you get out, these purple flowers, which are smaller, are lotions. They will moisturize your skin." She smiled, pointing to the huge robe that hung by the doorway. "When you are done, put that on and I will stand ready to assist you with your clothes."

When Mardina turned and left the room, Leanna took it all in with a look of wonder on her face. This had to be the most amazing bathroom she had ever seen in her life. Soaps that looked and smelled like actual flowers? It was amazing.

With a gleeful smile, she decided not to waste any time. Stripping out of her gown, she stepped into the bath. The water was so perfect. Hot enough to soak all the stress away, but not so hot as to burn her skin. The water was easily waist deep.

For a moment, she allowed herself to lie back and relax in the water. It felt amazing. Then, knowing she only had so much time before the women might think she had drowned, she moved to the side where the waterfall was and picked the white flower. Pulling the petals back, she inhaled the scent and smiled at the pleasant, but not overwhelming fragrance.

Pulling the small center from the flower, she marveled at how it just seemed to soften and become spreadable. Leaning back into the waterfall, she let the water wet her hair. Then stepping out a bit, she began lathering her hair, then rinsed it before doing the same with the pink bloom for her body.

When she got out of the tub, she dried off and applied a decent amount of lotion to her body before donning the robe and going back into the chambers where the women eagerly waited to help her dress.

Leanna allowed the woman to pull her to the wardrobe, which had floated into the room behind her when she entered. She had argued for a time as the lady took measurements, but finally gave up when she realized her protests were falling on deaf ears. She wasn't sure she had understood the reference to *her people*. But she knew better than to attempt to argue further with this lady.

The seamstress opened the wardrobe with a happy flourish. It had a wide array of dresses, in a variety of colors, and a few different styles. Every dress was long and reminded her of the kind of clothes worn back in medieval times, except for maybe being of a much better quality than she would have thought was possible in the mortal realm.

The first dress Mardina pulled out was a beautiful, free-flowing burgundy and lavender silk gown with sleeves that were as long as the dress but slit up the side all the way above the elbow. The collar was round cut and hung low enough to give a slight tease of a woman's cleavage, but not so much as to betray her modesty.

When Leanna moved to admire it, the seamstress smiled, holding the dress up and said, "This one will complement your complexion perfectly. I think it will please the king."

Without any argument, Leanna allowed the seamstress to help her get into the dress. Then the older lady stepped forward. "And now, if it pleases my Lady, I will work some magic on your hair." Her smile was so kind, Leanna found herself returning it and nodding her agreement. She handed her a little vial and requested softly, "Drink this, please? It will cleanse and refresh you."

Following the woman's instructions, she looked at the vial, noticing it seemed to be nothing more than water. It had no memorable or bad taste and went down smoothly. She soon found herself sitting in front of a vanity she had not even realized was there before. It was beautiful, with intricate artwork along the border of the mirror that portrayed Dragonflies and Faeries.

As she sat there, seated before it, she took the time to appreciate its beauty while Mardina bustled around, transferring dress after dress, and a few really beautiful pant suits that reminded her of belly dancing outfits, with jeweled tunic-style tops, instead of the unsuitable bra-like tops she would have been too modest to wear. Leanna watched in awe as the clothes were moved from the floating wardrobe, into the one sitting against the wall by the bed.

When Leanna noticed the number of clothes going into the wardrobe, she stammered, "Oh, I shouldn't need that many. I'm only staying a night or two. I should be done with the original sketches by then, then I'll do most of the work at home."

Mardina turned and tilted her head to the side for a moment, contemplating her words before saying, "Well, I am sure you will probably visit more often, now you've come. These will simply be ready and waiting for you during those visits."

It was then the hairdresser announced she was finished. When Leanna turned to look at herself in the mirror, she stared. Her hair had been left down, flowing in soft ringlets down her back, except for thin braids pulled up on the sides to frame her face. Silken cords, in matching shades to the dress, had been woven into the braids completing the ensemble and making the reflection in the mirror, one that almost made her think she was looking at someone else.

The lady in the mirror was beautiful. She was elegant and poised. Not anything like what Leanna thought herself to be. She had always considered herself pretty, but not anything spectacular. This woman she was staring at looked like royalty. Her heart fluttered and tears came to her eyes. It was more than her hair. Her skin was suddenly so perfect. She was baffled.

Her skin had always been good. She didn't have too much trouble with acne or wrinkles, but there had been a few blemishes. And she'd had a small scar on her forehead where she'd had an accident on her bike as a kid. And another, on her chin, where she had tripped going into school as a teenager and hit it on the pavement.

Both scars, as well as the blemishes, were gone. She stared, speechless. She looked *years* younger; and by years, she wasn't thinking a few years. She was thinking a decade. She was thirty-five years old. In her opinion, she didn't look bad, by any measure. But she had the hint of crows' feet starting just a tad around her eyes. After the past few years, could anyone not understand why? Now, her skin was smooth and flawless. She was reminded of how she had looked when she was nineteen. What was in that drink? And why did she suddenly feel like this was actually a bad thing?

Vlameir sat on the throne which had belonged to his father before him. He rarely sat in it himself, because he had never cared for sitting idle as his parents had once done. When he had inherited the crown, it had not been because of any untimely death of either of them, but instead, as Elves were blessed with eternally long lives, they had chosen when they felt it was time for their son to ascend to the throne, thus stepping down and surrendering it to him. He had been a grown man, serving in his father's military as a captain when the decision was made.

It was earlier than was expected. At the time, he was still a young man by Elven standards; No more than sixty cycles. He had always imagined his parents would wait to bequeath the crown to him until he had seen well over a hundred.

He vividly remembered the day he was crowned, happy because he always wanted to work to implement changes the kingdom needed—equal rights for the women of his Realm, as well as the other creatures of Fae.

It was also sad. He almost mourned his parent's choice. It meant he would not be reunited with them for a hundred years, or until he found his mate; whichever came first. It had been a day of both celebration and melancholy. He looked back through the memories with a sad pain in his heart.

There was still so far to go, but so much in his seventy years ruling. Now, knowing he had finally found his mate, there was so much more they could do together once she accepted her place at his side. He also felt an edge of excitement at the prospect of a reunion with his parents, He was both excited and worried about their reactions to the changes he had made. More than that, he was enthusiastic to see how well they would receive Leanna.

It was that moment when his attention was drawn to his friend. Torlek was pacing the floor, with a somewhat dismal look on his face. Amused, he simply watched him for a few moments before asking, "Is there a reason why you are working your hardest to wear a crater in the marble, my friend?"

Torlek stopped moving and turned to face Vlameir with a brooding expression. "You aren't even going to give her a choice, are you?" his question was blunt. But honestly, knowing him the way he did, the Elf expected no less.

"Her choice will be me." He answered in a soft low voice. "Already, I feel the way her soul is reaching for mine. She needs only a little time to realize it. By the time she knows her leaving indefinitely has been made impossible, she will no longer care."

The Dragon sputtered and gawked at Vlameir. "You *already* gave it to her?" He growled, turning to pace once more. "I can't believe you! *What are you thinking?* She is not one of your subjects! She is *Human!* She will not see what you have done the same way as your own kind does.

"She is your mate. I give you that. But she comes from a world where her will is her own and she must be allowed to make up her own mind." He shook his head and turned back to face his friend again. "I only hope when she realizes what you've done, there is room in her heart to forgive you. If not, then, my friend, as the humans would say; It is really going to *suck* to be you."

Vlameir rose from his throne swiftly and opened his mouth to reprimand his friend for his show of disrespect, but at that moment, the doors to the hall were opened and Leanna was ushered in.

As Leanna followed the man who reminded her of a butler into the parlor, she took a deep breath. She felt so out of place and insecure. Even after staring at her reflection for what felt like well over an hour, she knew any moment, she would wake up and find she had dreamt it all. She stopped awkwardly in the entryway, trembling ever so slightly without knowing exactly why.

Both men were staring at her with open admiration. She sensed the blush rise on her cheeks and bit her lip bashfully as the gentleman who had brought her down announced her arrival.

She looked first at Torlek, who offered her a small smile. When her gaze moved in Vlameir's direction, it was to see him striding to her with an almost desperate hunger evident in his eyes. Somewhat intimidated, she started to take a step back, but forced herself to stop. She had nothing to fear from him. He had promised this to her, and she believed him. He was an honest man. He had given his word. She could trust him.

Yet, even as she reminded herself of his honest vow, she could not quite ignore the soft voice in the back of her mind, whispering, *Can you really? Are you sure?* For some reason, she had an odd feeling her life was no longer her own.

No sooner had the thought come to her mind, than she brushed it aside, instead, looking deep into the Elf King's eyes. Such a light, translucent blue. They reminded her of the Glaciers she had seen once on the Discovery channel. She always wanted to visit such a place, but there had never been time. Being a wife and mother came first. Then, after the loss of both, she went through coming to terms with no longer being either.

Vlameir reached out to take her into his arms. She went willingly as the warmth of his touch went through her, and she felt as if that warmth was beginning to fill the gap left by the loss of those she held most dear. Even as she told herself this was moving too fast and she should push him away, she instead found herself leaning into his embrace.

It had been so long. So much had happened in the last several years, she all but forgot she was a woman. She had forgotten how it felt to be held this way. Her heart sped up when his voice spoke softly in the shell of her ear. "My beautiful Leanna. You're such a vision. I suspect these clothes are better suited to your form than those of your world."

At his words, she chuckled, "These clothes would be better suited to *anyone,* your Highness. They're amazing. Comfortable, as well as beautiful." As she spoke, she took a step back, so their eyes again met. "I still feel like I'm in the midst of some fictional, fantastic dream."

Vlameir stood silent before her, a solemn look on his face as he reached out a hand. "Come with me, Leanna. Let me show you my world. Let me show you exactly how real it all is." He paused before adding in a softer tone, "Let me show you how easily you could become a part of it."

His words flowed over her in such a way she felt her heart flutter, she opened her mouth to respond, but stopped short when Torlek spoke up, "Shall I meet the two of you out front? With my wings?"

A little startled at his tone, Leanna turned her head toward him, meaning to ask if he was upset over something, but was cut short when Vlameir dismissed him.

"No, old friend. You may take your leave for now. I wish to give her a closer, more intimate view of our home." Then, without giving the Dragon a chance to even sputter, he tightened his grip on Leanna's hand, and led her from the room, swiftly leaving Torlek behind.

Seven

Vlameir took pleasure in guiding Leanna through the castle, watching her reactions. Every bit of his home fascinated her, and he lost track of all the questions as she marveled at everything from the beauty and precision of the architecture to the artwork and furniture. He noted the eye she had for the older pieces. Her appreciation for the artwork and carpentry of his ancestors touched him in a way he had not expected.

He truly felt as if the only reason he had not found a mate yet, was because he found most of the Elven women of Fae had lost the appreciation of their ancestry. Indeed, he reasoned with himself in that moment, perhaps he lost appreciation to a degree himself. Her admiration renewed his.

He led her through the corridors and into each of the main rooms on the ground level of the castle. In several places, she was greeted by other Elves and Fae. Some were workers, some were royalty; all were enchanted by her easy grace and friendly smile. Every moment that passed more than solidified his belief he had made the right decision. She would stay. She would be his queen. In time, she would know and accept this as her home. She would be happy here. He would make sure of it.

A nagging feeling of guilt hit him as he watched the innocent excitement flit across her face when he led her into the Ballroom. He knew he was deceiving her. Right now, she had no idea she was trapped here. He felt underhanded and dishonest, but he needed her. So did his people. In time, she would understand. He hoped, in time, she would love this world enough, she wouldn't want to leave.

He smiled as she moved away from him and into the center of the expansive room, twirling happily in the middle of the dance floor. "This is beautiful. What it must be like to dance here!" Blushing, she sent a small smile his way as she seemed to remember herself. "I'm sorry."

Vlameir strode toward her with a grin. "Don't apologize. This room is meant for dancing." He didn't even pause before sweeping her into his arms and his eyes held hers captive as in a soft, yet firm voice, he commanded, *"Music."* All at once, the soft, beguiling tones of some invisible orchestra began to fill the room. Slowly, he led her into a waltz, all the while, giving her his complete attention.

The feel of her in his arms made Vlameir long to tell her the truth. Guilt tried to rear its ugly head, but he pushed it away again, instead focusing on the light in her eyes and the smile on her lips. He gave himself over to the moment and pushed all other concerns aside. He would deal with the hurt feelings and distrust later. For now, all that was important was the fact she was here. She was his.

They danced the entire song and when it ended, Leanna pulled away, short of breath. "I haven't danced like that since Max and I got married." She laughed breathlessly, "thank you. I forgot how wonderful it could be."

Vlameir inclined his head. "That is too long for you to not dance. You should dance much more often. I will endeavor to make it so."

Leanna laughed louder then. "Oh, well, but it isn't like I get much opportunity to do ballroom dancing." She shrugged, "I don't even go out these days. I am pretty much a hermit and I'm okay with that."

He reached out and took her hand. Softly, he began to trace its contours, slowly, as if memorizing it. When he spoke again, it was in a sad voice. "You are so much more than a hermit, my dear. I wish you could see in yourself what I see when I look at you." He smiled when she simply stared at him. "Indeed, I wish you could know what I saw the very first time I beheld you. Perhaps, in time I shall be able to make you understand."

Leanna looked away at his words. He watched her closely, willing her to return his gaze. Instead, she bowed her head, closing her eyes. "I understand your words, Vlameir. I also understand your body language. Please believe me; I am flattered. But I can't stop the feeling I am being unfaithful to the man I married."

As soon as she spoke the words, she opened her eyes, and his breath caught at the tears he found glistening in their depths. "I am attracted to you too. I mean I'd be a fool not to be. You're beautiful."

She smiled then, but it was sad. "I married my high school sweetheart. I thought I'd grow old with him. I know he's gone. I know he wouldn't want me to deny myself the chance to feel love again."

She took a deep breath and wiped the tears from her cheek. "But I cannot simply rush this. I'm not ready for it yet, even though you are everything any woman in her right mind would want." When she stepped away from him, he felt a deep pain lance in his heart. "I'm sorry, but I'm not sure I will ever be open to love again."

Vlameir could feel the magical moment they'd just shared slipping through his fingers. He wanted to demand she let go of her husband's ghost and give herself over to this new, special thing that was trying to grow between them. Yet, even as the desires of his mind wanted to demand this of her, his heart knew the only way he could win her over would be to give her the time she asked for.

With a slight nod, he offered simply. "Dinner will be served in the main dining room. Do you remember where I showed you?" At her nod, he continued. "Your maidservant will let you know when it is time. I shall introduce you to the officers of the Court then."

He wanted her to shrug his dismissal aside and tell him to show her more. Instead, she thanked him, and left his side as fast as her feet would carry her. The ache in his heart grew. She was working under the assumption that she was going back to her home after she painted him. How could he tell her now that she would never see that home again? Once she knew this truth, how would she ever believe that he had no intention of rushing her?

Even as he entertained the thoughts, he chided himself. She would not believe it because neither did he. A gnawing sensation in his gut reminded him of his cruel deception, even as his mind sought to justify his reasoning. He honestly had not thought his decisions through past the point of recognizing her as the heart his soul was meant to find. Beyond that, he had considered nothing.

He sat in the corner of her room watching her as she paced the length of it. He wanted desperately to reach out to her, but he doubted she was ready. He knew she missed him. He had known the Elf King would find her and recognize her soul as meant for his. Those were bits of knowledge which had come to him when his soul had left his body behind. Being a child had given him certain insight into such things—like what she needed to find to move on and find happiness again.

From there, he had started searching. When he had found the entry into the Fae Realm, he knew he had to do his best to lead his mother here. It was where she belonged. It had been difficult to draw her here. But once she had seen the cottage and the land surrounding it, she had fallen in love.

He remembered feeling sure she would. She was an artist. Nature and beautiful architecture had always appealed to her. The property had both. Even the ruins of the manor house were intriguing to look at.

He hoped the king had not messed everything up by taking his mother's choices away. He shared the Dragon's concern that she would feel betrayed when she discovered she could not leave. He even wondered if perhaps he should reveal himself to the king and discuss with him how to break the news to her.

He pondered the thought for a few moments before deciding against it. No, not yet. He would not be helping the situation by revealing himself to anyone. She had to find herself wanting to stay here on her own. She needed to find love with the king on her own. He could not force anything.

At this point, he worried that if he did show himself, she might accept staying here, but not for the reason of loving the king. Instead, it could very well be because of her ability to see her son.

Daniel admitted to himself, he wanted to be seen by her. But she wasn't ready. First, she would have to be back to a place where she was happy in her life without him. Because even though he could visit this place reasonably often, his spirit could not always stay here. There was so much for free souls to do. Staying in one place was not part of the Grand Design.

He watched as she moved to her sketchbook. A small smile found its way to his lips. He had been worried after he died, she would never pick her art back up. That would have been a shame because she was so talented. To see her with her art pencils and sketchbook eased his mind. Maybe it wouldn't be too bad once she found she had to stay here. Perhaps she would even be relieved. It would make for a simpler, happier life, he thought.

Eight

Leanna followed the same butler down a second time that day. When he had knocked at her door, she had tried to tell him he did not have to show her the way again. She was sure she could find it.

At her words, he had offered her a small smile, answering, "Then perhaps you will let me accompany you, simply for something to do?" he chuckled. "It isn't very often we have new company. Everyone else around here knows the lower parts of the castle very well. It makes my job a little obsolete when there is no one who needs me."

His charming demeanor, along with his request, made Leanna smile as she accepted his offer. She had not even considered the fact he might feel he wasn't fulfilling an obligation if she refused him. "All right, kind Sir. I will let you show me the way on one condition." When his eyebrows rose in silent question, she supplied, "I need to know your name. I can't very well go around, referring to you as the butler boy, now can I?"

He laughed then, gracing her with a charming smile. "Drock, my dear lady. My name is Drock. But I am one of the king's guards. But I suppose you could think of me as a butler; for lack of a better word, so I would answer to that title if you so choose to call me by it." He cleared his throat," Although I have not been a boy in nigh on four hundred years.

Shaking her head, Leanna answered, "I like Drock better. It helps to keep me from feeling like such an outsider." She felt a moment of melancholy coming over her and made a noticeable effort to push it aside.

Drock noticed it and offered her his hand. "You are not an outsider here, my Lady. Indeed, I am sure the people of Fae will be all too happy to think of you as one of their own. The kingdom has been needing you."

Leanna smiled at his words. She found herself truly wishing it were true. To finally feel as if she really belonged somewhere and not be alone would have been nice. However, she doubted it could really be possible. As nice as Drock's words were, she didn't belong here. She was mortal. Like it or not, that made her stick out like a sore thumb. She didn't voice her thoughts as she imagined he would strive to argue, if only for the sake of her feelings.

As he led her down, she admired the beautiful paintings of different scenery and a few portraits. At the top of the last landing, she stopped and stared. This portrait was a woman who had an almost ethereal beauty about her. Her skin was as close to alabaster as it could be, with just a hint of pink coloring her cheeks, making her seem a little more real. Her eyes were a slate gray, with highlights of amber streaking through them.

The artistry of the painter who had done this portrait was amazing. Leanna could almost see the woman's personality shining through. If the subject had picked that moment to move, she would not have been surprised. "Who is this?" she asked softly.

Drock, who had already started down the stairs, stopped and turned to look at the portrait. His face instantly softened. "That is King Vlameir's mother; Queen Mother, Jaylyn."

Leanna noted the way his voice softened and quirked an eyebrow in his direction. "By the sound of your voice, I assume she must be a very good person." She queried, "Why do you call her Queen Mother?"

Retracing his steps, he stared at the portrait with a smile. "Because, as her son has assumed the throne, she is no longer Queen, per se. But she is still his mother, so it is a term of respect." He turned to face Leanna. "And you are correct. She is a wonderful person, with an amazing heart. One day soon, you'll meet her. Then, you'll see firsthand how kind and beautiful she really is."

She smiled at his word, but she honestly doubted she'd still be here when his parents came back. From what he had told her, they had gone on an extended sabbatical when he had assumed the throne. Unless they were suddenly coming back, she didn't expect they'd return in a day or two.

Her sketches would be done by then and she'd be returning home to work with her paints to build his portrait.

A strange feeling hit her at that moment. Suddenly, she wondered if she'd ever go home. No sooner had the thought come, than she brushed it aside. That was ridiculous. She was a guest here, not a prisoner. Vlameir only wanted her to see his home. Once he showed her around, she could judge better where the best place for his portrait to be set was, and she could get to work. In a few days, she'd be back home in her little cottage... Alone... with all her memories.

A moment of dread hit her. She had nothing there besides a new house and a million memories from a life she no longer had. In the blink of an eye, she had lost everything she had believed to be the meaning of her existence. Her husband, her son, both were lost to her now. If they could see her and the level of her pain, they would encourage her to move on and be happy. So, why couldn't she? It was a question she had yet to find the answer to.

Pushing the sadness that loomed over her away, she turned her attention back to Drock and couldn't help but notice the sympathy in his eyes. Releasing a pent-up breath, she spoke softly, "If I am lucky enough to meet the Queen Mother, I will consider it an honor."

His face lit up at her words and he bowed slightly before turning to finish leading her down the stairs, where Vlameir was waiting, watching her. As her eyes met his, a deep longing hit her heart. A part of her wanted him to demand she stay. Would that be so wrong? It would be a fuller existence than going back to her lonely little life, in her lonely little cottage.

Taking his offered hand, she forced herself to push the sadness away. For now, at least, she could pretend the fairytale was reality, and the sadness in her life was only the dream. Couldn't she? What could it hurt?

When they entered the formal dining room, the first thing Leanna noticed were the tiny lights, hovering all over the room. They flickered like candlelight but were not attached to any candles. They reminded her of lightning bugs, except they didn't move around.

As Vlameir led her toward the table, the people seated around it rose. She smiled warmly to the ones who made eye contact. She had been afraid they would not be very friendly, but their smiles seemed genuine. When he pulled back the seat closest to his, she tilted her head a little before taking it.

The first person she saw besides Vlameir, was a beautiful, smiling lady with long silvery-blonde hair and lilac eyes that were just a shade lighter than her dress. Leanna couldn't help but return her smile.

Vlameir spoke at that moment, introducing her to the others in the room. "Ladies and gentlemen allow me to introduce Leanna, from the mortal realm. She shall be staying with us for a time. Please make her feel welcome as I would like her to think of our home as her home."

Almost immediately after his introduction, the beautiful Elf across the table leaned forward a bit and spoke happily. "My name is Elise. I am so happy you've come. I want to hear all about your world."

No sooner had she spoken, than the male sitting beside her shook his head and chuckled. "Never mind her. Elise, she is not your new toy." He rolled his eyes, then smiled at Leanna. "My name is Norwicke. Elise is my younger sister, and she can sometimes be a little overwhelming in her excitement."

Leanna returned their smiles and shrugged. "Oh, I don't know. I found her excitement welcoming." She paused, biting her lip. "I wasn't sure I'd be accepted very well here."

Elise gasped, "But why not? Our culture has always had an open acceptance of humans deemed worthy to come and integrate into our world. Cousin Vlameir has always been particularly good at allowing them to come when deemed worthy." Her smile grew, "Although, you are the very first he has ever chosen to bring across himself."

Leanna gaped at that proclamation. For a moment, she was lost for words. Vlameir had never been the one to bring someone over before? Really? But then, why her? What made her so special? Turning to look at him, she stared at the beautiful man before her. He was turned to the side conversing with a server in a lowered voice. He had been honest with her about hoping something more would grow between them. But could she trust that connection to be unbreakable? Her heart wasn't sure it could survive another tragedy like what she had endured already.

The woman sitting beside her who had been silently watching their exchange chose that moment to speak,
reaching out and taking Leanna's hand as she did. "Don't
let the gossip from the twins bother you, my dear. Although
what they say is correct. For Vlameir to have chosen to
bring you across, you must have endured some deep heartache." She smirked. "My nephew is nothing if not astute in
his judgement. It is how he strives to keep those who live
here safe."

She leaned a little closer and Leanna felt a slight push
in her mind, making her eyes widen as all her memories of
her life came rising to the surface. Her high school romance
with Max. The day they said I do. The birth of their son, and
then the pain of losing them both were pulled to the forefront of her memory as if she had no control.

Gasping harshly, she tried to pull her hand away as the
tears threatened to break free from behind her lashes, but
when her focus came back to the woman holding her hand,
it was to see tears reflected back at her from the woman's
eyes; Eyes that widened for an instant, as if startled.

"You're... But you... How?" She seemed to be somewhat shocked herself as she stared into Leanna's eyes.

But then the moment was gone as the older lady
reached out and touched Leanna's cheek even as she
kissed her palm. "Forgive me. My brave, brave girl. You are
more than worthy to be here. In fact, I am quite certain, you
belong here." She shook her head and moved to wipe the
tears from her own cheeks. "I should never have doubted
his heart. I am Adrianna; his mother's sister, and I tend to
be a little over-protective."

Her gaze slid from Leanna then and her face became
even more solemn. "I apologize, Vlameir. You needn't glare
so outrageously at me."

Leanna turned to see Vlameir shaking his head in what
she could only think of as disbelief. She could well read
the fury in his eyes as he spoke. "Aunt Adrianna, how dare
you? I have promised her she is in a judgement free zone.
So, at the first opportunity, you do your best to make me
a liar?"

Adrianna straightened in her chair and pulled her
shoulders back, looking him dead in the eye. "I was not
striving to make you a liar, Nephew. I was merely search-

ing to see what it was about her that has won you over so completely."

She glanced back at Leanna, speaking in a softer voice. "I am sorry, my dear. I see now how my actions were a complete intrusion and I beg your forgiveness. I have no explanation for my actions besides the simple fact that Vlameir has not ever even considered entering a soul bond before. Now, he has as much as declared that the bond between the two of you grows without even the words for it being spoken." She gestured between Leanna and Vlameir. "That has never happened between our race and a mortal. I was curious. I knew that for him to find himself bonding with a mortal woman, she would have to be something beyond special."

Her smile was sad, but genuine. "The depth of the pain and loss you have endured would kill a normal person's belief in love and magic. But here you are. Your heart still sings with it."

Leanna heard Adrianna's words and felt her heart begin to beat rapidly as they began to sink in. He was soul bonding. With her? But he had told her that if nothing came of it, he would accept it and they could simply remain friends. Even as she tried to assure herself that was still the case, his aunt's words belied that possibility.

Turning to stare at him, she could see it. The truth of what his aunt said was in his eyes. He was already bonding to her. That wasn't even the scariest part. The worst of it was that if she was honest with herself, she would admit that already, the very idea of leaving him—of going back to her tiny little empty cottage was not something she wanted to do. Her heart hurt and she fought back a sob, even as she pushed away from the table and ran for all she was worth from the room.

She ran so desperately, she didn't even hear his voice, crying for her to stop. All she knew was she had to get away from him. She couldn't stay here. If she did, then she would only be inviting more heartache in. She couldn't do that. She couldn't live through it again. To love someone. To have them become her entire world. Only to lose them. It was more than she could bear.

She had to go home. Now. Tonight. This very minute, lest she let herself fall too deep and not be unable to walk away when the time came. She ran blindly, not even really paying attention to where she was going.

Before she knew it, she was at the top of the tower where they had entered the castle earlier that day. She was almost to the tower's edge before she felt his hand close around her arm, pulling her back.

"STOP!" Even as she wanted to slap his hand away and keep running, the authority in his voice pulled her back and made her turn to look at him. Tears streamed down her cheeks and she glared at him in silent anger.

For what seemed an immeasurable amount of time, they simply stood there, looking at each other. She willed herself to calm down and then sank slowly to the ground, knowing he would follow her there. He sat so close to her she could almost lean into him. She wanted to. Her body ached to feel his touch, but still she fought it.

Instead, she asked in a bitter voice, "This bonding your aunt spoke of. It's already happening, isn't it?" at his nod, she stifled a sob. "There's no stopping it, then?" She refused to meet his eyes, even though she could feel his gaze hot on her face. She would not look him in the eye. If she did, she feared she'd already be lost.

But she wasn't expecting his low growl. Her eyes flew open to meet his then, and her heart stuttered at the pained look on his face. "Would it be so terrible? Is your heart so broken over the loss of your husband and son, you cannot see your way clear to let your soul join with mine?" His palm rested gently on her cheek, turning her face so she could not look away. "I do not ask you to forget them. I do not ask you no longer to love them. But is the idea of loving me too so repulsive? Am I horrible to desperately want you to love me?"

Closing her eyes, Leanna shook her head. "No. But you don't understand."

She had no sooner spoken the words than Vlameir answered, "I am trying to. I have even sworn to myself I would give you as many centuries as it takes for you to love me too. But I cannot lose you." His words broke with a desperation she had not heard earlier, and she met his gaze again. "I had all but given up on ever finding you. Don't you understand? I thought love was not meant for me." He half-laughed, half sobbed as he pulled her into his lap.

"Then there you were, running across that damn bridge and it was as if I saw a rainbow for the first time. Everything I had always believed to be out of my reach was suddenly there. At the first sight of you." His lips found her forehead, then moved to kiss each eye. Slowly, his mouth explored her face, kissing away her tears, but stopping when they reached her lips.

Her eyes remained closed as he asked, "Can you find a way to let me in? Can you try to love me?"

Her eyes opened again, and she leaned into his embrace, even as she tried to explain. "I want to let you in. For the first time since Max died, I want to feel you there. But I'm just so scared."

He wrapped his arms around her, trying to offer her comfort and a feeling of security. "What could you possibly be afraid of? I am not an ogre." He tried to lighten the mood a little with his jest and was rewarded when she slapped his chest.

"It's not funny," she answered. "I'm not afraid of you. I'm afraid of opening myself up and loving you, only to lose you too. Don't you understand? I can't go through that again. I don't ever want to feel that again."

Vlameir cradled Leanna in his arms, rocking her gently as if she were a baby. His hand brushed tenderly through her hair as if to sooth her. He seemed for a moment to be searching for the right words to say. At last, he spoke. "Leanna, I am an Elf. While I am not completely Immortal, I do not suffer the same vulnerabilities as mortal men. I won't get sick for many centuries. I can die if I were wounded in battle or such. But it is also unlikely. Even more so since our world is not at war and has not been in a true war since long before your world's Shakespeare died. I cannot promise you there is no risk at all, but I can assure you the chances are much slimmer here."

Leanna sniffled and tried to ignore the moment of feeling like a fool before she pulled back from him and tried to sit up. He helped her silently and waited patiently as she composed herself. When she looked back at him again, she hated how red she knew her eyes had to be from the tears.

Vlameir stayed silent as she worked to compose herself. He hated the pain she was still going through. He would have given anything to erase those tears from her eyes. But he knew it was a moot point. Even in the Realm of Fae, time could not be turned back.

"So, tell me," she said softly, "What would you have me do?" She watched him closely as he mulled over her words.

His answer was spoken in a hushed voice. "I would have you give what is growing between us a chance. I would ask you not to fight it. If you have a moment of fear or concern, share it with me. I do not ask you to ignore your concerns. But I want a chance. Just a chance to show you our love is possible. I want you to see how beautiful it can be. How beautiful it will be."

Leanna watched him for a moment before nodding. "Okay. I will give this a chance. Sliding off his lap, she moved to stand and offered him her hand. "Do you think maybe we could eat in my room tonight? I do not really feel like trying to go back down there after that scene in front of all of those people. Besides, if what you want is for this," she gestured between them, "to become what it's supposed to be, then we need to spend more time together; just the two of us. Right?"

With a smile, Vlameir agreed, rising. Taking her hand, he led her back down the stairs to her chambers. Once there, he called for a servant and ordered a small meal brought up for the two of them. Within moments, a tray was brought in, loaded full of cheeses, fruit, meats, and fresh bread. A flask of wine and two goblets were readily available as well.

Vlameir spread it out on the floor in front of the fire with an extra blanket thrown under it, along with some pillows from the bed. If they had been outside, she would have sworn it was the best picnic she had ever attended.

As they ate, they chatted about life. Vlameir told her of goals he still hoped to achieve while he was king. He told her of all the improvements they had made in the rights of their women, so their contributions were taken seriously. He told her how hard it had been at first to get his subjects to take him seriously.

She watched the way his face lit up as he told her of his goals and aspirations. She was proud of his accomplishments and told him as much. She blushed when he turned the subject to her.

"What about you? What was your dream, Leanna?" His eyes almost glittered with his smile. She felt secure in the knowledge he wasn't only asking. He really wanted to know. What astounded her was not that he wanted to know, but that she wanted to tell him.

"When I was a little girl, my favorite thing was drawing. I had to know how to draw everything. I wanted to make the horse or rabbit or tree look real. I wanted my pictures to be the kind that the people who looked at them would actually wonder if they could walk right into and actually become a part of."

"When I was twelve, my mother bought me my first canvas. I mean, a real canvas, it was huge. Twelve by eighteen, I think. She gave me oil paints and told me the sky was the limit. I could paint anything I wanted."

Vlameir lifted an eyebrow when she paused. "What did you paint?" He was interested in knowing. She could tell and was grateful for his attention.

She smiled. "I painted her. I got her to sit for me, and I worked for hours to get it right. The color of her hair, the shade of her eyes. The slant of her lips when she smiled." A giggle escaped her. "My mother was so patient with me while I worked on that picture. She even put up with me and my silly insistence she did not look at it until I finished. It took me three months before I was happy with it!"

He smiled indulgently, asking, "And your mother? What did she think of it?"

Leanna sighed, She and Dad both said they loved it. He insisted on hanging it above the fireplace in the den." Her smile slipped a little. "I always thought they did it to humor me. It's still there, though, and Mom always says she'll hang me by my toes if I try to take it down."

Vlameir's jaw dropped. "Hang you by your toes? Why, that's positively abusive! How could she even conceive—"

"Hold on, cowboy." Leanna interrupted. "She wasn't serious. That's only a figure of speech. It isn't something she'd ever really do."

At her assurance, he relaxed visibly and chuckled. "You worried me for a moment. I'd never believe with how nurturing of a person you are, you could have had a mother who would be so mean."

Leanna laughed then, wholeheartedly. "Oh, my mother is an amazing woman. She encouraged me always. The only time we ever had a real difference of opinion was when

I made the decision to get married straight out of school. She didn't think that was a good idea and she blamed Max for my letting go of my dreams. She believed she knew I was giving it up for him." Her expression became a little melancholy and she let herself relax back onto a pillow and looked up at him. "I guess, in a way, I was. I loved him and I wanted a family. I didn't even recognize it as letting go of one dream to have another. I always thought the time would come when I could do it again."

Vlameir, leaned over her, and brushed a stray hair away from her cheek. "Leanna, you can paint anything and everything you wish now. I will never try to hold you back or make you choose. I only ask that you let me be a part of it. Let me be part of you."

As Leanna stared up into his beautiful eyes, she found herself wishing for exactly that. Unable to deny it any longer, she accepted that this man was supposed to be a part of her life. The entire reality of it was more than only an idea. It was destiny. In a moment of total clarity and acceptance, she did what she had yearned to do since the day she had met this beautiful, perfect man.

Reaching up, she framed his face in her hands and slowly, hesitantly, drew him down and softly touched her lips to his. The kiss was tender and slow. Vlameir let her lead, never trying to push to deepen it, but instead letting her pick the pace of how this first kiss went.

He followed her lead obediently. Until she deepened the kiss and slid her fingers into his hair. When she did that, his arms wrapped around her and he pulled her closer. He held her close, his own hands tangling in her hair as well as hers did in his. When his tongue met hers, she moaned, spurring him to roll them over so she lay beneath him and their kiss became charged with a kind of electricity that left her all tingly and aching for more.

He felt amazing. His chest pressed flush to hers, his hair acting as a curtain shielding them from any intruder that might walk in and witness their kiss. Even though they might know what was happening, the actual intimacy of it would be hidden from them. She could feel herself slipping and becoming hungry for more.

It was that realization that made her stop. She wanted this. She wanted him. But she wanted it to be what it was destined to become. That meant stopping before it went too far in this heated moment.

When Vlameir pulled away, she half expected to see anger flashing in his eyes. Instead, all she saw was affection. He rested his forehead against hers for a moment, before retreating. "Goodnight, my Leanna. Rest well, for in the morning, we will begin our search for the place to do your painting." He shot her a grin. "And you can expect me to steal a few more of those kisses."

With that, he was gone, leaving her staring after him and feeling as giddy and anxious as a teenage girl.

Nine

For what seemed like hours after Vlameir left, Leanna found it impossible to sleep. Her mind kept going back over their conversation. She kept remembering the way he held her close and tried to calm her as she cried. She thought of how he tried to console her and how he promised her heart was much safer with him.

Turning onto her side, she stared out the huge window. She had a clear view of the moon from where she was. It was full and bright and beautiful to behold. Some people might even feel lulled to sleep with it watching over them, but Leanna became even more restless.

Tossing aside the covers, she grabbed the robe the seamstress had given her and put it on. It was as long as some of the dresses they had given her. It completely covered her nightdress, falling easily to her ankles.

Moving to grab her sketchbook and charcoal pencils, she sat down before the window and opened the book to a blank sheet. Pulling a pencil out of its container, she stared at the blank page for several moments. It was odd, but in her mind, she could see him, standing on the balcony with the moon behind him as he met her gaze.

With a determined nod to herself, she pressed the pencil to the paper and began following the lines in her mind. She knew the curve of his face. She remembered every line, as if she had traced him before. His unflawed symmetry was something she had not been able to forget since the first moment she had seen him.

The soft silkiness of his hair was perfection. She worked to make it visible through the artwork. She felt almost possessed in her desire to capture him correctly. It was almost two hours later when she looked up from her work. The sky was still dark, but she knew there would not be much more time left before sunrise.

Setting the sketchbook aside, she stretched and debated trying to get more sleep. Her stomach growled a little in protest of being neglected. Next to the bed were a pair of slippers that reminded her of house-shoes, so that was what she used them for. Maybe a trip to the kitchens and a glass of milk might help.

She wandered cautiously down the stairway, following a path back toward the formal dining room, where dinner was served earlier. Although she had not seen every room on the ground level, she imagined the kitchens should not be too far away from that, right?

As she descended the stairs, a blue, luminous light caught her gaze. It was coming from a room down the corridor, in the opposite direction of her intended destination. Hesitating, she considered if she dared be so nosey. Whatever was going on down that corridor did not concern her.

The temptation won out when she noticed the light flicker momentarily. Too curious to deny herself, Leanna started down the corridor. It couldn't possibly hurt to be certain there was nothing wrong. After all, something could have caught fire.

Heading cautiously down the hall, she reached the room the light was coming from quickly. Stopping just short of the entryway, she leaned around and peered into the room. Her eyes widened as she realized she was staring into an immense library.

Stepping into the library, Leanna took in the huge bookshelves, strategically placed in such a way which complemented the shape of the room as well as the vaulted ceilings. There were grand staircases, leading up to walkways that gave access to the upper shelves.

Although she was stunned and awed by the sheer beauty of the library, what really captivated and amazed her was the tiny little workers, flitting around on sparkling gossamer wings, returning books to their rightful places, and tidying up the room, which to Leanna's eyes, already seemed immaculate.

"Wow..." the whispered word escaped her before she even knew she had uttered a word. Several of the tiny, winged creatures turned to look at her before exchanging glances with each other.

Finally, it seemed wordlessly, it was decided between them who would address her. One tiny creature, no bigger than a sparrow, with silvery wings and hair to match, glided down to where Leanna stood, and greeted her with a smile. "Good morning, my Lady. You surely are an early riser. Is there anything we may assist you with?" The Faery's skin had a lavender tone to it that seemed to complement the silver of her hair and wings. Her dress, as well, was a dark shade of purple.

Realizing she was being addressed, Leanna recovered, blushing furiously at being caught staring. Her mother had always told her it was one of the rudest things a person could do. Shaking her head, she half bowed as she sputtered out an apology. "I'm so sorry. I didn't realize anyone would be up yet." She wrapped her arms around herself, adding. "I was having trouble sleeping. I had thought maybe a glass of milk would help." She chuckled a little. "When I made it downstairs, I saw the flicker of lights down here and curiosity got the best of me."

The Faery smiled, answering, "It's quite all right. The library is always open. Please feel free to come look for a book whenever you need or want to. My name is Ellora. I am the librarian for the evenings. My brother, Elwyn usually oversees things during the day. He would be most willing to help you with anything you might need as well." She smiled then. "Indeed, we look forward to you and King Vlameir's joining. I can see, you've already begun to bloom."

Leanna stared at Ellora with an odd expression, not sure how to react to her words. What did she mean? Joining? Bloom? Before she could respond, another Faery, with white and pink wings, along with matching hair, joined them, effectively shutting Ellora up. "My name is Riorran, my Lady. Might I show you to the kitchens? Truly, instead of milk, might I make you a cup of hot peppermint chocolate? It would do better to help relax you, I'm sure.

Curious still, but not sure they would tell her anything more on the whole blooming comment, Leanna instead smiled. "Yes, thank you. I think the hot chocolate might be nice." Looking back to Ellora, she thanked her softly.

Ellora smiled and half bowed. "Come back anytime, *Highness.*" She seemed to accentuate the word, with a mere

tad of a flourish, as if daring the other Faery to say anything.

Leanna wanted desperately to stay and drill Ellora
about what she meant, but instead, she let it go and followed the other Faery away with only a backward glance
at her new little friend. Perhaps there would be time before
she had to leave to talk to Ellora more.

Following Riorran from the library and to the kitchens,
she resigned herself to being in the dark about what exactly was going on. She knew Vlameir was someone special
to her. She knew he wanted a romantic relationship. Hell,
she did too. But fear she told herself was irrational, held
her back. She couldn't help it. After the past years she had
endured, she wasn't sure it was a response she could overcome.

Once she had tasted the amazing peppermint chocolate
and engaged in small talk with the cook, who was already
beginning preparations for breakfast, she felt the weariness
seeping into her bones. With murmured words of appreciation for the drink, she excused herself and made her way
quietly to her room, pausing for a moment to admire the
translucent glow that came from the library.

A small smile came to her lips as she ascended the
stairs, thinking about all the amazing things she had seen
since she had come here. And tomorrow was a new day.
What treasures might be found when they left the castle
to look for the perfect scenery for her to begin painting his
portrait

Ten

Leanna woke a little later that morning, feeling refreshed and for the first time in a long time, looking forward to the day ahead. There was a smile on her face when she saw the sunrise. Rising from the bed, she moved to the wardrobe and picked out one of the pairs of pants and a matching tunic shirts She was almost afraid to wear them because the material was so beautiful. But the comfort and fit of the fabric helped her decide to go ahead and give it a try.

After selecting a comfortable pair of ankle boots that reminded her of moccasins, she left the privacy of her room and began her descent to the dining area where Vlameir had told her they would meet in the morning. When she reached the base of the stairs, he was already standing there, waiting, basket in hand.

She took it in with a raised eyebrow before smiling at him. "Are we having a picnic for breakfast?"

Vlameir returned her smile warmly. "As well as enough for lunch. I thought perhaps you'd like an early start. There's a lot to see." He paused before adding, "We'll be riding my horse today. I hope you like horses. He's excited to meet you."

She nodded happily. "I love horses. Although I will admit to not being the best rider." She had ridden a few times, but not enough to consider herself an expert. She also noted he said they were riding his horse. So that meant she'd be on one horse with him. Her heart fluttered a little at the thought. For a fraction of a second, she considered canceling their outing. Then her mind wandered to the kiss the night before and the thought came to her, *Now why would you cancel a chance to relive that?*

Without even hesitating, she looped her free arm through his and clasped her sketchbook and bag with drawing supplies closer with the other. "Well then. Let's not waste any daylight."

When they stepped out of the castle, she saw the horse Vlameir had mentioned standing on the landing and the breath she had been holding whooshed out of her in a huff. He was black, with white streaks flowing freely through his mane, tail and down his chest, as well as the tufts of fur around his hoofs. He was also bigger than a Clydesdale. "Oh wow... He's bigger than anything I've ever seen. Are you sure he isn't a distant relation to Torlek?"

"I resent that." His voice rang out as he stepped around the horse in his human form. "I'll have you know that although Titan and I are friends, we are certainly no relation." He smirked and bowed before her with a flourish and a wink.

Vlameir cleared his throat. "Okay now. Don't be getting cheeky." As he spoke, he took Leanna's sketchbook and drawing supplies and put them into the saddle bag. "I saw her first, Torlek. Go get your own human."

Without so much as a missed beat, he secured the picnic basket at the back of the saddle, then turned and placed his hands on Leanna's waist. Bending only enough to bring him to her eye level, he asked softly, "Ready?"

Unable to form words while staring into his beautiful eyes, she simply nodded. A gasp slipped from her lips as Vlameir effortlessly lifted her up into the saddle. Then in one graceful and fluid movement, he easily lifted himself and settled into the saddle behind her.

Reaching around her, he settled one hand on her abdomen and pulled her back into him slightly while taking the reins with the other. "I've got you." He said softly into her ear before spurring Titan into a prance away from the castle, leaving Torlek watching after them with a small smile of his own.

As they rode, Leanna found herself taking it all in... the mountains in the distance, the forest flanking their right and the view of the lake to the left. The beauty of it was amazing to her. It was like the best parts of the scenery in her world all came together in this one. It seemed to her as if all of it was within reach. She started to ask which way they were going but stopped herself as he directed Titan toward the forest. A small smile graced her lips as she let her head rest back against his shoulder.

He knew where he wanted to take her. For once in what almost seemed like forever, she knew she didn't have to worry about what came next. It was a freeing feeling. To let someone else take charge for once. All she had to do was sit back and relax. There was a little hesitancy on her part to let it be, but her inner control freak was tired. She was tired. It was a relief for once, to know this was out of her hands.

As they rode into the forest, Leanna let her senses simply enjoy the sights and scents. She could smell the fragrance of the evergreens. She could hear birds singing, coupled with water from a nearby creek. It was a paradise stretching out before her, and it took her breath away.

The sound of the flowing water grew gradually louder until, almost suddenly, the trees seemed to part, and in their wake was a waterfall, complete with a pool, filled with clear, translucent water, and flanked by big beautiful blooming flowers. Roses, Iris, Honeysuckle, Lilies, and Ivy all filled her senses. Looking at the sight before her, she knew without a doubt this was where whoever had designed her bathing room had used this as the inspiration in their creation. The horse took them straight to the river's edge, where some of the flowers were within reach.

Vlameir slid off Titan easily, then turned and reached up toward her. "Let me help you down." Leanna let him help her off the horse, holding onto him for a moment to allow her legs to adjust after the lengthy ride. His arms were strong and held her steady as she found her footing.

When she finally pulled slowly away, it was to turn and take in the beauty of the place. She didn't think she had ever seen anyplace so beautiful. "This is amazing. I've never seen anything like it."

Vlameir stepped up behind her, and Leanna could feel the heat of his body from his closeness. She fought the chill that ran through her when he spoke so close to her ear. "This is my favorite place. I come here when I need to get away from everything." She felt his breath, like the touch of butterfly wings against her cheek.

Taking a step away from him, she turned to meet his gaze. The connection she felt to him was growing stronger by the minute. She could feel it. It was as tangible to her as her own skin and as undeniable as the truth of the rising and setting of the sun.

Before she could let herself give in to the desire to touch him, she turned and moved to Titan's side. Retrieving her sketchbook and tools, she said, "Why don't we eat breakfast and I'll start letting my hands become familiar with your lines."

As soon as she said it, she regretted it. Familiar with his lines? To someone who did not understand the way an artist thought, that would make absolutely no sense. His chuckle made her blush even as his words made her smile. "I am going to assume you are talking about the shape of my face."

She found herself laughing a little as she nodded, turning back to face him. "Among other things." She offered softly. She didn't even try to hide her blush. There was no point. He'd already seen it.

Vlameir unsaddled the horse, and set the saddle, as well as the picnic basket, on a nearby rock. Then, emptying the saddlebag, he pulled a large blanket out. Moving a little away from the water, he spread the blanket out on the ground.

Leanna set her things down on the blanket's edge and moved to retrieve the basket. When she turned back, she drew up short, catching Vlameir watching her closely, a lustful look in his eyes that made her breath catch. For several moments, they simply stared at each other. Then, she looked away, garnering her resolve, she moved to kneel on the blanket and opened the basket. "Let's see what we have here for breakfast."

She removed two napkins, two clay cups, a bottle filled with juice, and some sweet rolls. There was also some strawberries and cheese. "This looks good," she said as she set it out. There was more, but she remembered he had told her there was enough for lunch as well. As she sat back to survey her handiwork, she caught herself staring at it intently to keep from gazing at him like a lovestruck baboon.

Vlameir had been standing aside, watching her prepare the meal without saying a word. Truth was, at this point, words failed him. He was finding it harder and harder not to take her in his arms. He wanted so desperately to do exactly that. His soul cried for hers. Everything about her, from the way she moved, to the fall of her hair, the scent of her skin, called to him, making his senses yearn for her.

Biting his tongue, he moved to sit across from her and reached out, taking a piece of cheese. Breaking it in half, he popped on into his mouth, willing himself to stay patient. He had survived this long without even knowing she existed. Now he had found her, they would have an eternity together. He could be patient. She deserved that from him.

He watched as she bit into the pastry. Her eyes closed as a moan escaped her and he smiled at her reaction to the food. Leaning toward her, he asked softly, "Do you like it?"

Her eyes were still closed, and she smiled. "Yes. It's delicious. It reminds me of honey rolls, but it has a fruity taste." When she licked her lips, it was all he could do to stop himself from moving to taste them himself.

Instead, he tore off a piece of it for himself. "It is a honey bread. The reason you taste fruit is because the flour used to make it is made from dried berries. It adds a very distinct fruity flavor." He took a bite from his portion and chewed slowly. It was a bread often given to young couples after they shared their marriage bed for the first time. The irony was not lost on him as he considered the implications the cook made by packing such a treat in his basket. It was a blessing of sorts. His people were telling him they embraced his choice of mate.

The problem was, she did not know the significance of it, and he was hesitant to tell her. They had only just shared a first kiss. Did he dare tell her that already his kingdom was prepared to call her queen? Wouldn't that frighten her away? He smiled at her, silently resigning himself to the truth of having to wait. He'd share the significance with her soon enough. For now, he would enjoy the moment.

Eleven

They had been at the spot for a few hours. For a time, they talked of hopes and dreams; wishes and goals. She told him of once wanting to be a famous artist when she was younger. He shared his desire to bring all the races of Fae together in peace and acceptance. He shared how close they were, as well as how far there still was to go.

Leanna told him how the mortal realm seemed always to be at odds with each other politically, racially, and in almost every other way that mattered. "Our leaders spend so much time arguing over things that mean so little that they never make time to come together for the things that are important." She sighed.

"One side believes there is nothing wrong with the way we treat the planet. The other thinks we are on the verge of destroying not only ourselves, but every other creature in the world. So, they argue. Meanwhile, the Polar Bear is starving because the Ice Caps are melting, and no one cares enough to get past their petty grievances to try to change anything."

Once she picked up the sketchbook and began doodling, Vlameir fell silent, seeming to content himself with his own thoughts while she concentrated on perfecting his image. Her hands moved over the paper as she found herself tracing the face she saw onto the paper. The angles and lines meeting together to form what was in her mind a most perfect specimen.

Her eyes rested on him again as he sat before her, staring out toward the waterfall. What must he be thinking? Did he have any idea how deeply she was falling? This instant attraction she felt for this man was one that was sweeping her away. She feared she was quickly losing herself to him, and he probably didn't even realize it.

For a moment, she forgot her drawings and instead found herself staring at him openly, wishing she was as brave as she had always wanted to be. Indeed, she mused to herself, if Max hadn't been the outgoing person he always was, she probably would still be single and resigned to forever be an old maid.

Catching herself having a stray thought about Max without the inevitable pain of loss that always followed, surprised her. She waited for it to rear its ugly head, but instead of pain, she only felt a fond memory. He had been good for her. Her life was richer because he had been in it and now, sitting here, drawing practice doodles of this Elf King, she realized that if things had not happened as they had, she might not have ever ventured into this world or met this amazing man.

Before she could look away, Vlameir caught her staring and his own eyes widened for a moment before he closed the gap between them and claimed her lips in a fiery kiss that scorched her very soul. It was possessive and engulfing. She clung to him like a lifeline as she gave in to the fire consuming her. Her fists knotted into his tunic as she kissed him every bit as deeply as he had her.

When he broke the kiss, his forehead touched hers. "I've been longing to kiss you all morning," he confessed. "But I didn't want to seem pushy or needy, like a child."

She found herself chuckling and brushing a stray lock of hair away from his eye gently as she stared up at him. "Why would you think you'd seem like a child to admit you wanted to kiss me?"

He took a breath and Leanna heard the tremor in his voice when he spoke, "Because I need you as badly as a babe needs his mother's milk. My every waking thought is caught up in you." He confessed. "The first thing I wonder when I wake up is if you are awake. Did you sleep well? Were your dreams plagued by me as mine were with you?

"Most of all, I wonder how much longer I must stifle my desires. How much longer before you admit to yourself as well as I, that you need me too?" He turned his head from hers, even as he continued to hold her body close to his. "The thought consumes me. It rules my every waking moment, and it is beginning to drive me mad."

Leanna stared at him, wondering why she wasn't terrified at this moment. He had as much as admitted to being obsessed with her. She should be scared out of her mind, shouldn't she? But she wasn't. She knew why too. If she were honest with him as well as herself, then she'd admit to him that she was as tormented as he was. She wanted him every bit as badly, and she was very nearly ready to beg for the kiss he had just given if he had not beaten her to it.

Taking a deep shuttering breath, she whispered softly. "I do need you. It scares me. No, the whole thing terrifies me. I feel as if I'm caught up in a whirlwind and I have no control. But I can no more deny it than I can lie to you." She touched his cheek softly, turning his face back to hers. "I am so afraid that my first instinct is to run away. But the truth is I want this. Please don't let me run away. I don't want to run away from this." Leaning forward, she touched her lips to his again, softly. Her eyes were open, searching his as she made a silent offering of herself to him.

His response did not disappoint her. For a moment, he froze, as if afraid to move for fear she'd pull away. Then, recovering himself, he closed his arms around her, holding her close, with a gentle touch, like she'd break if he held her too tightly. The kiss became more, bringing a level of intimacy with it that swept them away.

She felt his hands span across her bare back and knew he was lifting her top slowly. He did it in a way that kept her from really feeling threatened, but she still knew she was not ready. Bracing her palms against his chest, she pushed him away slightly.

His passion-filled gaze met hers for a moment and she seriously considered throwing caution to the wind and going with what her body wanted. But her heart, she reasoned, would need more time. She feared his disappointment, but she knew if she rushed into this, then she would run away from him. This was not something she could rush. Not if she wanted it to last.

His eyes met hers and they simply stared at each other. When she opened her mouth to speak, he raised his hand, placing a forefinger to them. "Leanna, I want you for an Elf's lifetime. That is very nearly an eternity." He smiled, cupping her cheek gently. "I am not in any hurry to ravish your body. Although, touching you does feel amazing."

She felt herself blush, even as she smiled her relief at his words. Moving to hug him tight, she nuzzled her face into his neck, whispering, "Touching you feels pretty amazing to me too. But can we just enjoy that for now?" she asked sincerely. "I want to take this slow. I'm afraid if we rush it, this thing we have won't last."

She felt Vlameir rest his cheek against her head as he cradled her close. "I have no objection to taking it slow, if we can lay to rest the pretext of nothing being between us. I will not abide that any longer. My own Court can see with their own eyes the affection which grows between us." He placed a finger under her chin, tilting her head back so their eyes met again. "Is that agreeable to you?"

She nodded, offering him a smile. "Yes. I can agree to that."

His own smile grew, and he asked in a soft voice, "Of course, you know what this means?"

Quirking a brow in his direction, she asked, "What does it mean?"

She barely had time to register the mischievousness in his expression before he pounced, pushing her down to the ground and covering her body with his own as he kissed her breathless. When he lifted himself up a bit, he smiled down at her. "It means I can kiss you whenever and wherever I want."

His laughter was joined by her own as she slapped his arm playfully. "That's not very proper behavior, for a king, your Majesty," she bantered playfully, to which, he chuckled before growing solemn and kissing her gently again.

When he finally answered her, his words made her heart flutter. "It is perfectly proper behavior for a king who has chosen the queen he loves." She felt the sincerity of his words as well as saw it in his expression. He meant it. He meant every word of it.

The rest of their afternoon was spent enjoying each other's company. All Leanna's intentions to continue drawing were abandoned for the day.

Twelve

When Vlameir and Leanna made it back to the castle, there were people waiting in the foyer. Leanna stared at the beauty who greeted him without so much as even glancing in her direction. She bore a resemblance to him that Leanna was fairly sure meant she was his sister, with platinum blond hair, and sea blue eyes that seemed endless.

Standing slightly behind her was a man unlike anything she had ever seen, including Torlek. His hair was the darkest shade of black save for one white streak running down the length of it, which was actually exceptionally long, almost to the middle of his back. His skin was nearly gray, and she wondered if she were to touch it if it would indeed feel like marble. His eyes were a shade lighter than his hair and for a moment she felt very unsettled by his appearance.

Then she noticed his ears, and the fangs when he smiled at Vlameir when the king's attention turned to him and she remembered what he had told her about his sister marrying a Dark Elf. He had not lied to her about how his appearance could make others uncomfortable. She could well imagine how the appearance of those like him would be where many a storyteller in the mortal realm would use as inspiration for the bad guys in their stories.

Standing aside and observing the group before her, she saw an affection between them and felt a little spur of pain at being the outsider. How long had it been since she had truly felt as if she were a part of something that special?

Brushing aside the jealousy, she chided herself for feeling it at all. Vlameir was offering this very thing to her. She shouldn't be feeling jealousy, but instead an enthusiasm over being able to become a part of it. The thought of feeling as if she belonged somewhere again was something she longed for.

When Vlameir released his sister from their embrace, he turned, holding a hand out to her, "I want you to meet my sister, Hanna, and her husband, Roerik." When she took his hand, he pulled her forward, turning his brilliant smile to his sister, "This is Leanna. She's from the mortal realm," he paused, "but she is mine, as I am hers."

Hanna's eyes widened as she took in his words, turning to gaze at Leanna for the first time. When her smile filled her face was the first Leanna breathed. "Welcome, Sister. I am relieved he's finally found you."

Leanna felt herself blushing and looked down, even as she took Hanna's hand. "I must admit, I still feel a little confused and hesitant over all of this. But I cannot deny how I feel for your brother. It is a bit consuming."

"The soul bond always is." Roerik chose that moment to speak up, moving close to his wife and bowing deep to Leanna. "But the bond is something no Fae-raised being can miss, after the first few days, it begins to shine forth from the lovers." He smiled affectionately at Hanna then, adding, "Sometimes the lovers do not even see it until others who are closest to them do. That was the case between Hanna and me."

Vlameir chuckled at Roerik's words. "I remember the first time I noticed the glow that each of you had when you looked at each other. "Your faces just lit up, as if you suddenly understood every mystery in the world." He turned his gaze to Leanna, who was watching him, and his own face softened, "I was completely enthralled with the change that came over them when they were together. And it was captivating to watch how connected they became. They seemed to know whenever the other came into a room without even seeing each other."

Hanna looked between the two and smiled. "And now, I can see the same glow beginning to blossom between the two of you." She stepped forward, touching Leanna gently on the shoulder. "Welcome to our family, Sister. I understand this must feel as if it is moving extremely fast, but our people tend to know when love between soulmates begins to grow."

Leanna smiled weakly at Hanna before looking away. She knew what she was feeling was real, but Hanna was right. It did feel so sudden. Especially after being without

Max for so long. She felt at odds with herself over the entire situation. On one hand, it had been years. Enough time had passed that no one; not her family or her friends would even think to accuse her of not respecting his memory.

On the other hand, she felt the only way she would ever truly be able to move forward with her life, was if her son and husband gave her permission. That posed the biggest problem. How could the dead give her permission to move on? She honestly felt stupid pondering the question. Honestly, the fact they had died should have been permission enough. Shouldn't it?

She vaguely heard Vlameir suggest they move to the sitting room and visit. Knowing what he had told her about Roerik's aversion to sunlight, she imagined he couldn't be very comfortable in such close proximity to the windows and doors, so the others turned and made their way to the darker and more comfortable living room.

She didn't know all the terms and fancy words tied to a fairytale castle. For all intents and purposes, the room looked like what would be called a living room in any ordinary house, if somewhat larger by such standards. There was what she guessed to be a ten-foot-tall fireplace on one wall. The room was as awe-inspiring to her as any fancy castle in the mortal realm ever thought to be.

There were three different sitting areas. Two focused with couches, facing said fireplace. One was a bit closer, and the second was farther back and a little closer to the third.

The final sitting area was arranged around what looked to be a golden harp, and another instrument Leanna recognized as a grand piano. She smiled upon seeing it. Perhaps if it indeed was one, she might convince Vlameir to allow her to play. It had been years, and she was sure to be terribly rusty. But still, it would be nice.

As Vlameir ushered them to the sitting area closest to the fireplace, before turning to the nearby servant. "Would you be so kind as to alert Torlek to my sister and brother-in-law's presence? I'm sure he would love to visit with them as well."

Leanna watched as the man nodded with a small smile and turned, quickly exiting the room. It was then Roerik laughed heartily. "You only call him so you can watch him stare at me like I'm some fancy trinket to add to his collection again! I swear," he turned to Leanna, explaining, "If I ever disappear and the lot of you can't find me, I dare say, go look in his lair. Chances are, he's spirited me away to hide amongst all his jewels."

Torlek laughed as he entered the chamber. "I cannot help that I have a fascination for your skin, my friend. It tends to sparkle, as a jewel; and you know Dragons have a fascination for jewels." He raised his hands in mock surrender. "But I promise, I shan't try to steal you away. Indeed, I have not mistaken you for an actual gem since that one time I had too much Faery wine, and I have since promised not to imbibe in your presence again."

Vlameir and Hanna's laughter joined Roerik's, and Leanna could not help but smile at the easy banter between her four companions. She quirked an eyebrow in Torlek's direction. "Wait, are you saying you mistook Roerik for a jewel?"

With a shrug Torlek answered, "His skin glistens. I *knew* he wasn't an actual gemstone. But the drunk me... Well, the drunk me, in full Dragon form... Well, it gets confused." He scoffed at Roerik, "I promised you it would never happen again. Didn't I?"

Roerik laughed in earnest then. "Of course, I do believe you, old friend. But who would I be if I didn't heckle you about it from time to time?"

Torlek lifted an eyebrow, smirking, "Who indeed? I can only list a few enemies who would give me half the hell you have since that incident." He took Roerik's offered forearm in a show comradery and it was only then that Leanna realized they were truly only speaking in jest.

Still, she found herself asking, "Did you truly mistake him for a gemstone?" She couldn't keep the disbelief out of her voice, though she tried.

Torlek laughed and sank into the chair nearest hers. "I had just finished off my third bottle of elderberry wine by myself. I didn't have the foggiest clue that the lump, lying on the balcony of the princess's room was a Dark Elf, sleeping, out in the open." He chuckled, turning to Leanna with an innocent smile. "I honestly only meant to sleep on her balcony myself, then make my way to my caves come morning." He gestured to Roerik. "And there he was. All curled up in a ball, naked as the day he entered this world... all shiny and glistening in the moonlight.

"We Dragons have one weakness, Leanna. We love shiny baubles. We can rarely resist them when we are in our Dragon forms." He lowered his voice, as if telling her a special secret. "You should see the treasures I have gathered during the course of my lifetime. I guarantee, when I meet my Lady Dragon, and I show her my collection of jewels, she won't be able to resist what I have to offer." He chuckled. "I will surely win her completely on the day I show her."

Leanna couldn't resist the temptation to ask, "But what if when you find the lady you want, she isn't a Dragon? What if your jewels are less impressive to her than an offering of your heart?"

Her question caught him off guard and he sat back in the chair and seemed to ponder her questions in earnest.

Hanna watched him every bit as closely as Leanna did. After a moment, she turned to Vlameir, "I do believe you have found yourself a wise woman. She seems to understand more in matters of the heart than many." She smiled warmly at her brother. "I am so very glad for you."

Leanna looked down at her lap as she felt her blush rise in her cheeks. She didn't quite know how to respond to such simple praise. It was only a kind-hearted statement, but in many ways, it meant more to her than she was even sure she could express accurately.

Looking to change the subject, she looked toward the musical instruments. "Who plays the harp?" she asked curiously.

Vlameir turned to look at it, answering, "It's mine. I began playing tunes on it when I was only a boy. My father thought it was a waste of my skills, but luckily, my mother, encouraged me."

Leanna smiled at his words. "And the piano? Is that yours?" she asked Hanna, who immediately declined.

"Oh, no. I sing, and I can play the flute a little. But I've never mastered how to play such an instrument. I can attest I wouldn't have the slightest clue where to begin."

"So, who does play it?" she asked, confused. Why would they have a piano if no one played?

Vlameir stared intently at Leanna. "Do you play, Leanna?" his expression was more than only a little curious, and she found herself pondering what exactly was in his thoughts.

She did not have to wonder for long. After a moment, he began to tell her a story that made her heart flutter nervously. "When I was child, there was a Seer in the castle. She was similar to our aunt, in that she had a talent for knowing things. She told my parents that the woman I would soul-bind with was not anywhere near here, but that where she was, she was playing an instrument like this one, and she was creating the same songs I was."

He closed his eyes for a moment before adding, "I would always get so angry when I tried to compose what I heard in my head. It was never quite right. Something was always missing. So many years—indeed, almost a century passed, and as it goes with Seers, sometimes they are right, sometimes they are wrong. One never knows for sure when they are looking into futures. Perhaps, she was wrong about your playing music linked to mine. Instead, your artistry was coming out in your paintings."

His eyes again found hers and he asked again in a voice so soft, she was not altogether certain she heard him right. "Do you play, Leanna?"

Her heart was thrumming in her ears as all the different tunes she had heard as a child came back to her in a rush. Tears brimmed, blurring her view as she considered the magnitude of what he was saying. This was all too much. She was already accepting that he was something special to her. But to hear that he had actually been hearing the same music in his head that she had. Was such a thing even possible? There was no way... Was there?

Finding her feet, she approached the piano slowly, waiting to wake up as she did so. This could only to be a dream. Things were falling into place too easily. It really was too good to be true.

Reaching out, she traced the lines of the instrument as she walked slowly around it, before coming to the bench. For a moment, she simply stared at it, pondering if she even still had enough knowledge of the songs to attempt to do them justice. And what if her songs weren't his? Would he change his mind about her being his soulmate then? Would he make her go back to her world, where she was alone?

Deciding to go ahead and take the chance, she leant down and pulled the bench back, moving to sit down and then slowly opened the keyboard and ran her fingers reverently over the keys.

When she looked up, she saw Vlameir had taken his place at the harp and was watching her intently. Drawing a shaky breath, she murmured, "It's been so long since I've played, I'm not even sure I even remember any of them."

The beautiful Elf who sat across from her, leaned the harp back against his shoulder, and answered softly, "Just think of the one you loved the best. If it is as the Seer said it will be, it does not matter how long we have forgotten the melody. It remembers us."

With a slight nod, Leanna turned her attention to the piano. This moment defined it all. If they didn't know each other's song, then chances were, he would give up on the idea that she was his soulmate. A momentary pain lanced through her heart in response to the unbidden thought. She had only begun to catch herself hoping that perhaps there was something real between them.

With that possibility looming over her, she reached into her memory for the song that had always struck the deepest chord with her. As she began to play, the music filled the room, bringing with it the depth of loneliness that had been in her heart over all these years. The sorrow and pain, mixed with the hope for renewal poured from her, into the music.

As she played, she felt the core of the song reaching into her soul and filling her with promise as a deeper melody began taking hold. Suddenly she realized the song had become so much more than it had always been before. She heard the tones of his harp, playing in accord, bringing a new soul into the song.

Tears coursed freely down her cheeks as she realized he knew the song, and he played it as passionately and heartfully as she did. All doubt she had held within fled as she gave herself over to the melody. Her heart felt full. She could feel the air filling her lungs as she breathed deep of the new life she now knew without a doubt was hers.

She would always miss her child. She did not forget the love she had for her first husband. But now she realized that opening her heart to love another was not sacrificing or forgetting anyone or anything. Her heart was filled with new hope and love. Instead of thinking it would push any other love she had away, it opened it up, and blended it into a perfect semblance of completion and tenderness.

As the song ended, she lifted her hands from the keys, hardly aware of their trembling. Her eyes sought for and found his. The depth of emotion she found in his own eyes was her undoing.

No one else existed in that moment. She wasn't even aware of the other people gathered in the room anymore. She had no knowledge of who stood first. She didn't know which of them made the first step to close the distance between them. All she knew was suddenly, she was in his arms, her lips were pressed to his, and she couldn't hold him close enough. His fragrance filled her senses, encompassing her very existence. He was hers. He was truly hers. She would never be alone again. In that moment nothing else mattered.

Neither of them had seen the many other onlookers who had gathered in the room as they performed. Neither of them realized the tears that had gathered in their audience's eyes. Neither of them even stopped to care when Torlek and Roerik began to usher every curious set of eyes out of the room. The door closing, affording them privacy for whatever intimacy occurred between them was completely unnoticed as they both lost themselves in the undeniable realization, they had each found the other side of their soul.

Thirteen

Vlameir didn't dare let go of Leanna, lest she disappear. He had prayed too long, hoped too hard, and now that she was his and finally believed and trusted in what he had been telling her all along, he wasn't willing to take the chance of losing her.

He led her swiftly from the sitting room, through a hidden panel that opened up to a series of staircases leading to the rooms on the second and third floors, eventually leading to his chambers. Walking swiftly through them, he hardly even noticed he was nearly dragging her behind him as he led her through the hidden staircases.

When they arrived at the panel that led to his rooms, he paused before the door and released a pent-up sigh before turning back to face her. He caressed her cheek with his forefinger and spoke in a soft voice. "Leanna, I don't think there is any mistaking the truth now of how much I want you. I want nothing more than to take you into that chamber, lock all my doors and refuse to allow anyone near you for at least a week while I memorize every single curve, freckle and blemish on your body." He paused, smiling almost awkwardly as he added, "I want to count every strand of your hair and worship you endlessly."

Then his expression became somber. "But I do not want you to feel as if you have no choice but to enter this chamber with me. If you feel you need more time, I understand, and I will respect your wishes." He worried she heard the tremor that was buried in the undertones of his voice, betraying the level of emotion he felt as he spoke. Would she think him weak for offering her this?

His worry was laid to rest when she stepped into his arms and pressed a kiss gently to his lips. When she leant back, she gave him a smile that took his breath. "I want nothing more than to be in your arms, Vlameir. I feel as if

I've been foolish this entire time and hesitant for no reason."

When he heard her words, he pushed the spring on the panel and was rewarded, when it slid easily aside, allowing them entrance into his rooms. Once again, taking her hand, he led her inside and released her to look around as he slid the panel back into place. As he turned back toward her, he was struck by how beautiful she was. His heart filled with a feeling of such love and awe in the realization she was his.

Stepping closer to her from behind, he let himself feel the softness of her hair as he admired the way the silky tresses slipped through his fingers. Leaning down just enough to touch his head to hers, he inhaled the fragrance of her shampoo and smiled. "You smell of roses and mint, and it intoxicates me." His arms came around her and he pulled her closer, enjoying the way their bodies fit together.

She moaned in response and sighed as he nuzzled her neck, placing a tender kiss behind her ear. When she spoke, her soft voice trembled. "I sat down at that piano, thinking I was going to lose you. I was so afraid you wouldn't know my songs, and then you'd realize I wasn't who you thought, and send me home."

He pulled away from her neck, resting his head on her shoulder for a moment as he contemplated her words. His deep baritone vibrated through the room when he answered, "That wouldn't have happened. For one, my soul has always recognized you, and my heart was already given."

He paused then, before adding, "Leanna, at the moment I let my heart begin to beat for you, our love was set in stone. Nothing in either of our worlds can change that now. It would not matter if our music had not come together. I am already yours. I was yours from the moment you came across that bridge, and face to face with your first real Dragon." He chuckled. "Your expression is etched forever in my memory."

At his words, Leanna turned so they stood face to face and reached up to trace his cheek with her hand. He turned, placing a kiss in her palm, drawing a sigh from her. "I think that's why I was so hesitant to accept this. I think I recognized you too. And I fell in love immediately." She closed her eyes on a sigh, before turning her gaze back to his. "That's why I resisted so hard. I felt like I was betraying Max by the way my heart wanted so desperately to open up to you." She looked down at the opening of his tunic, her hands resting against his chest. "Forgive me," she whispered.

His hands came up to cover hers, and he answered softly. "There is nothing to forgive. I feel no anger that you had a good life without me. My heart hurts at the sadness you have had to endure, and I will spend the rest of my days doing everything to make the rest of our life together happy and full."

When she looked up into his eyes at his words, he saw the tears glistening within them. "Make love to me, Vlameir. I want this. I want us."

He needed no more encouragement. Silently and effortlessly, he lifted her into his arms and carried her the remaining steps to his bed. Laying her gently upon it, he made short work of ridding her of her shoes first, taking a moment to massage each foot as it was freed of the shoe. Then, he leaned over her and his hands came around her waist, tugging gently at the drawstring of her pants before sliding them down her hips and tossing them aside.

Leanna gasped when he climbed slowly onto the bed over her, her legs parted to allow him room. His hands slid slowly over the naked skin of her legs. Her moans were the only sound in the vast chamber.

He watched her, smiling at her reactions to his touch as he memorized the feel and curve of her skin. When his hands came to the hem of her tunic, he paused, eyes meeting hers, waiting for her permission.

Her heart fluttered for a moment at his thoughtful patience, and she nodded, raising up and lifting her arms so he could rid her of the top. When the offending garment was no longer between them, his eyes feasted on her, bared down to her underwear for him.

His appreciative expression gave her a bravery she had thought she'd lost. Her hands went to the clasp of her bra and she opened it slowly, sliding it off as well so she was bare to his view. She watched as his gaze darkened at the sight of her.

Slowly, his eyes moved back to hers and he removed his own tunic and tossed it aside. She watched as he undid the ties of his pants, slowly releasing them to pool at his feet before stepping out of them. Leanna had a moment to fully appreciate his beautiful form as time seemed to slow. She had considered him a little too lean to her liking when they had met, but now, as he stood before her in his full naked glory; a silent ethereal beautiful statue that made her think of the perfect specimen for the male of any species.

His muscles were toned and perfect. His physique was extreme perfection. Even the way the tips of his ears tapered up to a point made her breath catch. His long shiny silver-hair cascaded in sleek waves to his waist, as well as down his back. His chest had only a slight dusting of the same silvery hair across his pectoral muscles and she felt the urge to slide her fingers through it, feeling if it was as silky soft as the hair on his head.

As her gaze traveled down to the evidence of his own attraction to her, her breath caught in her throat. Biting her lip to silence her moan at the distance between them, she moved onto her knees, and with shaking fingers, slid her panties down her legs, then tossed them aside, along with the last of her uncertainty.

Her decision made, her eyes again met his and she reached out to him, ignoring the moment of fear that tried to make her conscious of her nudity and ashamed of the slight bump of her belly, grazed with the stretchmarks that gave evidence of her already having a baby. No sooner had the thought brushed the edge of her mind than she shoved it away. She loved her son. She felt no shame at the marks left on her body from birthing him. It was part of who she was, and Vlameir had already told her he wanted all of her.

Her resolve strengthened, she gave him a small smile as she widened her arms in her offering, letting him have full view of the woman he wanted. Her bravery was rewarded as he moved to her, swiftly pressing her back on the bed as his lips melded to hers, stealing her breath with his passion. Her moans filled the room as his hands moved slowly and purposefully over her naked flesh.

Vlameir groaned at the silky feel of her skin, and how responsive she was to his touch. Her moans were enough to have him fighting to control himself. He wanted their first time together to be perfect. It would not do to find himself spent too easily.

Wrapping his arms around her, he sat up, pulling her into his lap. Her legs were spread and instinctively, she wrapped them around his hips. His eyes searched hers, looking for any sign of hesitancy. Instead, what he found there was a desire as deep as his own.

Holding her close with one hand, the other reached down between them, sliding down her lower belly to the trimmed nest of curls that covered her treasure just enough to make him imagine what the sweet bloom hidden beneath must look like. Slowly, his forefinger spread the lips of her sex, allowing him to find what he searched for. When, he took the sensitive bud between his thumb and forefinger, twisting gently, he was rewarded by her arms tightening around him, pushing herself closer still and gasping when his middle finger slid into her moistness. He smiled as she bent slightly toward him in response to his thumb still rubbing her nub while a finger toyed with her. In answer to her moans and whines, he became a little more forceful, rubbing and teasing, until she cried out his name.

"Vlameir! I-I can't... I need... Please! I want..." Her cries were muffled as his lips found hers again, even as he lifted her easily, then pulled her down to fill her with his throbbing shaft. He thrilled in watching her head lift; her eyes rolling back in a kind of recognizable ecstasy as he filled her deeply.

She was tight and moist. Her moans filled the room as he let her set their pace, moving over him in such a way that he felt as if together they would reach the stars. His own guttural groans echoed hers and sounded like music to his ears.

He'd waited for her so long. To now have her in his arms, to know without a doubt she was indeed his made the entire moment more special. He loved having her in his arms. He clung to her as they rode the waves of completion; cresting together as one before landing together, wrapped in each other's arms, continuing to kiss and cuddle for hours.

When Leanna finally drifted off to sleep, Vlameir continued to cradle her close, watching her sleep, his heart full and content for the first time in two centuries. She was everything to him. It was her existence that made his bearable. Grabbing the blanket that had been pushed aside during their lovemaking, he pulled it up over them,

With a rare show of his special magical talent, he flicked a finger at the fireplace and the fire, which had been dwindling, instantly came to life, bringing a decent level of warmth to the room. With a small smile, he looked back at his love. There were so many things he could not wait to show her. So many secrets of his world he wished to share. He would make sure she never regretted choosing to be with him. Truly, he vowed to spend his very existence making sure she never knew sadness again.

Vlameir dozed off some time later, Leanna still nestled safely in his arms. But he felt the spirit studying him even before his eyes focused on the small child. He knew instantly, it was Daniel at the foot of his bed. He took a moment to study the boy as he was engrossed at looking at his mother.

When he spoke, it was with a quiet calm. "Do you want me to wake her? I'm sure she would want to see you, to know you are here." He felt a slight reluctance to share the fact that spirits were able to walk freely in this realm, with her. But looking at the young boy, he knew he'd never hide something like this from Leanna.

Daniel looked from his mother to the Elf addressing him. He studied him closely for a moment, before shaking his head. "She's not ready. She's still battling to truly let me go." He turned a small smile back in her direction. "But having you with her will help. She is ready to be happy again. That's a start."

Vlameir felt an almost protective feeling toward the boy arise within him. The child was extremely mature, despite his youth. "Are you certain? She'd be so happy to see you."

Daniel turned back to him again, and the Elf saw the tears glistening in the boy's eyes. As he spoke, he began to fade. "She will see me. Soon. But not yet. She deserves to have her newfound love a while longer before being distracted with me."

As the boy faded completely into nothingness, Vlameir heard his final request, "Take care of her. As much as you have already helped her, her feelings are still fragile."

The Elf King, lay there, holding Leanna to him, with a small ache in his own heart. The child was so very selfless. He could tell how badly the boy wanted to be reunited with his mother. But he was choosing to wait for her sake.

Blinking back a few stray tears which had found their way into his eyes, he drew a deep breath before placing a tender kiss on Leanna's forehead. He chastised himself for being surprised. After ten minutes of knowing the boy's mother, he had known she was special. Why had he not realized how special the boy had to have been as well?

With a small chuckle, he turned more fully toward Leanna, cradling her sleeping form lovingly and thanking the heavens for her. With a sigh of contentment, he let himself drift back to sleep.

Fourteen

The Drowmonger came awake with a start as the first shadow broke free of him. Screaming out, "No!" he moved swiftly, trying to catch it, only to come up empty. For almost one hundred and sixty years, he had slept peacefully, secure in understanding his people were knowing peace. He had made every sacrifice he could have thought of to ensure the Shades could never return.

Of course, some sacrifices had not been his own, but it was just. It was necessary to protect all the Races of the Fae Realm. The child whose line would have spawned his soulmate had been dealt with and disposed of over a hundred years ago!

There was no way Vlameir had found someone to which his soul would bond. The Mage had declared there was no one else in the kingdom who could have produced an heir who would be compatible with him. He had taken every measure to ensure the child they had sent away would never have offspring able to find their way back to this place.

So why now? Why did he feel the bond between the Elf King and his soul-bound bride sliding firmly into place through their intimate connection? He could feel the way the lovers were now becoming so tightly joined that nothing in the Fae Realm could ever defeat it.

Rising from his resting place, the Drowmonger paced for several minutes, contemplating what had to have gone wrong. He searched for any other reason. Any other reason besides the one he dreaded to be the one. It was the only reason there could be. Had she told him? Had she led him to where the babe had been sent? His student and lover... The Light Elf, who had sworn her undying allegiance in exchange for the knowledge he had given her; had betrayed their cause? Surely not! She knew as well as he what was at stake.

Desperation coursed through him at the very thought. She had wanted all the knowledge he possessed on how to destroy one's enemies at the blink of an eye and he had agreed at the time. but when all was said and done, neither he nor she could bring themselves to destroy one tiny infant. It was why they had decided to make her memories of him unfavorable. To help keep this very thing from happening.

Anger and frustration made an electrical current course through him and sparks flared from his fingertips as he growled lowly at the feeling of being trapped. before saying her name; *"Adrianna!"* He knew a moment of fear as he realized the Shades were headed straight for her. Being imprisoned within his sleeping body, they had been privy to all his knowledge and trickery, as well as to who had aided him.

He reached for her consciousness desperately. He had to warn her. Even though he knew she did not remember their partnership, he said a silent prayer to the powers that be she would have her memories restored in time to save herself from the silent killer that now hunted her. He added into his call a magical summoning that she would hear, no matter where she was. He had after all, once been her lover. If they could not solve this problem together, they would both pay dearly for this breach.

Adrianna was pacing her bedchamber, considering fleeing into the mortal realm when his call hit her as hard as any physical blow could. Memories she could not trust came rushing back to her as the deception the Mages had planted in her mind crumbled away. Denial made her head spin, but somehow, she knew the memories were real. She had once loved this man. He was not her enemy, but... he had been her lover and they had a pact together. They had made a sacrifice... But what?

Then realization hit. The Shades were free. Her love was trying to warn her. They would resume attacking now. Innocents would die of chronic, unfightable madness. No sooner than she had the thought than the first shadow snuck up on her. Silently and undetected, it stretched itself, then shrank down to a tiny needle size sliver and slid past her defenses and into her mind. Crumbling to the ground, she cried out at the pain that overwhelmed her, attacking her senses as if her very veins had been filled with liquid fire.

She had known the moment she had touched Leanna this was coming. The girl was a descendant of the baby she had sent through the veil to the mortal world all those years ago. A small smile crossed her lips as she breathed through the last of the pain and moved to sit up.

Taking deep, gasping breaths of air, she let the shame of her past petty actions fill her. No... This was all her fault. She was a fool. Her love for the Drowmonger had made her blind to the evil in his heart. By the time she had realized the depth of his malicious nature, it was too late. She had already given him everything he needed to control her. She couldn't let him control her again. She could hear him trying to reach her telepathically, but she shut his voice out. He would not gain her aid. Not this time. But the only way she could be sure he could not, would be to take herself out of the equation.

Otherwise, she could not ignore his call forever. These few decades he had been asleep had been a small reprieve from what she remembered of his hateful control and she had rather enjoyed the small freedom afforded to her from it. Now, however, with his waking, she knew it was only a matter of time before she was no longer able to resist his call. To do so would kill her.

Closing her eyes, she rested her head against the footboard of the bed, "I'm sorry, Vlameir. I'm not a very good aunt." Her words were a mere whisper as she tried to breathe through the next wave of pain.

Leanna woke up in Vlameir's arms. Breathing deeply, she lay beside him, taking a moment to observe his sleeping form. His hair was braided and thrown over his shoulder. His lips were soft; parted in sleep. Even in his slumber, he exuded authority. She found herself smiling as she inched closer to him, relishing the feel of his skin, so smooth and warm.

It had been so long. She considered if it was really a feeling she missed, being in someone's arms. But as she thought it over, she realized, this was more than only a happy feeling of being cuddled up to someone. This was a feeling of completion. There was no underlying sense of urgency or need to be productive. Snuggling closer still, resting her head on his shoulder, she considered the last time she had felt so relaxed.

It had been a long time. Truly, ever since Max had died, she didn't think she really had a moment where there wasn't some underlying current of anxiety she had endured. Every day had been an exercise in trying to cope with the fear of when the next tragedy would strike, all the while putting on a brave face and hiding that fear from her son... from her parents... from everyone she knew. Indeed, it had been an all-consuming thing.

But now, in this moment, lying next to Vlameir, watching him sleep, she knew peace. She knew where she belonged. The panic and anxiety which had kept her feeling for so long that the safest place for her was hidden away from everyone was gone. She no longer felt it.

She had almost drifted back to sleep when Vlameir's deep voice roused her. "I like waking up with you in my arms, Leanna." He took a deep breath and held it a moment before releasing it. "I've never been in a more comfortable position."

Unable to keep the chuckle from escaping her, she smiled. "Sure. Any moment now you're going to tell me your arm fell asleep and could I please give it back."

She had barely gotten the words out when he shifted, and rolled, pushing her onto her back. In the fraction of a second, he was over her, holding her in his arms, smiling down at her. "Oh, believe me, dearest one. If I found I was uncomfortable, at any point, I can easily reposition us to another more suitable position." He leaned down, kissing her lips gently, before whispering, "This one is nice."

Leanna opened her mouth to respond, but instead gasped as his lips found hers again, deepening the kiss, and making her ache with a need to make love to him again. She returned the kiss, letting all the caution she had been allowing to rule her, slip away.

His touch was gentle, but commanding, all at the same time. She felt protected, cherished, and secure in the knowledge that this man, holding her, cared for her in a way she would never be able to doubt.

Just as his hands began to explore her, awakening all her senses, a knock sounded at the door. Breaking the kiss, Vlameir rested his forehead against hers, whispering, "Ignore them. Maybe they'll go away."

After a few moments, he was almost sure they had left, but as he leaned down to renew their kiss, the knock sounded again, followed by the panicked voice of his aunt. "Vlameir, I must speak with you. This is important. I don't have long and there are things you and Leanna need to know."

Both of them turned to the door and stared for a moment, before glancing at each other. The panic in her voice was impossible to miss. Reluctantly, Vlameir pulled away from Leanna and grabbed a robe from beside the bed, handing a second one to her as he began dressing.

As he turned to the door, he called out, "Just a moment, Aunt Adrianna. We will be right with you." Tying the sash to his robes, he checked to be certain Leanna was presentable as well, before opening the door to allow his aunt entrance.

She moved swiftly inside, looking around the room with an anxious expression. Her eyes touched on the bed before she turned and moved to sit on the large sitting area on the other side if the room. Her face was filled with worry as she turned her gaze to her nephew. "Oh, my dear boy, I'm so sorry. I had no idea what I was really doing w-when I did it." She stammered, wringing her hands nervously.

Glancing at Leanna, he moved to sit across from his aunt. "Now, now, Aunt Adrianna. What is so pressing that it cannot wait until morning?" He was a bit surprised at her behavior. He had never seen her this way before and although he was not sure what it was that brought her to his door this time of night, his intuition told him he wasn't going to like it.

Adrianna sat there for several minutes, taking deep breaths to calm herself. When she finally spoke, it was as if she was telling them a story. "When I was younger, I met the most amazing Mage." She turned and smiled sadly at Vlameir, "You were only a small child then." Her voice drifted off for a moment and she simply stared at the floor, as if trying to find the words to continue the tale.

"I fell in love with him before I knew the truth of what he was. I was starved for his affection and I would have done anything to win his love. Such is the way of a naïve female, who believed if she could prove her love, he would love her in return."

It was then Adrianna's eyes moved to look over Leanna. Her smile was sad and resigned. "Of course, destiny finds a way to right all the wrongs we try to impose." She stood then and moved to grasp the younger woman's hands. "I am so glad you found your way, my dear. I think I always knew it wouldn't matter what I did in my stupid youth. Love always finds its way, after all."

Vlameir stood and moved to stand beside them, "Aunt Adrianna, you are beginning to worry me. What are you talking about?" She had never acted in such a way and he couldn't understand what she was trying to tell them.

Adrianna's eyes filled with tears. "I was trying to prove myself, you see. It was back when unions between our races were forbidden." Her smile was sad. "I thought by doing this for him, I would win his love." She drew a ragged breath, 'I was wrong. And before I knew he was not capable of returning my love, I had already done the deed."

Leanna put a hand on Adrianna's shoulder when she began to cry again. "What did you do? Surely we can fix it."

The Elven woman took Leanna's hand and placed a gentle kiss on the back of one. "My dear child, you already have. And you don't even know it."

She looked again to Vlameir and reached out to take his hand. "I owe you the biggest apology, Vlameir. I have done a horrible disservice to you. To prove my love to the Drow Lord, I was tasked with the chore of getting rid of the child from whom your soulmate would be born. He wanted me to kill her. But I could not."

"I thought by simply getting her away from the Fae Realm, I would be getting rid of your chances of finding your soulmate." Her eyes looked between the two of them, before she continued, "I was wrong." Looking back at Leanna, she squeezed her hands. "Welcome home, Leanna. You are the descended granddaughter of Ellaria Nightshade. I took her from her family when she was only a babe."

She cleared her throat, and took a few deep breaths, steadying herself before continuing. "He had wanted me to kill the child, thus killing any chances of you being able to stay on the throne, Vlameir. But I couldn't bring myself to take the baby's life. Instead, I made arrangements for her to be adopted into the mortal realm."

"I never knew her line would find its way back to us." She smiled at Leanna. "But here you are. You've come and the two of you have found each other." Her expression became melancholy, "And at the consummation of your love, the Drow Lord has awoken. Even now, his magic summons me. He seeks to punish me for my betrayal, and I know no other way to protect you." Her eyes were wildly darting around the room as if searching for some hidden enemy.

Turning back to Vlameir, she handed him a small book. "My diary from that time. It is all I can do for you now, to make up for my selfish, stupid mistake. I hope it is enough to help you fight the coming battle." She squeezed Vlameir and Leanna's hands, whispering, "Please forgive me."

Before either of them could anticipate her next move, she turned and ran out onto Vlameir's balcony. Both he and Leanna gave chase, but she had flung herself off the edge of the balcony before they could reach her."

Looking over the edge of the railing, Leanna, cried out at the sight down below them. "Oh my God! Vlameir," she turned and found herself caught in his arms as he held her close.

"I know. I'm as shocked as you." He answered softly. His mind was reeling, and he found his heart was pounding in his ears as he tried to process all his aunt had said before taking her own life. The Drow Lord was someone he had heard stories about as he had been growing up. But that had been all it was. Stories. Horror tales told around campfires in his youth. They were said to be strong magical beings, Fathers of the Dark and Wood Elf races, but separate still, because they were mean and spiteful creatures, with no capacity to love in their hearts.

He had never even met any Drow. Indeed, it was believed that they had either gone so far to ground that they had died, or discovered yet another Realm to call their own, free of sharing with others. Truly, they were said to live so far beneath the earth's surface that no one ever encountered them anymore.

Looking down on the broken body of his beloved aunt, Vlameir had a horrible feeling that his peaceful land was about no longer to know peace. He was so deep in his thoughts, he almost missed Leanna's words.

"I should go home. I'm disrupting things and I do not want to be the cause of anything bad happening. Do you think Torlek would mind taking me to the portal? I'll simply go back home and that way whoever this Drow Lord is won't have a reason to try to start anything—"

Vlameir crossed the room to her side, taking her hands in his own. "It's too late. You heard my aunt. He has already awoken and knows you are here." He paused, and a look of self-loathing crossed his face as he added, "and I apologize, but you cannot go back home. Not now. Not ever."

Pulling away from him, she tugged her hands free from his grasp slowly. "Why? What do you mean?" Her question was softly spoken, as her eyes searched his.

Vlameir covered his face with a hand, before running it through his hair in a show of building frustration. "I have never considered myself a selfish man. But the first night I beheld you, I knew you were the other half of my soul." His eyes searched hers for any hope of forgiveness, even as he admitted why she would damn him. "As soon as I got you here, I had the Castle Mage give you a potion to slow your aging to the same rate as a normal Elf.

"It turned back time, just a little. I'm sure you noticed you looked a tad younger the next day." He watched as she considered his words, before adding with a shrug, "That in itself does not bar you from going back to the mortal realm. But what I failed to mention to you when you came across is that time moves differently here. To you; you have been here mere days. Meanwhile, back at your home, it's been the better part of four months."

At his words, Leanna's breathing became ragged, and she started pacing the floor, reminding him of a caged gazelle. "Four months? I've been away from my home for four months? Are you kidding? How in the world—How dare you! Why wouldn't you tell me this? I don't understand."

Holding up his hands, he tried to step closer to her, but she backed away from him swiftly, "Don't touch me! Don't you *dare touch me!*" She could not fight the tears that came so swiftly. "I trusted you. I believed you were..." her words stopped as she fought to suppress a sob. "I am a fool!"

Vlameir was swift to respond, "But you even admitted there really was no one waiting for you. You said you were mostly all alone now. Why do you care about going back to a place where nothing waits for you?" He hit his chest passionately. "I'm right here, and I would die without you!"

Leanna shook her head, backing away from him, tears streaming down her cheeks. "I should have had the choice!" she yelled back angrily. "It was *my* choice! When were you going to tell me? After I had been here long enough that *everyone* I knew on the mortal realm was either in *geriatrics, or dead?*" she groaned. "I cannot *believe you!* You don't even respect me enough to give me the choice!"

Fighting against every part of her that wanted to continue lashing out at him, she fled the room, running blindly to get away from him. Some part of her wished she could flee from the truth of the pain he had just inflicted in his harsh words of no one really waiting for her. That was beside the point!

Leanna ran through the halls of the castle as fast as her legs would carry her. She ran, not even realizing where she was going, her tears blinding her. When at last she ran into a dead end, she simply leaned brokenly against the wall before sliding down it, giving in to the sobs that wracked her system.

She didn't know how long she continued to cry. Her heart broke for Vlameir's deception, but more for how accurate he had been about who would even miss her. Her parents would mourn, she knew that.

But they would not search. She had pulled so far away from everyone all on her own in the last couple of years. Losing Max, then Daniel, had made her feel as if the best thing she could do to keep from feeling the pain of losing anyone else was to keep them all at a distance.

Kinsley was the only exception to that. They had been friends for too long. Kinsley would look. Not only would she look, but she would not stop. Poor woman would probably search the ends of the earth to find her.

"Lady Leanna?" the voice startled her, and she swung, ready to lash out at whoever was hovering. When she saw it was Drock, she relaxed. "Yes, Drock. It's me. Just testing my sanity, I guess."

"My Lady, are you unwell?" he asked softly, adding, "Should I send for a Mage?"

Holding out her hands, "No! Please don't." she half growled. "Last time one of those did anything for me, I was suddenly altered without even knowing I would be. I'd prefer to not repeat such a thing if you don't mind."

Drock's gaze became sympathetic. "Oh, I take it the king has finally informed you about not being able to leave." His words were soft.

Leanna's shoulders drooped. "You knew he didn't tell me?" she drew in a deep breath, then releasing it, stood facing him fully. "Does everyone know? What was going to happen if I decided early on I wanted to go home? Were you and the other guards going to stop me? With force if necessary?" She knew her words were accusatory, but she did not have it in her to be kind."

Drock looked at her with a sad expression. "I do not condone my king's actions, my Lady. But I know his reasoning. He did not want to lose you. He had hoped you would decide on your own to stay."

Leanna turned away, closing her eyes against the pain of the truth that she had very nearly already decided on her own to stay. "I probably would have chosen to stay on my own, Drock. But don't you see? That's what hurts, though. I wasn't given a choice." She sighed dejectedly before turning back to him. "I'm lost. Can you show me back to my chambers, please?"

His eyes were worried as he bowed his head in acknowledgement of her request. "Of course. Follow me." He paused for a moment, as if wanting to say more, but then seemed to decide against it and turned away, walking at a moderate pace.

Leanna was thankful for his acceptance of her desire not to talk any longer and instead followed behind him silently. It was not as far of a walk as she had thought it might have been with how she had ended up lost so easily.

When they reached her door, he turned and bowed to her. "My Lady, if you have need of anything, please call on me."

With a nod, she turned to enter the room. "Lady Leanna?" at his voice, she stopped, and turned back to meet his gaze. She waited as he continued. "I know you are angry at the king. But if I may, in his defense," He held his hands out, entreating on her sympathies. "He had all but given up on finding you. I know, he was working to come to terms with letting the kingdom go." He smiled sadly. "Then, there you were, and I've never seen him so happy. He's a changed man, because of you." His eyes pleaded with her to understand, "Try not to hate him for too long. He fell in love with you at first sight."

After speaking his mind, Drock did not dally. He bowed deeply to her, then turned and left her, leaving her with her own thoughts.

Turning, she opened her door and entered her room, looking around to be sure she was alone. Realizing she was, she breathed a deep breath of relief and moved to sit on her bed.

It was then, she saw it. The book Vlameir's aunt had left them. Lying atop it was a note from him.

Leanna,

I realize you are angry with me. I did not make the right decisions where you were concerned. Torlek told me I was doing you a disservice by not being forthcoming with you from the start.

I have nothing to say in my defense, save the fact I was terrified you would not choose me. The scariest part of that is my heart had already chosen you. Please read through my aunt's journal. It is basically written for you.

If after you have read it, you cannot find it in your heart to stay, I will procure the needed antidote to the Youth Serum so I can return you to your home. My only wish is for your happiness.

Yours Eternally,
Vlameir

Fifteen

Leanna sat on her bed, reading Adrianna's diary. Her mind was all over the place at the other woman's revelation. Finding out Vlameir had no intention of letting her go home had been hard enough. But now, through reading this woman's journal, she had found a hidden story behind who she really was. It was scary in and of itself. She did not see how she could possibly be related to an Elf. That would mean that she should have been born here, wouldn't it? Or did that mean, she shouldn't even exist? No sooner than she would begin to ponder one question, another one would pop up in her mind.

A sick feeling hit Leanna in the gut, making her have to lower the book, take a deep breath and calm herself. If this was true, then that meant she was descended from a woman who was an Elf and belonged here. This was her true home, her true heritage.

She felt out of sorts and at a loss as to what emotion she should even be feeling. Part of her was furious for her ancestor because it was horrible that a child should be stripped away from her true path in life and thrown into another.

But she felt confusion over also feeling thankful she had gotten to experience the life she had. How could she dare to feel slighted or punished when she had been happy in her human life?

So far, from what she had read, she knew that Adrianna had fallen into a deep infatuation with a Dark Mage, who was from a different race of Elves. He had always kept her at an arms-length, while teaching her how to hone her magical skills.

The Mage had taught her how to channel magic in such a way, it gave her dominion over the elements, as well as some aspects of mind control. She had easily become infatuated with both the power he opened her up to, as well as with him.

He was beautiful and unique, unlike any creature she had encountered earlier in her life, with skin the color of deepest night and eyes that reminded her of the light that shown from the moon. Indeed, the stars themselves seemed to be reflected off his skin. She considered him an amazing mentor and instructor and caught herself frequently wishing he would become her lover.

On and on, the sections in the journal continued spouting praise for the mystery Elf who was changing Adrianna's world. A few times, Leanna found herself only skimming pages that really said nothing pertinent about him other than her infatuation.

When Leanna turned to the page where her heart stopped, it was from reading the lines; "He says I must prove my love. I'm afraid, because what he is asking of me is a betrayal to everything I have been raised to believe. But my heart hurts at the idea of him leaving and the prospect of never seeing him again."

The next entries outlined the plan to steal the newborn baby away from the unsuspecting parents and take her to be sacrificed to some weird creature that was said to live deep in the woods.

Pain gathered in Leanna's chest as she read the horrible plan Adrianna was being asked to take part in. How could anyone do that to an innocent? Just the concept turned her stomach. The burning of sacred runes into the child's skin was the worst of it. Leanna imagined the torturous pain the poor infant would have been subjected to.

The rites the diary spoke of made tears flow freely down her cheeks. She had only just met Adrianna, but she couldn't have imagined the lady could ever be capable of such barbaric behavior. It would not have mattered how much Leanna loved someone. If they had wanted her to prove that love by completing such a heinous act, she would walk away from them, never looking back.

As she read on, she soon discovered the plan Adrianna actually followed was, by all means, still on the brutal side, but not as horrendous as the original plan. The child had been marked with one simple rune, which once healed looked like a birthmark. The rune was the marker for Destiny, and it had been placed on the back of the baby's shoulder.

Adrianna had used healing balms and incantations to eliminate the pain that had been caused to the child and erase the incident from the babe's memory. Then, she met and bargained with a strange creature, known to her people as a Bakru, who was able to deliver the child to the mortal realm and safely into the arms of parents who would love her as their own and help her find a full and carefree life.

As Adrianna's story went on, she described the price she had to pay to see the child to safety. The Bakru, while willing to help her see to the baby's safety, had demanded a steep price in payment. Every single bit of magic she had grown into and learned how to harvest, had to be given up. He stripped her of every special power she had, save one. Her intuitive sight had been spared. It was neither a defensive nor aggressive power. In reality, it was, in the Bakru's mind, a useless gift. Adrianna had quoted his exact words to her: This is less of a price to be paid, and more of a punishment, for the squandering of your gifts. Love cannot be added into the narrative when it comes to magic. Too high of a price will always be paid. Be glad, it is only your magic I demand for this boon. By all rights, I could have demanded your soul and made you my slave.

The final entry into the journal had been a simple letter, addressed to Leanna:

My Dearest Leanna,

This letter reaching you, means I have surrendered my life to keep the Drow Lord from using me against you and my nephew. As much as I would like to believe I have grown past his influences during this time he has gone to ground, I cannot say for certain he cannot still control me. He is, honestly, a master manipulator, and has a way of making the person under his influence believe what they are doing is all their idea.

I cannot let him use me in that way. Not against Vlameir, or anyone else I love, for that matter. Beware of him, should your paths cross and you find you are alone in his presence. He is a seductive creature who will make your heart ache for things you believed were lost to you. He'll promise to bring those things to you in abundance, but you must be on your guard.

He cannot be trusted, and you must guard yourself extra carefully, my dear. For you are the only soul that will open Vlameir to all his untapped potential. The magic which will grow from the love in your two hearts is the kind that can bridge the gap between races and create a new life for both the human and Elf races. The Drow Lord sees that as a threat and will want to eradicate you as a means of keeping my nephew from reaching his full potential. He draws power by feeding hatred and distrust between your many peoples. Do not be fooled into thinking he would not lead others to do the same in the mortal realm as well, if he could.

I hope Vlameir can find it in his heart to forgive me. I did what I did in my youth, foolishly believing I could make the Drow Lord love me. I did not see at the time that I was playing such a dangerous game. Please look after him and never forget, you belong here. It is your birthright, as is the kingdom of the Elves of the Forest Moon.

Another tragedy that came from my actions over a century ago, was the decimation of the Forest Moon Clan. You are the descendant of Ellaria Nightshade. She would have been the queen of her people.

The Rune I placed on your great-great grandmother was worked magically into her blood. It is a Rune symbolizing Destiny. The mark she bore was to be passed down through her descendants. You have that same mark on the back of your shoulder. It was why the portal opened up to you so easily. It was the reason I knew you beyond a shadow of doubt when you came to dinner.

Then when I touched you, I saw more than only your memories. I was given a view into the life Ellaria had before you and I knew you were her granddaughter. I knew you'd come home.

The Forest Moon Clan left their homes and scattered after the abduction of their king and queen's daughter, leaving their world behind. The entire kingdom was so stricken by grief, none of them had the will to try to carry on. It is one of the reasons the forest here is now such an untamed place. The village that was there is abandoned now. Ellaria's parents placed a charm on their castle when they left it. No one can open the gates except for one of their bloodline.

Leanna, claim your birthright. Take back your kingdom and help unite the Elves who scattered, taking their talents for magic forestry with them. Your people will come back if they know you have come. Also, with you and Vlameir united, our world will flourish and peace between all of the kingdoms can finally once and for all, be reached.

Again, I ask you and Vlameir find it in your hearts to forgive me. Please tell my sister when she comes home, I am so sorry for being a weak-minded fool and not making up for it sooner.

Sincerely and affectionately,
Adrianna

Leanna sat, stunned, staring down at the book in her hands. In such a short time, she had gone from being a mere mortal, entering the Fae Realm as a visitor, to becoming the soul-mate to the king... and now she was discovering that she was half Elven herself and the true heir to a throne all her own.

She wondered for a moment if perhaps she shouldn't pinch herself, if only to prove she wasn't dreaming, before shaking her head. She knew full well, she was awake. She didn't have the kind of dreams where people committed suicide before her very eyes.

Setting the book down, she stood and walked slowly to the full-length mirror which stood in the corner, waiting patiently for her to gaze upon it. As she neared it, she stared blindly at a point in it, considering all she had just learned. The birthmark Adrianna had spoken of had always appeared to her as a very strange mark indeed. Her mother had it also. What they had always found so odd about it, was they were always exactly the same. There were never any subtle differences in them. Well, now she knew why.

Pulling down the collar of the robe, Leanna turned and examined the mark again. Was it even possible? Could what Adrianna told her in her letter even be true? And who was to say that a fortress would magically open up, the moment she appeared at its gates?

Almost as if summoned by her turn of thoughts, a knock sounded at the chamber doors. For a moment, Leanna stayed silent. Then called out, "You can come in."

There was a slight hesitancy. Then the door opened and Vlameir entered the room, looking somber. He stood meeting her gaze through the mirror. The sharing of their emotions was immediate. Then he broke the silence. "I am sorry, Leanna. I had no right to take the freedom of your choice from you." He paused and held her gaze in the mirror's reflection. After a moment, he cleared his throat, asking, "So, what did you find in her journal?"

Seemingly chilled at the mention of the book, Leanna pulled her robe back tight against her, turning to face him. She walked slowly to his side and stared up at him. He seemed to hold his breath as he opened his arms to her. She paused, looking from his open arms then back to his face. Softly, she whispered. "Please don't ever lie to me again. Okay?" she paused for a moment, before adding, "And for the record, I do not care if there is something you are terrified I cannot handle. Don't keep me in the dark about anything which concerns me."

When he nodded, she gladly stepped into his arms when he opened them again. Drawing a shuddering breath, "As to what I found out in the book," she answered softly, "It was more than I bargained for."

Sixteen

Vlameir read through the same book while Leanna paced, stopping every so often to look his way, watching his facial expressions for signs of his emotional reactions. She didn't dare to speak a word. Instead she tried to busy herself straightening things around her chambers.

As he neared the end, she moved to sit beside him, watching his face as he finished reading. She noted his face was stoic as he finished the letter his aunt had left in the end. When he slowly closed the book and turned to look her in the eyes, his expression turned sad. "I wish she would have had more faith in my ability to keep her safe from the Drow." His words were softly spoken and pulled at Leanna's heart.

Reaching out, she took his hand in hers. "I know. I feel her reasons were to keep him from being able to use her against you. He must be extremely dangerous for her to have felt this was her only choice." Unwillingly, Leanna's eyes moved to the balcony and involuntarily, she shuddered. The sickening crunch of Adrianna's body hitting the ground kept playing over and over in her mind.

Vlameir's guards had long since taken the body away, erasing all signs of the suicide. Everyone already knew about it. After Leanna had fled to her own chambers, she had the nagging feeling of being watched. Part of her even worried that in some small way, she might have been blamed for the Lady Adrianna's death. Of course, she knew that wasn't the case. But all the same, she still felt that way.

She hated this feeling. It was a nagging sensation of being watched and judged by her every movement. How many people even knew of Adrianna's suicide? Was it all over the castle? The very idea made her feel ill. She had no desire to open herself up to other's speculations yet.

Although Vlameir had appeased her desire to stay secluded, he had been steadfast in his argument that no one would blame her for his aunt's death. He dismissed the very idea as insane.

If she were honest with herself, Leanna knew he was right. But some part of her could not help but feel somewhat responsible. If it had not been for her coming here, after all, the Drow Lord, as Adrianna had referred to him, would not have awakened.

When she voiced this thought to him, Vlameir did not hesitate to correct her. "If what my aunt says is true, he would have awakened within the next few years anyway; and he would have been even a worse threat because I would not have found my mate. Without you, I would lose my throne. As well as my desire to live." He paused, running his hand through his hair, "Don't you see, Leanna? The fact you are here makes us stronger against him. You must see that."

When Leanna looked down at her hands instead of agreeing with him, he moved to her side, kneeling down before her and taking them in his own. "My love. You are the missing link to recovering the people lost to us from the fall of the Forest Moon Clan. When the babe was lost to them, their entire culture crumbled. Her parents were so lost to their mourning, they lost the very desire to rule, and their Clan simply chose to all walk away."

"When it is brought to light that you are returned to your rightful place, they will come. They will rebuild. The alliances between our people will strengthen us and the power to defeat the Drow Lord will end him once and for all."

When she still didn't meet his gaze, Vlameir squeezed her hands gently. "Leanna," his use of her name made her look at him. Smiling gently, he explained, "My aunt knew that this enemy will be grasping at any means he has to gain the upper hand over us. As much as I hate that she ended her life, I recognize she did it to take herself out of the equation, so he cannot use her against us." He sighed before adding, "Don't let her sacrifice mean so little, okay?"

Weighing his words, she knew he was right. Taking a deep breath, she nodded. "You are right. I know this." With a shake of her head, she glanced at her art supplies, lying forgotten on the table. "To think this all started by my coming here simply to paint a portrait." She smiled sadly, looking back to him. "and I haven't even started it."

Vlameir's face broke into a huge smile and he leaned forward, gently kissing her lips, before whispering, "You'll have a dozen lifetimes to finish that painting. We are only starting our new lives together."

Returning his smile, Leanna squared her shoulders. "So, I guess we need to go find this lost village and see what it takes for me to open this fortress up, huh?"

Vlameir nodded. "Yes. And I know just who knows the way to it."

Torlek whistled softly as he set the book down, having read the journal from front to back. He had paled considerably when he got to the letter Adrianna had written Leanna. Now, as he looked at her, he smiled. "Well, now... I always knew you were royalty. Fancy that?"

Leanna rolled her eyes at his comment and shook her head. "Leave it to you not to be surprised by all this," she muttered, not without humor.

The Dragon shifter shrugged with a smile. "I am older than you would believe, your Highness. I remember the days when all of the Clans, including your Clan were all thriving civilizations." He smiled sadly. "I helped search for your ancestor when she was taken, and I remember the queen's tears when she realized her baby was forever lost to her." He tilted his head as he stared now at Leanna. "You look very much like her. I'm surprised I didn't see the resemblance before. Of course, I doubt I would have put two and two together. It seemed like it happened so long ago now."

Vlameir had been leaning against the wall, waiting patiently as his friend read the journal. Now, he pushed away from it and moved to stand beside Leanna and Torlek. "Do you remember the way to their castle, my friend?"

Torlek sighed before nodding. "It has been a long time, but I still visit the area from time to time." He looked to Leanna. "It is very overgrown by the Forest, but I am sure, the fortress will welcome you and come back to life straightaway when you arrive."

Leanna glanced between the two men in confusion before laughing at their absurdity. "The way you talk, you would think the stones of the building were alive."

Torlek laughed before answering, "You are in the Fae Realm, my Lady. Of course, the castle is alive."

Leanna's face fell and all humor vanished as she stared in something akin to shock. "Seriously?" That was a new idea.

Torlek raised an eyebrow at her, "How else do you think the castle will know it is you? It isn't as if your body has a magical key hidden on it that even you haven't seen." He held out his hand to her. "No, my Lady. The stones will remember the scent of your ancestors. Now, let us go begin putting together your destiny, shall we?"

Leanna hesitated for a moment, considering. Vlameir stepped up beside her and took her hand and she glanced down at their fingers linked together before turning her face back to Torlek and taking his offered hand as well. "Well, I've never really been the kind to turn down a good adventure."

Seventeen

When Leanna climbed onto Torlek's back, it was with a sense of resolve. Her mind was still trying to process what all had occurred over the past week. She'd barely come to terms with the fact that Dragons and Elves both existed and in fact, lived in a Realm, accessible from a bridge found on the land she had just bought.

Now, on top of those revelations, she had to come to terms with the fact that she was one of them. Or a great grandmother had been, which meant she was too, as well as also being royalty. At the thought, Leanna caught herself smirking. To think of herself as royalty was a bit far fetched to her. She didn't think she was anything special.

Then, she considered that there was still a possibility this was all only a dream; an amazing dream, to be certain, but still... The whole thing seemed too crazy to be real. What could possibly be the chances?

No sooner had the thought escaped her than she dismissed it. She chastised herself to stop depending on logic to wrap her mind around all that was taking place. She knew that any and all logic she would call on could not be applied here. This was beyond logic.

Instead of letting herself try to make sense of it all, she instead looked out over the forest Torlek was just beginning to fly over. A feeling of peaceful acceptance came over her. This was her world now. She belonged here. Exactly how any of it had come to pass, was no longer relevant. If they believed she could gain access and reopen this kingdom, she gave herself in to that belief. Why shouldn't she? Faith was a small leap when it came to this new life she was becoming a part of. She had already found herself believing in the miracles that had flooded her life in the small time she had been here.

She shared a love with a man she had never dared to believe was real. He had written the other half of the songs she played in her head since she was a child. Her heart was full for the first time since before she had begun her journey through the loss of her husband and son.

A small smile flitted across her face as she let the beauty surrounding her finally capture her attention. The trees almost seemed to hum with a life and vibrance that called to her in a way that made her breath catch in her throat. Suddenly, she could feel their essence. As if realizing these things she had always viewed as plants were not only alive, but conscious, intelligent, and possessed not only the memories of the things that had taken place in the past, but also the intellect to share them with someone who knew how to listen.

No sooner had the realization come to her, than she felt the gentle touch of their consciousness reaching out to her, showing her images of the lives her ancestors led. Through the visions they brought to her, everything else seemed to fall in place. Their memories seemed to join with hers, giving her the knowledge of the path to the castle and the understanding of who she really was.

A sense of calm came over her. She found herself biting her tongue to keep from calling out to Torlek, to correct his path to a quicker route. Neither Vlameir nor Torlek knew what she had just experienced. She sensed Vlameir knew something was different by the way he was holding her, but he was not linked to her telepathically as these trees now were. Indeed, the link that had just formed with them was spiritual.

She knew a sense of coming home when Torlek began to descend toward the ground. She watched as the wall of vines and brush came into view. To someone not knowing what to look for, it would merely look like a collection of roots and foliage that had simply grown too high to climb.

As Torlek landed, Leanna didn't even pause. She lifted her leg over his back, and slid down his side swiftly, landing on her feet and starting forward, not even hearing as Vlameir cautioned her to wait for him she felt the pull of the place so fully.

Torlek and Vlameir exchanged a glance and the Dragon immediately shifted down into his human visage. As he moved to the Elf's side, the king handed him his dagger. Both men prepared to defend Leanna, even as she raced headlong into possible danger unknowingly.

As she walked closer to the wall, she took in the intricate carvings, hidden within the foliage. It blended so well with the wood and leaves, not just anyone would have seen it. Taking the beauty of it in, she smiled slightly as she followed the path the carvings created, pointing her in a direction only she seemed to understand.

There was something so familiar about it. She felt as if a part of her knew this place even though she had never been here; never in her wildest dreams had she imagined this was anything real. Growing up, she had an affinity for different fantasy stories. The kind that centered around Faeries and Dragons and enchanted forests were her favorite kinds. But she had never believed they were real.

Now, in this short amount of time, she had discovered she not only had a soulmate in a Realm she'd only barely discovered existed. In that short breath of time she had not only learned the reality of the Realm, as well as the fact she was meant to have lived here. This place before her was her home. She could feel the truth of it inside her heart.

Torlek and Vlameir followed closely behind her but did not try to dissuade her from her direction. Instead, they watched her closely and tried to guard from any unseen traps or danger that lurked in the woods.

Soon, the three of them came to what looked to be a giant, fallen tree with part of its trunk hollowed out. The tree was so huge, even lying on its side, there was no clear way over it that could be seen. However, it was not the tree that drew Leanna's attention, but what was inside the hollowed-out part of the trunk which made her curious.

Inside the tree, was an elderly woman. In spite of being notably old, she had a certain energy about her which Leanna regarded with awe. The woman sat cross-legged on the ground, a strange set of runes thrown on the ground before her, along with several crystals. Her hands moved slowly, hovering over each rune in turn.

When she looked up, her keen eyes, moved immediately to Leanna and a huge smile lit up her face. "Well, there you are. I've been searching for you ever since I woke up. You're a hard one to pin down, child."

Leanna opened her mouth to respond but could not quite find any words. Instead, Vlameir asked, "What do you mean, trying to find her?" his voice was curious, and his hand had clasped Leanna's, as if holding it would keep her from venturing any closer to the stranger.

The older lady turned her gaze to Vlameir. "Hello, Elf King. Fancy seeing you in our neck of the woods." She smiled softly as her gaze took him in. "And to answer your question; I felt her. The moment she crossed over that first time I woke up. But she was gone; like a shooting star; here one moment, vanished the next. It was quite titillating, I tell you."

She turned back to Leanna, continuing to speak excitedly, "I began scrying as soon as I felt your presence again. The castle is so excited. Everything has been put in order and announcements of your arrival have been made."

Leanna had been nodding at the old woman's words but stopped short at her last words. "Announcements?" she repeated softly. "Announcements to who?"

The older lady smiled, and her eyes seemed to light up as well. "Your Clan, dearest. Your people scattered when your ancestor was taken, that is true. But your people have always had faith you would return." As she spoke, the woman closed the distance between herself and Leanna. "I am known as Gwendolyn and I am the consciousness of your castle, I am your advisor."

Before Leanna knew what her intentions were, Gwendolyn had placed her hand on the back of Leanna's neck and pressed her forehead onto hers. What followed was a kind of psychic connection that drove both women to their knees.

Gasping, Leanna felt herself transported into the memories of all her ancestors. She saw the forest Elves, from their earliest memories of existing in the forest, making their homes within the biggest of the trees and living in harmony with the wildlife of the forest.

Her people were hunters and fishers. They worked to protect the land from the darker creatures of the Fae Realm which meant harm.

The sheer magnitude of information flooding Leanna's brain had her fearing it might very well explode. It was like a massive 3-D journey into something like Tolkien's novels, but instead of a binge watching of unedited versions of the movies, it was more of a simultaneous instant download.

Physically, the only thing Leanna knew was when she lost her battle to stay standing and felt the pressure on her knees when they hit the ground. Reaching out, she clasped hold of Gwendolyn to keep from slipping directly into a fetal position on the ground.

The farther the memories went, the more she knew the information was vital to her success as a leader of her people.

As the memories continued, she saw into the lives of her ancestors and the love they had, not only for each other, but also for the baby as she became the center of their world.

When the memories of the babe's kidnapping came, Leanna felt the sting of the tears against her cheeks at the sense of loss her people felt. The despair they fell into was palpable and her heart felt the pain first-hand.

As the vision began to recede and Leanna slowly became aware of her surroundings, the first thing she knew was the knife brandished in Vlameir's hand as he demanded in a stern voice she be released.

Torlek also had sword in hand and was standing; ready to attack if needed.

Her eyes widened as she wrapped her arms protectively around Gwendolyn. "What do you think you're doing? How dare you!" Indignation was recognizable in her voice. "She was showing me my ancestry. My history! And you would attack her?"

It was Gwendolyn who answered her. "It is fine, my queen. They only seek to protect you." The Mage offered her a beautiful smile. "They could not have touched us. My magic surrounded us as you were incapacitated. No one, enemy or otherwise could touch you during your vision."

Vlameir sheathed his dagger and nodded to Torlek, who in turn, put away his sword with a grimace. "You cannot get angry because we simply chose to attempt to protect you."

Leanna regarded Torlek for a moment, weighing his words before offering a resigned nod. He was right. Even though she had realized what was happening, that did not mean either one of them had. She honestly could not hold their alarm against them. Especially since if their roles had been reversed, she probably would have panicked as well.

Gwendolyn chose that moment to speak. "Well, now that's done, there are only a few minor details to take care of. Then you will be able to assume your rightful place as Queen of the Forest Elves as well as future wife of the King of the Light Elves. I believe, the joining of the two kingdoms will strengthen all."

Leanna and Vlameir exchanged a troubled look, before Vlameir questioned the old Mage. "What more needs to take place? She hasn't already endured enough?" A slight edge had seeped into his voice, giving a clue of his protective stance when it came to his mate.

Gwendolyn offered him a soft smile, holding up her hands in a sign of truce. "The Bakru. His magical camouflage should be lifted, so her people can recognize who she is and there can be no doubt of her true heritage."

Leanna stared at the Mage for a moment before asking, "My camouflage? You mean I don't even look like I'm suppose to?" her frown grew when she turned to Vlameir. "I feel like I'm about to have a serious identity crisis. What's wrong with the way I look?"

Moving to her side, his hands rested on her shoulders as his eyes bore into hers. "Nothing. You are perfect. Your heart will be what your people believe in when all is said and done—"

"But it will help to gain their attention if you have the same ears as them." Gwendolyn interrupted softly. When Vlameir turned an exasperated expression her way, she elaborated, "Not all Elven born trust humans." She shrugged. "I mean, look at what the majority of them have done to the world we share." Her eyes held some sympathy when she turned to look at Leanna, adding, "Some are fine with the few humans who have moved to our Realm, but would react very differently if they believed one of them was being given a position of power."

Torlek chose that moment to pipe up. "As much as I wish I could argue her points, my Lord, I am unable to give an honest argument over the fact. It would be best to allow the Bakru to remove his glamour. Her people cannot argue the fact of her heritage if the truth of it is staring them in the face."

Leanna sighed and looked at the entrance into the fortress that was of her family. She felt a moment of melancholy over it. This was her heritage, and it had been robbed from her. This was a piece of her life that should have been for both her and her son. Daniel should have been here too. He should be revered as a prince to the people who were about to be called back home.

Taking a deep breath, she released it on a sigh as she squared her shoulders and looked at the Mage. "So, where is the Bakru, and do I have to wait for him to remove the glamour before I can see my castle?"

Gwendolyn bowed deeply. "I've already summoned him, Majesty. As to your castle... of course, you may see your home now." She smiled at Leanna warmly. "It has been very excited about your return."

Leanna raised an eyebrow at the Mage's words, but instead of asking her to explain, simply shrugged. "Okay, then. I would like to see my castle, please."

Again bowing deeply, Gwendolyn turned and raised her arms in a dramatic gesture, facing the only closed off part of the hollowed-out tree they were standing in. Her arms crossed over each other over her face, then with a sweeping gesture, the wall of wood began to shimmer, melting away to reveal a beautiful garden, filled with flowering trees, vines and plants.

The scents of the blooms filled Leanna's senses, and she felt a calm sort of peace come to her. The worry and frustration she had felt over all the talk about her appearance being a glamour to be removed, dissolved as she took in the beauty of where she was.

Beyond the gardens, with their beautiful flowers and amazing fragrance, stood an ancient tree. The circumference of its trunk was big enough Leanna imagined that if fifty people stood with arms around it, outstretched to touch each other, they would barely be able to surround it.

Mesmerized, she crossed the distance toward it. At first glance, it seemed to be simply a tree. But as she drew closer, she saw the steps that began to form in a spiral, around the front of it, leading to a doorway. Stopping, she stared at it, catching her breath at how spectacular it was. When she spoke, it was in a hushed whisper. "My castle is a tree?"

Gwendolyn chuckled at her words. "Well, you are a Forest Elf, my Lady. I'd wager a boon even when you were in the human realm, you still preferred to be close to nature." Her smile grew. "How often did you find yourself talking to the trees?"

Leanna found herself returning the smile almost shyly. "All the time, actually." She glanced up at Vlameir, adding, "I used to tell the trees all my secrets I didn't dare share with any walking, talking soul. It was the reason I bought the cottage on that land. The trees gave me such peace. When I first saw the property, I imagined they were singing to me." She chuckled absently, "I-I must sound nuts."

At her words, Vlameir grabbed her hand and pressed it to his heart. "NO! No, you don't sound crazy, my love. You sound as if a part of you knew that by being there, you would find your way home." Raising her hand to his lips, he placed a tender kiss on each finger. "I'm so glad you found your way back to us. I would be forever lost without you."

Smiling through the sheen of tears that sprang up at his endearment, Leanna bit her lip as she turned back to the Mage. "Show me my Ancestral home, Gwendolyn."

The older woman smiled and nodded, "Come right this way, my dear." Turning, she led them up the steps spiraling around the ancient tree.

When Leanna had first seen the steps, she thought it would be quite a climb to get to the entry. But in less time than she would have imagined, they were standing before it.

Swallowing her anxiety, she stepped up to the door and instinctively placed the flat of her palm against it. She didn't know how she knew, but part of her simply had the knowledge that all she needed for the door to open was to let it recognize her.

It took only a few seconds before the tree seemed to groan, as if waking from a long sleep. In a few more moments, the door seemed to magically shift and slide open, like doors on an elevator.

The expanse of the view which greeted them was anything but the view of an elevator, however. A huge open balcony greeted her, an intricately carved wooden staircase with a banister flanking either side of the entrance. Carvings of birds, Faeries, and Elves bearing what appeared to be a specific coat of arms greeted her view, making her smile.

As she looked around, she noticed there were several stairways. Some led to floors above, while others led down to floors below. But amid the different staircases were huge corridors, with entryways into various rooms. With a deep breath, she chose which entryway to walk through, and squaring her shoulders, walked right through it without any hesitation.

As soon as her eyes lit on the thrones sitting side by side, she knew it was the throne room. But when her eyes traveled up to the wall behind it, she felt a wave of fresh emotion well up within her. The wall behind the seats had been carved into the likeness of the last king to hold the throne, with his queen beside him with their child in her arms. The beauty of it made Leanna feel robbed.

Moving closer, she studied the faces of her ancestors. When she spoke, her voice was no more than a whisper. "This isn't fair. I had the right to know my family. My true family. How dare that monster take it all from me."

Turning, she stared into Vlameir's eyes as she addressed them all. "Summon the Bakru. The sooner his glamour is removed, the sooner I can take my rightful place here and we can unite forces against our common enemy." She took a deep breath before adding, "It is time our race was united against any and all enemies."

Vlameir watched the woman he loved speak with such authority it made his heart swell with pride. She was worthy to be queen of her people, and of his. He had no doubt of it, but hearing her words reinforced his resolve. She would be queen of the two Elven tribes and also, his wife. Together, they would begin uniting all their people as it was meant to be.

Eighteen

After the Mage sent summons to the Bakru, she also called forth a few of the other Mages and villagers whose families had not traveled too far from them. As they began arriving, the castle was abuzz with a life all its own. Lights magically illuminated high above them from an unknown source, giving an almost ethereal glow to each of the chambers.

Leanna had already dragged Vlameir around the castle, looking through every available space and taking everything in, twice. She marveled at it all and went back and forth between excitement and trepidation at the very idea of being a ruler over such a place. Now, as she sat in the privacy of her chambers, with him, she was half petrified at the very thought of what was taking place all around her.

Vlameir had sent Torlek to gather a group of guards from his kingdom to come assist in guarding and watching over things as the Forest Elves began making their way back home. Gwendolyn had suggested Leanna stay out of sight until the Bakru had taken care of removing her glamour. She did so; reluctantly at first. then fearfully as time ebbed on ever slowly. "What if he doesn't come, Vlameir?" Her voice trembled with the evidence of her trepidation. "Or what if he refuses to fix me?"

At her words, Vlameir pulled her into his embrace, and held her tightly against him. "Hear this now! You are perfect! There is nothing wrong with you and you do not need to be *fixed*. Once your people know you, it will not matter that your ears are not shaped as ours."

He pulled back, forcing her to meet his gaze. "If the Bakru comes and can lift his glamour, then fine. If he doesn't, then we shall merely endeavor to let the people see how amazing you are, all on your own. But there is nothing wrong with you! You do not *need* fixing."

Leanna melted into his arms and held to him tightly. Her heart felt so full, she wondered if she would explode. He was her lifeline. She realized easily, all her bravery and resolution over the entire matter came from him. He was the embodiment of the meaning of bravery.

She realized in that moment the depth of his love for her was unlike anything she had ever felt before. Lifting her face toward his, she whispered softly, "Make love to me."

Vlameir's eyes sparkled as he stepped back from her. For a moment, she wondered if he would deny her, but then, he made the decision to stop any doubts he might have had. Her eyes never left his as she slipped the tunic dress off, letting it drop to the ground and leaving herself open and bare to his view.

The look on his face erased any insecurity she may have felt. He stripped his own clothes away, closing the distance between them and pushing her down onto the bed as his lips crushed hers greedily. She moaned into his mouth in response, meeting his passion with a full fire of her own.

A magical energy crackled between them like a tinderbox, simmering with their combined energies. Neither of them noticed the room became somewhat dimmer; the lighting seeming to garner initiative for what mood needed to be set by the actions of its occupants.

Leanna felt the kiss setting her body on fire. The burning began in her lower abdomen and spread through to the rest of her. She ached for him in ways she could not even consider finding words to try to explain. The depth of her love for him made her want nothing more than to give him everything. Greedily, she ran her fingertips over his torso, paying extra attention to the puckered skin of his nipples, before continuing her exploration downward, relishing his well-defined muscles as she went.

He rewarded her touch with a deep shudder, and his kiss became gentle, shifting from the hunger of a half-starved man, to one who was slowly savoring a long deep drink. As if coming to his senses, he began a slow, gentle exploration that had not even been present the first time they made love.

This time, it was there with such an intensity, it brought tears to her eyes and made her own movements echo his. She loved exploring him—touching, tasting, memorizing everything. She found a scar on his shoulder and gave it extra attention, kissing and nuzzling, and bringing a smile to his face.

When he pulled away slightly and gifted her with that smile, she whispered, "I love you." Her heart sped up as she wondered what he would say to her for speaking those words to him right now.

Vlameir wrapped his hand around the back of her neck, pulling her closer to him, resting his forehead against hers and spoke softly in words she recognized, but did not understand how. *"Is brea liom tu,"* She knew he had said *I Love you,* but she did not know how she recognized the words.

Shaking her head, she bit her lip. "How is it I understood you? That's a language I shouldn't know." Even as she asked, she continued to touch him. She felt like if she stopped touching him, he might disappear, like awakening from an amazing dream.

His own hands were moving in whisper soft movements over her skin, waking every inch of her to his tenderness. She ached to do more, but at the same time was enjoying the intimacy of the touch. It felt more like making love to her than any mere sex ever could. By the time he answered her, she had nearly forgotten she had asked a question.

"All Elven-born speak universal Gaelic. It was once the chosen language to communicate with all Humanity." He sighed. "Until the decision was made to close our world off to theirs and reject their progress, as they call it. They began dabbling in things that stole resources from their dimension of Gaia, and we made the decision to limit their ability to harm this side as well." His expression became a little hollow at that, "That is the biggest reason the language is almost all but forgotten in your Realm now. Only the Elders who have learned from their Elders even still know any of it."

His smile grew when he tenderly stroked the apex between her thighs, and she gasped. "You recognize the language because the part of you, which is Elven, was born knowing it. Just like some small part of you knew when we met that we belonged together."

At his words, his touch became a bit more demanding, rubbing her clit in a way that had her gasping and opening farther for him. His eyes moved down her body to where his fingers were touching her, and he growled deeply, before moving to kneel between her legs. *"Mine."*

When his tongue joined his hand, Leanna came apart, falling back on the bed, and giving herself over to his unspoken demand. He was right. She was his. Body and soul. His fingers parted her folds, giving his mouth better access and when he began sucking on her sensitive nub, her hands tangled in his hair and she cried out his name.

As if he were part of an orchestra, he took her calling his name as a reason to truly play some special instrument she had never had any clue he had. As he sucked on her flesh and his fingers probed her core, he began humming and the very vibration of it made her come undone, shaking, and crying in a release that she felt sure would take her life as the waves of ecstasy crashed over her.

The orgasm left her shaking like a leaf and spent. It was then she felt Vlameir climbing up her body, pausing only to kiss her navel, then suckle a moment at her nipples. When he was completely over her, she felt his member, engorged and pressing slowly into her wet core.

Her eyes opened wide as she lifted her hips slightly to help him slide fully into her. The heat she felt by his body joining with hers made her cry out. When he began moving, she moved with him and together they found a place even the heavens would envy.

When they were spent, they lay curled together, not even caring they had not pulled the covers back or slipped under. They needed no extra warmth. They had found all the heat they needed within each other.

Nineteen

The Faery light flickered to life, casting an earie glow to the now darkened room. Vlameir slept soundly through it, but Leanna had been just starting to doze off when the light moved closer to her.

Her eyes opened, momentarily alarmed to find herself staring at what appeared to be a lightning bug. But instead of the yellow light she was used to seeing, this one was a baby blue in color and seemed to call to her, moving back and forth before her eyes. Glancing back to Vlameir she considered waking him, because a part of her wondered if to follow this little light might be leading herself into a trap.

But as she looked at his resting form, sleeping so peacefully, she could not bring herself to wake him. Instead, she stared at his beauty for a moment before whispering, "You are so beautiful, my king."

Resigned to let him rest, she rose and grabbed the robe lying by the bed and donning it, followed the flickering light. Surprisingly, it didn't lead her from the room, but instead, to the fireplace.

Confused, Leanna stood for a moment, watching the tiny creature buzz around a specific area of the hearth, as if trying to draw her attention to it specifically. Try as she might, she couldn't see anything. Finally, she moved closer, and knelt beside it and looked closer. It took a moment, but once she noticed the small button, she reached out and pushed it hesitantly, silently praying there wasn't some trap door she was going to fall through.

In a moment, she heard a sliding sound. Standing back from the fireplace, she watched as a panel opened, showing a small, hidden compartment. Leanna's eyes widened as she took in the contents of the small cabinet.

"It's a hidden jewelry box," she whispered to no one in particular. There were necklaces and rings, and a thin, silver crown with a single dark green stone at its center.

"Everything here is part of your birthright." A soft, feminine voice that seemed to echo through the room intoned. Leanna whirled around to find a translucent specter of a beautiful Elf. She had long brunette hair with auburn highlights that flowed freely down past her hips and green eyes. She stood only a few feet from Leanna, a kind smile softening her face. Her entire form was surrounded in a blue aura, and Leanna recognized it as the light she had followed. "We have waited for so long for your arrival. Now with you here, our people will be reunited, and the land will thrive again."

Leanna looked at the spirit in confusion. "Vlameir hasn't told me about any of his people suffering. I mean, we know now about the enemy who plotted to keep us from finding each other, but from everything I've seen, no one has truly suffered."

The Elven woman nodded. "As yet, our enemy has not put his plan into motion. He has been biding his time, waiting for Vlameir to lose his rights to the thrown. Of course, now you have come, his original plan will be thwarted." Her expression became one of grim determination. "Now, he will be forced to come forward from the Shades and attack, if he has the nerve."

The woman's words confused her for a moment before understanding dawned; this woman before her was her ancestor. "You're part of my family from here?" Her question was spoken almost hesitantly.

The translucent woman nodded with a sad smile. "I've met your son. He would have made a fine prince. Just as his mother will be an amazing queen."

Leanna felt her jaw drop and for several seconds, she simply stared at her antecedent before recovering. "You've met Daniel?" tears sprang to her eyes. "Is he okay? I-I mean; is he happy?"

The spirit started to reach out to embrace her, but stopped short, as if realizing she wouldn't be able to touch her. She stared at her hand for a moment with a disappointed look, before letting it drop back to her side and giving Leanna a tender smile. "He is. He has been dwelling with us for a time in the spiritual plane. But I am fair-ly certain he has only been waiting to visit until you were ready." Her smile seemed sad when their eyes again met. "He's missed you. Honestly, we are all so happy you've fi-nally come home."

As she started to fade, she smiled at Leanna and whis-pered, "You're such a blessing, Leanna. May your life here be charmed with every happiness, my sweet granddaugh-ter." Then she was gone, leaving the younger woman, star-ing at the space where she had just been.

Barely a moment passed before Leanna heard the soft voice she had accepted she would never hear again. "Mom, I've missed you."

Leanna wanted to turn around, but the fear of him dis-appearing if she tried to see him was too great. Instead, her legs gave out from underneath her, and she sank to the ground. Pressing a fist to her mouth, she tried to stifle the sob that threatened to escape.

Afraid her voice would break of she spoke normally, she instead whispered, "I've missed you so much, Daniel."

The boy approached her side and knelt beside her. "Mom, I've been trying to watch over you. When I left my body, I was given three choices. I could stay with you, I would come here, or I could go ahead and go to heaven. I chose to come here because I already knew you would be here soon."

Finally, taking a deep breath, Leanna lifted her head to see her son sitting before her, looking strong and healthy. Gone were the dark bags under his eyes. His small form no longer looked like a skeleton. His appearance was one of vitality and happiness.

Leanna couldn't stop the smile that came to her face. "You look wonderful, honey." And he did. He looked like the happy healthy boy he had been before he had gotten sick. She wanted to wrap her arms around him and hug him tight, but she knew it was not something she could do. Her heart felt full. She had known he was no longer suffering, but actually seeing the proof of it made losing him a little easier.

Daniel stood, stepped closer to her and smiled. "I want you to be happy, Mom. I know the king loves you. I want you to give yourself permission to completely love him too."

He looked from her to Vlameir's sleeping form. "You're going to have more children and I will watch over them. Let yourself be happy without feeling guilt over me. You deserve this."

Leanna watched as he began to fade and felt a moment of alarm, unconsciously reaching out toward him. He raised his hand to calm her. "I'll see you again soon. I can't stay any longer, because this takes too much energy. But we are going to have many visits. I promise."

Lowering her hand, her shoulders sagged a little, but she took a deep breath and nodded. "Okay. I'll see you again soon." Sitting on the floor in silence, she watched as his image faded from sight. She was so lost in her own thoughts, she didn't notice when Vlameir knelt down beside her.

His hand rested on her shoulder and he queried softly, "Does losing him hurt so much now that you know he can visit you here?"

Surprised, she turned to look at him. "You saw him? I thought you were still asleep."

He chuckled softly, "I woke up the moment the former queen spoke. But she wasn't here for me; and neither was he," he explained. "I felt it was better to let you have your time with them uninterrupted." His hand caressed her cheek. "I knew you would tell me if you wanted me to join in."

Closing her eyes, Leanna leaned into his touch for a moment. Then she moved the remaining distance to him and wrapped her arms around him. "Thank you."

Vlameir returned her hug with a soft smile. He knew the reunion of mother and son had healed something he could not. "You needn't thank me. I knew your son would come to you. He found this place searching for a way to come back to you." He whispered, "I believe he is the one who opened the dimension for you to pass through. That bridge had been dormant for so long, I was shocked the day you went through. If I'm honest, I dare say it is because of him we found each other at all."

Smiling, Leanna hugged Vlameir tighter. "That sounds like Daniel. He always tried to find ways to help others be happy."

Vlameir considered her words and felt a wistful moment of unease, before asking, "And are you? Are you happy now?"

Pulling back, Leanna met his gaze and let the love she felt for him shine through her smile. "I am. I am so much happier. So much so, that..." she paused, searching for a way to explain. "Until tonight, seeing him, and knowing without a shadow of doubt that he is no longer suffering, I felt guilty for how happy I was becoming." She shook her head as she looked away for a moment. "So much so that I was still at odds about staying."

He sat back, resting his palms on the floor on either side of him, bringing his eyes level to hers. "You were considering leaving? Truly?" his expression was one of pain as he awaited her answer.

Leanna met his gaze and answered honestly. "I don't think I would have, no. But I had guilty feelings that I should." She reached out, taking his hand. "I don't think my heart could bear to leave you. But that same heart would make me feel guilty for my happiness. Do you understand?"

He squeezed her hand in response as he nodded. "I believe I do." He rose to his feet before pulling her slowly to hers. "There are a few more hours until dawn. Should we get some more sleep?"

She nodded and followed him back to bed, climbing in beside him when he held the covers back for her. When she rested her head on his shoulder, his arms wrapped around her, making her feel safe and cherished. She drifted off to sleep, completely oblivious to the small creature as it moved up onto the bed.

The Bakru looked from the woman to the king sleeping beside her. The time had come to undo his glamour. He had known when he had worked the charm for the Mage over a century ago that the fate she wanted to thwart would not be changed. Such destiny was not the kind to be changed.

Closing his eyes, he held out a clawed hand and whispered the incantation. Such things were hardly noticeable to the casual observer. The slight point to her ears became more pronounced. The slight tilt at the corners of her eyes would hardly even be seen. The original spell performed on her great grandmother had been such a simple thing. It did not amount to much, truly. Just a few simple changes.

Standing back and looking over the sleeping Elf now, he smiled in admiration of the woman. Truly, she was something to behold. The Mage had thought to eliminate the threat to their world by sending her ancestor to the mortal realm and keeping the lovers apart. Instead, what she had done was put the future queen in a place and position to become the person who was meant to be in order to fight the true threat and eventually rule justly beside the king.

With a twinkle in his eye, he wished the sleeping couple a happy life. He knew they had a long road ahead of them. There would be a war against the power that plotted against Vlameir. Even now, he could feel the threat of the growing Shades beginning to close in.

But the Bakru was a creature who existed beyond the restraints of time. He already knew all these happenings which were about to take place. He knew the way it would end. With a quick hop from the bed, the Bakru vanished from the room before his feet even touched the floor. In the air hung an echo of a blessing, left to bring luck for the two lovers with the rising of the sun.

Twenty

The Drowmonger paced the final length of the cave, just beyond reach of the light coming from the entrance. For nigh on two centuries, this hole in the earth had been his self-inflicted prison. He glared angrily at the light coming from beyond the entrance. He was free of the confines of his enchanted sleep, but still a prisoner to the sunlight. He could not leave the protection of his cave until the last rays of light had vanished from the sky. Darkness was his only respite.

Already, he was too late to save Adriana. He had known when they first met that their lives would never travel the same path. But he had loved her. She had been such a strong pupil and would have made a worthy partner. Her desire to be taught his magic had been so strong when she was young, her life so full of promise.

To take the baby's life would have been the easiest route for him. But it would have made him as evil as many of the other races of Elves already believed him to be. No, the decision she had made when she sent the child to the mortal realm had been the right one. But the spell chosen to alter her memory after had been a horrible choice. In the end, it had cost Adrianna her life. Pain hit his heart as he thought of the loss. He huffed in disgust, clenching his fists so tightly blood seeped through his fingers where his unkempt nails bit into the flesh of his palm.

The Drowmonger's face twisted in a bitter smile as he heard his children begin to arrive. Turning, he watched as the Drow who were loyal to the cause began making their way into his home within the cave. Some of them had smoke rising from the parts of their skin which had been exposed to the sun. The smell of singed flesh greeted his senses as he watched them making their way into the safety of the darkness.

Moving to his throne which rested against the ancient wall, filled with carvings of incantations of magic so dark, only a handful of Dark Mages would dare to attempt them. He did not even like to attempt most of them. They were borne from a place of animosity and greed.

The Drowmonger had once been among those dark souls. He had been filled with so much hate and evil, he had no qualms about using any of the incantations written on this wall. And he had very nearly wanted the Light Elves gone. For so many centuries, he had hated their kind. The anger and hate he had toward them knew no bounds. But then he had realized there must be balance within their worlds. For Dark to exist, so too must the light. He had tried taking over the kingdoms of all the races of Elves. He had thought if he became Leader to all of them, he would be able to defeat the Shades easily enough, because he would find a way to make them see what threatened their world.

After every Dark Mage who remained loyal to the Drowmonger had assembled in the depths of the cave, one stepped forward. He was the only one of all of them brave enough to speak directly to their Master.

The strong Dark Mage stepped forward, bowing deeply to him. His skin was as black as onyx, his eyes a smoky grey. His hair, which matched his eyelashes, was the color of the moon and fell without any wave or curl, straight down his back, to his waist. His build was strong, and he didn't even whine or cringe in response to the pain he had to have felt when the sunlight had been burning his skin. Instead, he didn't even pay his now replenishing skin any mind as he addressed his king. "Master, we await your command."

"Tell me," The Drowmonger spoke softly. "Has she made it safely to her castle?"

Doerin nodded. "She has. the king is with her and they plan to stay for a few days at least before they go back to his kingdom."

"And our warriors? They are in place?" his voice grew a little, not so soft as it had been a moment before.

The Elf answered, "Yes, Master. Even now, they sleep in the darkest bowels of the castle, undetected by any who thrive in the Light."

A hopeful smile graced the Drowmonger's face as he acknowledged his servant. "Doerin, it has been a while since we've last spoken. Tell me, how fares your twin brother, Roerik?"

An equally affectionate grin met the Master's. "He got married, my Master. To a princess."

The Drowmonger chuckled, "Does he love his Light Elf Princess greatly?"

Doerin nodded, answering, "Our sleeper is nestled deeply into her heart, and is a trusted friend now to the king, my Lord. I do believe everything is going as planned. Roerik has no clue how his magic is still linked to ours. He believes himself and the others of his ilk free of your hold. So he and his pretty princess should be joining Vlameir and Leanna as soon as the sun is down, completely unaware of the sleepers who already rest in the bowels of the castle."

"Good, my loyal son. Good. So, when you go in freely, tied to his magical signature, no one will suspect." The Drowmonger turned his attention to the ring on his forefinger. Pulling it softly from his finger, he handed it to the Dark Elf. "Tonight, upon the setting of the sun, use our link to him to break into the festivities. Upon rendering every magical being at their celebration immobile, bring me their newfound beloved queen... What was her name? Leanna? I want this newcomer in our land."

Doerin raised an eyebrow as he smiled, bowing. "Yes, my Lord. She shall be yours before the next Sunrise." He paused for a moment, before asking. "What will you have me do to Roerik?"

The Drowmonger shrugged. "Leave him to his fate. He has chosen his path. He is as stubborn as his Light Elf brethren." The elder shrugged. "If we had but the time, I'd bid you warn him of the Shades' escape." For a moment, he looked away from Doerin, and watched as a few remaining Shades crept across the walls, slithering like snakes in his view. He took a moment of comfort, knowing his people had found ways to thwart the Shades' invasions of their minds. But it took discipline and training, which took time and patience. It also helped if the people believed.

He scowled at how stubborn and unwilling to listen the rulers of the other kingdoms had been. His eyes pierced Doerin's. "We do not have such time. I must have the woman soon. Everything depends on having her swayed to our cause."

If the Drowmonger had been watching, he would have seen a flicker of doubt in Doerin's expression. Instead, he was preoccupied with what he now believed was their world's last hope. If the other Clans could not be made to listen soon, then it would only be a matter of time before the Shades would destroy the barrier between their Realm and the mortal realm.

He did not particularly care for the human race. They cared so little for their own world, they could not be trusted as a whole in this one. He found himself lost in his thoughts again for a time.

When his attention did return to his son, the Dark Mage bowed and cast his eyes away from him. His voice betrayed nothing of his emotions as he answered, "Your will is my command, Father."

Leanna awoke to a knock on the chamber door. As it opened, an Elf appeared, bringing a tray laden with food as well as something that looked like fresh squeezed orange juice. When the Elf looked up, he met her gaze and smiled. "Good morning, my Lady. The king bid me bring you breakfast. He said to tell you he'd be back to join you in just a few moments himself."

Sitting up slightly, but still covering herself with the sheet, Leanna offered the man a smile. "Thank you."

He sat the food down on the table, which was close to the window with a smile. Then he bowed graciously. "You are most welcome, my Lady. Everyone is most happy that you've come home to us." Then he was gone, leaving her alone to her thoughts.

Leanna rose from the bed and donned the dressing robe which had been hung right inside the armoire. Turning, she started toward the table but stopped as she got a glimpse of her reflection. Slowly, she turned back to the mirror and moved closer to it. Her eyes stuck to her reflection, wondering what was different.

The reflection was hers. That was not something she could deny. But there was something different. She was the same, yet not the same. Leaning even closer, she tilted her head, and pulled her hair away from her ears. There, almost unnoticeable, was the point to her ears which had not been there before. Gently, she traced the outline, feeling the skin which felt exactly the same as before, but now made her resemble any other Elf.

But the Bakru had already come? He had not said anything. He had sneaked in like a thief, left his signature by changing the shape of her ears back to what they were supposed to be, then crept back off in the dark?

Leanna frowned as she considered it. She couldn't quite understand why, but she had thought he would have spoken to her. Maybe impart some words of wisdom to guide her on how to become something she had never known she already was.

Her musings were cut short when the door opened again. When Leanna turned, it was to see Vlameir staring at her with a soft smile. No words were spoken as he shut the door and slowly closed the distance between them. He reached out and ran a finger across the line of her ear, smiling. "It's a subtle change. But it looks good on you." His voice was deep, and she recognized the desire burning in his eyes.

Taking a small step away from him, she whispered, "But breakfast will get cold."

He followed her, biting his lower lip for a moment as his hands found the opening of her robe, and tugged lightly on the sash, making the garment fall open. "It's under a stasis spell. Everything will stay at the same temperature it was in the kitchens until you are ready to eat it."

Leanna opened her mouth on a sigh when his fingers brushed against the swell of her breasts. "Oh, will it really?" at his nod, she asked, "Even if we leave it here and decide to pursue other things all day?"

Again, Vlameir nodded, as his forefinger began to make slow circles around the outside of her nipple, making it pucker in response. "Even if I decided to strip you naked and have my way with you up against this wall, the food would still be warm for us when we are ready for it." He smiled when she moaned, leaning down to capture her lips with his own.

She returned his kiss, before pulling away and resting her head against his shoulder while enjoying his embrace. "We keep this up, I'm going to start thinking I've been turned into some randy teenager a hormone explosion going on in my body."

Vlameir laughed, hugging her tightly before pulling back and closing her robe, using the sash to secure it closed. "I am some randy young Elf where you are concerned, beloved. There will never be a day or moment within the day when I do not desire you. I can only hope you grow to feel the same way."

She smiled at him, reaching up to touch his cheek before guiding his lips down to meet hers in a chaste kiss. "Don't worry about that. I already feel that way. I promise. I'm only worried my loyal subjects that I never even knew I had until recently will worry that I can't focus on other things that are more important than how quickly we can rid each other of our clothes."

Vlameir returned her smile and tilted his head. Your people will fall in love with you. They will know your heart is just and true where they are concerned and the love the two of us share will give them that much more reason to believe in your sincerity."

Leanna smiled at his words, but she couldn't stop herself from worrying out loud, "What about the enemy your aunt spoke of? How will we be prepared for him?" She bit her bottom lip as she let the worry seep into her eyes.

Vlameir took her hand in his, giving her an encouraging smile. "We are prepared for him, my love. I've already alerted the guards and I see no way he could sneak up on us undetected."

The sinking feeling remained in her stomach even though she tried to take his words to heart. She knew he had spoke with the guards after his aunt's cryptic warning. She believed Vlameir had taken every measure he could to prepare for the enemy before he could strike. For some reason, though, she couldn't shake the fear that this foe was a danger far greater than even Vlameir could anticipate.

Shaking the nagging feeling away, she returned Vlameir's smile, and led him to the breakfast. "Come eat with me. I want to continue touring the castle today. I also need your advice on how to behave when I meet my subjects."

At his deep chuckle, she raised an eyebrow. "*Don't laugh.* I'm a simple country girl. I'm already working double hard at not letting my Texas accent take hold and make me sound ridiculous."

When she admitted that, Vlameir had the decency to argue, "You have the voice of an Angel. I don't think anyone could ever be any other way but enchanted at your accent."

Biting her lip, she sat down at the table and picked up a piece of bread. "I only want them to like me. Believe it or not, I've never really been that much of a people person. It was one of the reasons I moved into that cottage, surrounded by nothing but all that acreage and no nearby neighbors." Her eyes showed her concern. "I don't really know how to be myself around people. I get nervous."

Vlameir smiled at her then and moved to kneel beside her instead of sitting down across from her. "Are you nervous with me?" His voice was a soft whisper. As he spoke, he took her free hand in his and kissed the flesh of her palm.

"Well, *now*—No. Not so much. But at first? I was honestly surprised at myself for being able to string together coherent sentences." Her breath caught as his lips lingered on her hand. "I still have moments when I'm not sure I won't embarrass myself around you."

He moved his attention at that moment from her hand to her lips. His kiss was gentle, and she felt reassured of his affection. When he spoke, his words brought a smile to her face. "You never have to be anyone to me, aside from who you are. I could never be disappointed or embarrassed by you. You have already proven yourself to be one of the most tender, caring souls I have ever come across. I dare say, your gentle nature is the most fearsome thing I've ever had the privilege to behold."

Leanna flushed in embarrassment at his words. "Now you're making fun of me." Her brows drew together in a frown as she began to turn from him.

"No, I'm not, Leanna. What I mean when I say your gentleness is a fearsome thing to behold. I mean it." His forefinger touched her chin, gently directing her to meet his gaze. "I feel sorry for anyone who believes they could ever do you harm. Because your mere beauty is enough to render a man speechless. I believe any man in your presence would be in danger of losing his heart. The only reason I am able to be so calm when you are in the presence of other men, is the knowledge that you've already given your heart to me."

Leanna was so moved by his sweet words, she found herself leaning toward him and kissing his lips gently. "I love you, Vlameir. I don't know what I did to deserve to find love a second time, but I am so grateful it's with you."

Vlameir took that moment to claim her lips again. Slowly, she felt the robe she wore being opened and shuddered when his fingertips traced the lines of her neck, trailing down slowly, skimming the curve of her breast and circling a nipple.

She sighed as she felt it tighten at his whisper of a touch. Moaning, she leaned into that touch, wanting more, even as she chastised herself for having no willpower where he was concerned.

He broke off the kiss, leaning his forehead against hers, "I know I shall never have enough of you. Damn being a king. I do not want to have to share you with the Courts, the Clans, or even the Mage, who is quite insistent on your learning everything you should know." His voice was deep as he pushed her robe off her shoulders.

Standing naked before him, garment pooled at her feet, she held his gaze, unashamed. Slowly, she pulled at his tunic, smiling when he lifted his arms to make the task easier for her. His chest, bare to her eyes, made her want him even more. Slowly, she pressed her hand to his torso, enjoying the feel of his skin before lightly pinching his nipple. She was rewarded when he groaned deeply and lifted her into his arms.

Her legs wrapped around his hips as he backed her against the wall, plundering her lips with an almost carnal passion that had her clasping him tighter to her to keep begging for more.

She did not have to beg. His staff pressed at her open core almost as soon as he had purchase with her against the wall. His hands pulled at her hips, centering her and helping to push her down over his hardness.

Crying out, she leaned her head against the wall as he paced himself, filling her deeply and repeatedly until both of them were barely hanging on to the growing completion they found only in each other.

As she lost herself, crying out his name, he growled, emptying his seed inside her and holding her close as his cock pulsed inside her depths. She marveled at how snugly he fit. She felt well and truly sated.

As he stepped back, she regretfully let her feet find the floor and sighed happily. "That was a good morning wake up." She looked up into his eyes and smiled. "Deliciously so."

He chuckled, "Was it worthy of, what was it you compared us to? Two randy teenagers?"

She shook her head, giggling. "No. That was much, much better."

He squeezed her hand for a moment before lifting her in his arms and striding over to sit in the chair. "Come now. You need to eat, clean up, and we need to quit this room soon. Otherwise, I am taking you to that bed and we will do nothing today which involves anyone besides the two of us."

Biting her bottom lip at the idea of staying in bed with him all day, she admitted to herself that would be her preference, but instead of voicing it, she smiled contentedly. "Yes, sir." She answered before taking a bite of the fresh baked bread he offered her. She didn't even think to complain about his trying to feed her. She was too happy.

Twenty-One

Invitations had been sent out the night before. Elf and Fae from all over the kingdoms responded, making their way to the lost Kingdom which had lain forgotten and hidden in the depths of the forest for so long. Magical travel in the Fae Realm was a mainstay to all of the different races of fae. Portals were not only used to travel between the human realm and the Fae. It was also strategically placed throughout their world, making it possible to travel hundreds, even thousands of miles with simply a thought and a hint of their magical signatures.

Magical signatures varied from each race. Each being carried with them, the trace of a signature that carried every part of their culture and heritage. Because of this, invitations to events, such as the introduction of Leanna could be planned and executed easily and efficiently.

Gwendolyn took care of all arrangements, sending out the invitations to the trusted members of each of the Elven Kingdoms, as well as personal invites to specific members who might have had different magical signatures from others, but were still trusted members of the realm.

When Leanna and Vlameir emerged from their chambers, the hall was already alive with many of the Kingdom's subjects, all waiting happily to behold their new queen. Leanna knew a moment of fear as she wondered if they would approve of her.

Gwendolyn scoffed at her, tsking loudly, before moving to her side and worrying over her hair for a moment, as she spoke softly, for her ears only. "You are better than any of them had dared to hope for. There will not be a single one of them who will not love you. Not with how brightly your heart shines. I believe, they will consider themselves lucky."

When the elderly Mage moved away, a man she had not noticed before moved forward. His hair was as long as any of the other male Elves she had met in Vlameir's kingdom, but instead of the white-blonde color, this Elf's hair was brown, with auburn highlights. It actually was only a few shades lighter than hers. "Your Majesty, please allow me to introduce myself." He bowed deeply in a show of respect before straightening and meeting her gaze with emerald eyes. "I am Quinlynn, and I am descended of the Captain of the Guard who protected your family when your grandparents ruled. If it would please you, I shall begin putting together a Sentry once again, to serve as the protectors of your Realm."

Leanna swallowed and stammered slightly. She looked from him to Vlameir, at a loss as to how to respond. At his slight nod, she spoke softly. "Yes, Quinlynn, thank you." She turned back to him with a small smile. "I must confess to you, where I am from, this is nothing I am familiar with, so I will be grateful for any and all assistance you are willing to lend me."

Quinlynn offered her a broad smile, and bowed again, "It is my pleasure to be of any assistance I can. Thank you, your Highness, for allowing me the opportunity to help you restore our home back to the rich heritage it once was."

She smiled at him and nodded. When Quinlynn stepped away, another stepped forward. Leanna graciously accepted and listened to each of her subjects as they each introduced themselves. Some came alone. Others brought their families.

Soon, the servers from the kitchens began bringing trays laden with food, as well as bottles of Fae wine. Music began to play, and when she and Vlameir took their seats, she found pleasure in watching the children dance around her happily.

She was bemused by them and the ready acceptance her people had shown her, even knowing she had been raised in a realm that did not know or even believe in their existence.

The festivities lasted throughout the day and into the night. Firepits were built in place at the four corners of the great hall, where magical flames lit the area and kept the chill out of the palace. Leanna had stared at them in wonder when they first came to life. There was four of them When Vlameir's sister, Hanna, and her husband, Roerik arrived, they joined happily into the merriment, listening to the music, and watching the couples dance across the floor.

Hanna turned to Leanna, asking, "Have you joined in the dancing yet?" Her blue eyes sparkled with happiness.

Leanna shook her head and gestured at the dancers. "I can't do that! I may have Elf blood in my veins, but I assure you, when it comes to the folk dances like what I've witnessed here today, I have two left feet."

Hanna, Roerik and Vlameir all laughed at her confession before Vlameir reached over, taking her hand. "I shall teach you the dances, my love. You'll know them all in a short time. They are really not all that complicated." He smiled, squeezing her hand before adding, "I promise."

She returned his smile with a tilt of her head. "I'll take you up on that. But you must promise not to hold it against me when I step on your toes."

Roerik spoke up then. "Oh, I know your plight well, Lady Leanna. When I was first accepted by Hanna's family, she endeavored to teach me their dances." His eyes rested on his wife's face for a moment and Leanna could see the love shining in his eyes. "My poor wife suffered horribly trying to ensure I learned each of them. I was a poor student. So bad. I must say, it was a wonder I didn't break any of her toes."

Hanna laughed wholeheartedly at his words before turning back and sharing a huge smile with Leanna. "Oh, it wasn't as bad as all that. Although, I will confess to a few nights after his lessons, I would relish soaking my feet in a mint and chamomile soak to help alleviate the pain."

Leanna chuckled at her words with a tilt of her head. "I'd be afraid, with my two left feet I might actually cause more damage than only a few bruised toes." Her gaze turned to Vlameir with a coy expression. "I'm certain you'd be horrified if you saw how uncoordinated I really am when it comes to dancing."

He returned her smile and leaned closer to her, placing a kiss on her nose. "There is nothing you could do which would change my opinion of you. If the love of my life cannot dance, then I shall simply enjoy carrying her when we must grace the dance floor."

Leanna felt the blush creep up her face at his words and squeezed his hand with hers. "I think I'd love that," she whispered.

As the festivities progressed into the night, no one noticed the darkness that seemed to spread throughout the hall. It clung to the walls. Shades seemed to be caused by the fading light of day but had their own lives, if one had the mind to pay attention, giving a somewhat muted tone to the chandeliers and torches. No one recognized the infiltration for what it was. It was a different kind of infiltration than what anyone knew to look for.

As Doerin entered the Ballroom, he and a few of the other Drow noticed the Shades, and whispered spells to bind them, even though the spells would not hold them indefinitely, but would keep them until long after the enchantment that froze the unsuspecting Elves was gone.

He hated not to be able to banish the Shades away from this place entirely. But unfortunately, the magic he had would only last through the night and into the morning. Until the other Clans could be made believers of the existing threat, there was nothing else he could do.

The attack came just as Leanna and Vlameir began to wish their subjects a good night. In what seemed like mere seconds, the horde of Drow morphed from the Shades that had clung to the walls, merging into the populace, and surrounding the people. As Vlameir and his guards were swiftly relieved of their weapons, Leanna found herself magically immobilized and the edge of a sharp blade pressed threateningly to her throat.

Before she could utter a word, she saw a kind of gray aura settle over every member of the Court like a blanket. Her eyes met Vlameir's as his limbs became as stone and he was unable to move. His expression as she was pulled away from his reach, one of panic, frozen on his face.

She glanced at the face of her aggressor and found herself staring at a Dark Elf who was a mirror image to Roerik, Vlameir's brother-in-law. When he saw the shocked recognition on her face, a rather bored smile spread across his lips.

He said nothing but tossed her easily over his shoulder and whisked her away swiftly. The last thing she saw as the dark Elves made from the castle with her in tow was Torlek in his human form, watching after them silently. When his eyes met hers, he held a finger to his lips, motioning for her not to give away his position.

Holding her tongue, she said a tiny prayer of thanks for Torlek not being under the spell that had befallen every other being in the castle. Trying not to give in to the tears which threatened, she assured herself silently that all would be fine. She knew it would. It had to be.

When the Dark Elf dropped her unceremoniously back onto her feet, she stumbled, and only barely caught herself to keep from falling. The hand that still held onto her wrist was the only reason she was able to avoid crumpling to the floor. Not daring to meet the cruel Elf's gaze, she looked away, then wish she had not as she saw what could only be described as a black slice taken out of the scenery. It was as if someone had taken a knife and made a slash in the very fabric which made up the land. But then, what was beyond it? Was it just a void? Or perhaps something like scientists from the mortal realm speculated what a wormhole could be? Perhaps a shortcut to a different place or time?

She barely had time to register what she was looking at it, when her captor began pulling her toward it. Recovering herself, she dug her heels into the ground and tried to pull away from him. "NO! I won't go with you! I refuse!" She half screamed. "Let me go!"

Without missing a beat, the Elf glared at her for a moment, before whispering, "Forgive me. I do not have time for your refusal." With a whispered spell, a blast of some unseen energy hit her, almost like a physical blow, knocking her down. Tears welled in her eyes as she realized, she could no longer move. She was helpless and useless in all of this. A sad ache engulfed her heart as she considered the possibility, she would never see Vlameir again.

Before she could understand what was happening, a dark kind of energy swirled to life around them and they were quickly engulfed by it. For what seemed like no more than a moment, she would have sworn they were swallowed into the bowels of a dark void.

Then it was over, and the absolute darkness cleared, replaced by a sort of twilight, which seemed to be the result of some kind of glowing stones, embedded in the walls and ceiling of what seemed to be a cave. As Leanna looked around, she found herself alone with the Dark Elf, in a place which indeed reminded her of a cave. The cool temperature and absolute darkness, aside from the translucent stones, told her they were deep in the bowels of the Earth.

She felt her control start to slip as she imagined being swallowed into a dark grave where Vlameir, Torlek and the others would never find her. Closing her eyes for a moment, she sought to center herself and remain calm. She knew in her heart, Vlameir would never stop looking for her. When she blew out the breath she had been holding, she heard the Dark Elf taunt her.

"Are you speechless, Princess?" His tone was weary and caused an ominous chill, which traveled down her spine. "My brother didn't know it, but it was his bond with your love's sister that made it possible for us to sneak in undetected. You see, it is his magic that allowed us in." he paused, "Although, I feel I must add, he did not intentionally betray you."

The doppelganger looked away from her for a moment, before adding coldly. "He may have a heart as deserving as *any* Light Elf, but like it or not, he is still descended from the Drow. His magic tends to weave through the darker strands of nature. My magical signature is close enough to his to pass for him. That made it easy for us to ride unhampered off his flow and enter your home."

Leanna simply stared back at her captor. As she searched his eyes, she found a feeling of calm settling over her. Suddenly, she was no longer afraid of what the near future held for her. She couldn't quite put her finger on it, but she somehow knew everything was going to be all right.

Instead of responding to him, she remained silent, and busied herself looking for a place to sit. When she found a rock that seemed sturdy and a comfortable size, she leaned heavily against it with a sigh. "Do I at least get to know the name of my kidnapper? I would think that's only fair."

The Dark Elf scowled at her. "My name is Doerin. I am the son of the Drowmonger, who is also father to Roerik, who you have already met." He smirked and tilted his head, as if trying to study her from a different angle. "I must say, you surprise me. You're way too calm, princess. I do not believe you should be. You are about to learn so much more than you bargained for." He chuckled mirthlessly, "In fact, I'm sure nothing the king or his people have told you could have prepared you for this.

Leanna had not even ventured to meet his gaze until that moment. When she did finally look up at him, he was taken aback by the clear lack of interest she showed. For several seconds, she simply met his gaze, with a straight face which seemed to bear little to no interest in his threats.

Finally, she asked softly, "And is that what you would have me know? What exactly should I learn by this little excursion?" Her eyebrow lifted as she contemplated him for a moment. "And tell me, based on what you know of the one who sent you after me, if it were you he or she wanted, how likely is it I would let you go?"

Her captor stood in stunned silence, taking her in, as if really seeing her for the first time. Then he chuckled lowly. "Oh, you are a clever one, Princess. I give you that." He clicked his tongue as he scrutinized her from head to toe. "You've managed just to slip in comfortably, haven't you? One day, you were a mere mortal. But now..." he gestured at her grandly, throwing his arms out to encompass her, "now we shall learn if you are prepared to join in a cause that will not only benefit your love, but also your friends in the mortal realm."

It was Leanna's turn to laugh. "Was that a compliment?" she asked softly before shrugging. "I grew up on a farm with my parents. Only special thing about me, I suppose was, I loved to paint." She shook her head, closing her eyes. "I keep catching myself waiting to wake up. It has all been so unreal, happening so fast. I can barely keep up. I do not know what you mean about me joining your cause. I'm not sure what I could even bring to such a thing." She gestured to herself. "I'm no warrior. I do not have a malicious bone in my body. I do know I won't lift a finger if it means I lift it to hurt Vlameir or his people." She closed her eyes, worrying over the very possibility that was what they expected of her.

When she opened her eyes again, she moved closer to the Elf, asking, "What does he want with me? Why does he hate Vlameir so much?" Without even realizing it, her hand had grasped Doerin's forearm, and he shivered at the contact.

With a hiss, he swiftly slipped away from her. "Do not touch me!" He backed away from her so fast, she thought she had hurt him somehow.

"I'm sorry," she stammered. "Did I hurt you? I-I didn't mean to." She tried to check his arm, but he stepped farther away from her.

His expression was one of near confusion. "You are descended from the world of Light. Why would you deign to touch me, Princess? As I am Drow, throughout our history, everyone in your Realm would say I am below you." He paused, then added, And no one hates Vlameir. Just by watching his interactions with the different Clans, one would say he seems to be fair and just. But this is not about him. This is about something threatening all of us, his Clan included."

Leanna shook her head at his words. "How do you figure you are considered beneath the Light Elves? Your own brother is the same as you, isn't he? He is married to Vlameir's own sister. Because of that, is she considered less than Vlameir?"

Doerin scowled at the mention of his brother. "You know little of our history, Princess. The Drow separated into two distinct factions many years ago. I live beneath the surface of the planet. I do not venture out into the sunlight unless I have no other choice... Ever." His lip curled, as if he were disgusted by having to explain it to her. "My brother," he went on to explain, "chose to venture out into the twilight back when he was coming of age."

At Leanna's confused expression, he elaborated, "When we are born, we are raised in the way of our parents. There are those who live in the shallow caves, just barely below the surface. It is lighter there and they can venture into the sun upon occasion. It takes time, and patience. But eventually, those Drow who live in the shallow caves develop an immunity which allows them to spend time out in the early morning, when the sun is first rising, as well as in the early evening, before the sun sets."

Doerin shrugged, "It is of little consequence. In the simplest terms, I chose the way of the original Drow. My brother did not. As a result, he is displaced and at odds with his own father, his blood kin have cut ties with him and he has been left to try to fit in with his wife's people." he scoffed. "Poor fool refuses to accept that he will never truly be one of them." He spat angrily. "His choice is his. I do not fault him for it. But I cannot trust him with the issues I know of or the business my father has with you. He chose his fate by choosing to lay eyes on the sun! It has made him as blind as the Light Elves."

Leanna could not stop herself from responding. "If you ask me, I think it is you who are doomed to the worst of the two fates. Frankly, I think he fits in quite well." She quipped, "I have met him twice now and both times, he was well received by members of the Court. He also seems content, while you growl and spew your discontent at your current situation."

She considered her words before adding, "If you are so unhappy with it, then why don't you choose to follow his lead? I'm sure, given time, the Elves above ground would welcome you as readily as they do him." She tried to keep the pleading note out of her voice. If she knew Vlameir as well as she thought he did, there would be no forgiveness for this Drow. He would not care if this was Roerik's twin or not.

The Drow seemed already to know this. From the look in his eyes when he looked at her, he was already resigned to something. Leanna wished she knew what his thoughts were at that moment and considered asking him. But before she could, she felt his hand wrap around her wrist like a band of steel.

"Enough of your fantasies, Princess. It is time!" With a snap of his finger, they disappeared from the spot they had been in, and the air was filled with the remnants of a sparkling static which left a telltale sign of magical teleportation.

As the particles cleared, a light sparked from the darkness, beginning tiny in stature, before growing. Suddenly as quick as a lightning flash lit the cave, it was gone. Growling, Torlek slammed a clawed fist against the cavern wall, cursing, "Damnation!" Angry purple eyes searched the fragments of the magic, left behind when the Drow and his captive had vanished.

He had been able to follow them up this point, remaining invisible in order not to alert Doerin to his presence. The sudden disappearing act was when he had lost them. Try as he might, he knew he could not track their signature. He scowled, knowing what that meant. They had gone further down into the bowels of the earth. Too far for him to sense their location.

He had listened, though. Leanna was smart to keep Doerin talking. It had given him enough of a clue what this was all about. He would return to Vlameir and give him the information. He only hoped it would be enough to help them find her in time.

Twenty-Two

Vlameir felt the anger rising within himself. How long had they been stuck as statues? He had been conscious of everything around him. He watched, helpless as members of the Drow rebels walked among them all, taunting and insulting many of the warriors with their weapons. Fury had built within him as he fought for what had seemed an eternity to free himself of the bewitchment.

As the first rays of sunlight began to shine, breaking the darkness and chasing away the Shades, the control of his limbs returned. Breathing deeply, Vlameir stretched his muscles and took a few tentative steps, before turning to glare in Roerik's direction. "Am I correct in assuming it was your brother and his men who breeched the castle last night and kidnapped Leanna after freezing us in this suspended state of helplessness?"

Roerik was kneeling next to his wife, checking her well-being. At the king's words, his shoulders dropped before he turned to answer him. "Yes, it was Doerin leading them. But the men and magic were the Drowmonger's."

Vlameir's eyes widened at the mention of the ancient Drow his aunt had said would be plotting against them, right before she took her life. He turned fully, raising an eyebrow at his brother-in-law. "I realize you and your brother are at odds, but why would he do that madman's bidding?"

Roerik took a deep breath and glanced hesitantly at Hanna, who had moved to his side, and touched his cheek gently, encouraging him. With a slow nod in her direction, he turned back to Vlameir. "He is our father, My Lord. He is the reason my brother and I are at odds. He is loyal to our father's insanity."

A pained expression engulfed him. "I am not. I have tried for so long to escape that monsters' clutches. But it seems I shall never know peace from him. For as long as my blood runs Drow, his magic can bend mine to his whims." He clenched his fists as Hanna embraced him, trying to offer comfort to her husband as he faced a fact that pained him deeply. "I had thought I had finally escaped him. When Hanna and I were able to find love and be together... I had finally believed I could no longer be used by his whims." His eyes opened and he bowed his head to Vlameir. "My being here was the reason he was able to get in. I am sorry. I will do anything I can to help recover Lady Leanna."

"You say they snuck in, using your magical signature, Roerik?" Torlek was walking swiftly coming into the chambers. Both Vlameir and Roerik turned to face him. "That may very well prove to be to our advantage as we endeavor to track them to Leanna."

Vlameir, moved to grip Torlek's arm. "Please, tell me what you know. The only relief I had while forced to stand as a statue was the knowledge you were not affected and could follow them."

Torlek nodded, saying, "I followed them into the first level of caves in the Night Abyss Mountains. Once they reached there, he teleported her farther in. I lost all sense of them at that point. But I do not believe she will come to any lasting harm if we can get to her soon enough."

Roerik groaned. "If he's taking her into the depths of the Night Abyss Mountains, then he is taking her to our father. She will not be safe for long once he has her."

Vlameir turned back to Roerik, growling "What does he want with her?"

The Dark Elf looked from Vlameir, to Hanna, then back. "My father and I have never gotten on well. He certainly never confided in me. If I were to give an opinion, I think he wants control over this Realm and all those within it. I think he believes if he controls our Realm, it would only be a matter of time before he could move in on the human realm as well. Binding her to him would be his quickest way to obtain that goal." He broke his gaze from Vlameir then and sighed. "In his mind, it would also be the quickest way to break your spirit."

Torlek threw his hands up in the air at that. "Of course! Why would this have to do with anything else other than world domination? Makes perfect sense. And sure, he must get the girl, too." He ran his hand over his face in a show of frustration.

Vlameir called out to his soldiers, barking orders to prepare for the journey to the mountains. The Night Abyss Mountains were where the darker beings of the Fae Realm lived. It was said that even in the middle of the day, no sunlight would ever touch its surface. It was a land fabled to be haunted by ancient spirits, believed to be older than the land itself. Most of those born of Light would not venture even close enough to view them, much less travel into their depths.

If the mountains' surface was intimidating, the caves were far worse. Voices from the past were said to echo within its nadirs. Darkness and shadow ruled there. No light would shine in the caves, save the ethereal glow of the Faery magic. Normal torches would not work, as flame could not live inside.

Vlameir remembered his grandfather telling the stories of the horrors within the caves when he was a child, of the expedition he had led when their people had decided to try to make peace with the Dark Elves in an attempt to bring security and prosperity to the Realm.

Fifty of his grandfather's best warriors accompanied him into the caves. Only two made it out. The rest were lost to the Darkness. That was the reason the mountains became known as the Night Abyss. Once someone was lost within their depths, they were never seen again. Their voices were said to join the chorus of the ancients who called it their home.

As the memories of his grandfather's stories poured through his mind, Vlameir realized the journey he was about to expect his men to follow blindly along with, could be truly perilous, before and if they even found Leanna. As desperately as he wanted to find her and bring her home, he knew he could not order any of his men to abandon their families and follow him.

Turning to address the warriors, who stood ready for his command, Vlameir addressed his men, offering them the choice. "We must travel into the depths of the Night Abyss Mountains. We're going to be going in blind." He took a deep breath and held it for a few seconds, before releasing it and continuing. "We do not know for certain what will be waiting for us there. In fact, I rather expect it will be riddled with traps. I must go after the Drow. They took Leanna. I will not stop until I am able to bring her home. But I will not force any of you to follow me. I respect every one of you. I recognize many of you have families, and I could not in good conscience ask you to leave them behind unprotected.

"Should we fail," he continued, "You will want to be in place to defend your loved ones." He looked out over the faces of his warriors, making eye contact with each of them, ensuring they understood his sincerity. "Those of you who choose to follow, make arrangements with those who stay to watch over your families in your absence. We leave in one hour."

Without saying anything more, he turned and made his way out of the castle. He didn't check to see who followed. He knew Torlek would be at his side. Out of the corner of his eye, he saw Roerik share a look with Hanna before embracing her as she began to cry.

"I love you." His sister spoke softly to her husband, kissing him before he pulled away. "Must you go?"

He pulled back enough to look down into her eyes before answering. "You are everything to me, Hanna. I do not believe my life had any meaning until you entered it. That is why I must go. It is my fault my father was able to infiltrate us. I must make myself useful in finding her. I was raised in the depths of those caves. I know them well."

Straightening her shoulders and wiping furiously to rid her face of tears, she offered him a brave face. "Then go. But I'll be waiting for you to come back to me."

He smiled and rested his forehead against hers. "I will return to you." His hand moved to her belly as he added softly, "both of you."

Vlameir caught himself, stopping to take them in. His jaw worked for a moment before he asked, "Sister, you are with child?" he cursed himself for feeling a tremble in his body as a mixture of both fear and excitement for her growing family ran through him.

Hanna nodded, answering, "We weren't going to tell you yet. I mean, we meant to. But after we knew you had found your mate, we decided to wait until you and Leanna were finally wed." She offered her brother a hesitant smile and he could tell she was worried.

He looked from her to Roerik. "You cannot go, Brother. You must survive this for Hanna and the babe."

Roerik opened his mouth to argue, but Vlameir raised his hand to stay him. "If anything were to happen to you it would not only be my sister who was angry with me over it, but Leanna as well. She would never forgive me for endangering the father of an unborn babe. You can simply draw us maps we can use to navigate."

"I have a better idea." Gwendolyn, the Mage, appeared suddenly. With only a glance acknowledging Vlameir and Torlek, she turned to Roerik and Hanna. "In the depths of our castle is a room of transference. It is filled with quartz, fluorite, amethyst, and obsidian. When companion stones are taken by the travelers, whoever stays behind in that room can transfer their energy to go with them. You would be there in spirit." She turned to Vlameir. "He would be able to see where you were, tell you which direction to take, but be safe from any and all attack, because his body would be here; untouchable by the enemy."

Vlameir looked the old Mage over. "Where were you when the Drow attacked?" He questioned curiously. He had no memory of seeing her anywhere right before or even after the attack. "Did you become frozen in place as well?"

Gwendolyn smiled sadly at Vlameir. "I am older than anyone you could possibly know, young Elf. My lifeforce is attached to the woods surrounding this kingdom. When the castle senses danger, my corporeal form is made spirit. Therefore, I cannot even be seen, except by other Mages. It becomes even harder at that point for me to be of any help." She gave him a knowing look. "Unfortunately, I was witness to all that occurred, but useless to stop it." She bowed her head, as if shamed. "It is how the castle protects me. I am sorry, it rendered me ineffectual at stopping any of the attack."

The men regarded her for a moment, each pondering their own reactions to her announcement as to basically being a spirit. But then, they turned their attention to what she had said about the transference room.

Vlameir spoke first, turning to both Roerik and Torlek. "Let Gwendolyn show you to the room. Gather the pieces we need with us to help connect us to you and give them to Torlek to bring back to me. Then you must prepare yourself for your part in this. I would much rather keep you safe, for my sister and niece or nephew."

He did not bother to add that he was also unsure how safe it would be to have Roerik with them. If the Drow had been able to get into the castle through a connection to his magic, who was to say they could not use his magical signature against his men while they were in the caves?

Vlameir had no anger at Roerik. It was not his fault he had been born Drow. It was his heritage. Just as Torlek was Dragon, and he was Light Elf. It was his background. It had no true bearing on who he was inside. He trusted the Dark Elf as a friend and brother. But until they managed to conquer this enemy, Roerik had to be kept in a place where his magic was not useful to this nemesis.

Turning, he continued to make his way outside. "Torlek, come with me." Raising his voice, he continued, "Anyone else who has already decided they are going with us, come now. We need to discuss which direction we will take. If any of you who are familiar with the better and safer paths, I welcome your council."

Wordlessly, many of the warriors followed behind their king. The men left behind began speaking with the wives of the ones who were leaving, making their plans on how to best stay together for safety.

Roerik kissed Hanna's hand, before they both turned to follow Gwendolyn to the Room of Transference. Relief was evident on both of their faces that they could help without parting from each other.

Twenty-Three

When Doerin and Leanna solidified in the cavern, he pushed her away from him so swiftly, she fell to the ground. Trying to shield herself, she twisted her wrist at the impact, crying out at the pain she felt.

He growled in annoyance at the sound. "Why are human females so fragile?" How can the Elf King even find you attractive? You are, by far, too easy to break." Even as he spoke, he knelt beside her and took her injured wrist in his hand.

Leanna scowled at the Dark Elf. "I'd like to see you get thrown off balance every time you turn around and see how well you fared, asshole. It doesn't help that you grab me every time you zap us from one place to another, then push me away from you like a hot potato when we land."

She started to pull away from him but stopped as she felt a warming sensation in her wrist. Looking from her hand, which was no longer hurting, to the Elf before her, she whispered, "You healed me."

Doerin cracked a smile at her, "I am a Dark Elf. I am also a Mage, and a healer. Being dark, does not make me evil, Princess. I realize you do not believe this. But no one here wishes you any harm."

She considered him for a moment before pulling her hand out of his grasp. She huffed as she made to stand, dusting herself off slowly before standing straight and studying him. "Thank you," she chuckled a little before adding, "but you still have the manners of a warthog."

Doerin rolled his eyes at her remark before laughing in a friendly manner. "Well, you're in luck. We've arrived at our destination. No more teleporting. Now you'll have to walk the rest of the way down." He pinned her with a smart-tass expression before adding, "That is, if you think your clumsy, human-raised legs will carry you down."

Leanna leveled a scowl in his direction, scoffing, "I can manage just fine as long as you don't try to manhandle me anymore before we get there." She groaned, turning away from him to face the path she was walking on. Fear coursed through her as she realized there was no view of where they were headed. It was darker than a moonless night down there. She couldn't see anything.

"How far down are we going?" She cursed herself silently for the tremble she could hear in her voice. The last thing she wanted was to give her captor anything else to gloat over. He had surprised her by not being the hateful, condescending captor she would have expected. But still...

He sighed, "It isn't as far down as you think. You are not a Drow, so your eyes will not see what I can. The village we are going to will make itself known to you once we have fully entered it. Until then, simply take one step at a time and focus on not falling, please. I made a promise not to harm a hair on your head. There are some steep ledges we will be going through, so pay attention."

For once, when he took her arm, she did not protest or hate it. Instead, she offered a soft, "Thank you." It was a relief to know she was not alone in the dark down here. She had never really thought of herself as being afraid of the dark, but this was not the kind of dark she was used to. This was the kind of darkness that made her feel as if she were all alone. This was the kind of darkness that could make philosophers doubt the existence of stars. If it had not been for the fact she could feel Doerin's hand on her arm and hear him breathing, she would believe she was alone.

At first, he said nothing. Then he answered, "You are welcome." His voice was different from how it been earlier. "When Drow children are young, their parents use certain spells and enchantments to light the child's way because their eyes have yet to grow accustomed to the depth of the dark here. It can be very unnerving to us when we are little. But over time, as our eyes mature, we are able to see what a surface dweller never can."

He paused, then said something in a language she couldn't understand. As his voice fell silent, an illumination began at some point away from Leanna. Curious, she watched as a soft glow began and traveled. Suddenly she could make out all hues of deep purples and blues, pinks, and greens.

She released his arm, and turned in a slow circle, taking in the giant geodes that were part of the cavern. Huge crystals bigger than skyscrapers—amethysts and quartz filled her vision. "Oh my Lord. I can't believe this. It's so beautiful."

Doerin watched her reaction with a small smile gracing his lips. "There is beauty in the dark, my Lady. if you can but open your heart to let it give your eyes the power to see." He looked around the cavern himself for a few moments before seeming to remember he was on a mission. "Anyway, now you can see better, we need to get a move on. He won't be happy if we keep him waiting much longer."

Leanna looked at him. Instead of arguing or fighting with him, she simply lowered her head with a small, "Okay." Turning, she looked back the way they were headed and could see for the first time, the lights from the village he mentioned. The way it glowed reminded her of what holiday lights looked like from a distance when one was driving through a town at night.

As they got closer, she recognized the glow not as lights, but from the gemstones all throughout the caverns. It amazed her to see them in such a way. It was as if each stone was giving out an aura. No, it was not as if. *It was.* Each stone had its own aura, giving off a light that complemented it.

She fought to remain calm. The closer they got to their destination, the sicker she felt. As beautiful as the place they were going was, there was something else there, and it made her feel horribly ill. That was the only way she could think to explain it. Her stomach was threatening to make her vomit its contents. She told herself it was only because she was uptight and worried about what was going to happen. But some deeper part of her felt she was unprepared by what was about to take place here.

They walked through what looked like the center of the village, straight to this huge fortress that looked to be made of obsidian. Some kind of flameless torches were placed strategically at the entrance, lighting the way to those wishing to gain entrance. Leanna noticed the light from said torches burned with a green flare. She wondered if there was a specific reason why, or if that was only the color of the light because of the quality of the oxygen, or maybe the material used to ignite the glow?

As they neared the entrance, she stopped, panting and covering her mouth with the back of her hand. As Doerin took in her expression, she held up her hand. "Just... I'm sorry. I need a minute... okay? I feel like I'm going to be sick."

He watched her with a raised eyebrow. She did look a little green in the face. He did not doubt she was affected by the nearness of the Shades. Although they were kept in stasis here, their energy could still be felt. He hoped that once she was enlightened, as his father wanted, she would be a welcome addition to the warriors who could fight the Shadow's evil.

He stood patiently as she gave in to her body's command and threw up over the banister. When she seemed to collect herself, he gave in to his urge to reassure her. "He isn't going to kill you, Leanna. I would not help him if that was his desire."

She looked at him, taking in his words. Then she asked, "What *does* he have planned for me?" She was more afraid now of the answer. She did not consider herself afraid of much. But if he planned torture, she would not be particularly good at that.

Doerin contemplated her silently. The truth was, he did not know the full extent of what his father had planned. But he did know that of everything he had spoken of, her death was not a part of it.

Considering his words carefully, he watched her closely when he finally spoke. "I believe he is hoping to gain your assistance in ushering in a new faction of civilization. One that cannot be harmed by the things they cannot see. Maybe your fresh blood will aid in the creation of a new life for all of our people."

Leanna went utterly still as she turned, regarding the entrance into the stronghold warily. She had no way to escape this. She knew if he were able, Vlameir would come for her. But she did not know for certain if he could even find her.

Squaring her shoulders, she took a deep breath and followed Doerin through the entrance. She would be brave.

She had faith Vlameir would come. This was simply a detour to their happily ever after. That's all.

"Considering you lived your life in the mortal realm, do you really believe that?" The voice was deep and reminded her of a voice that would easily be associated with the bad guy in a scary movie. It also seemed to come from all around her and was confusing. Without knowing where the voice originated, she had no idea where the enemy was.

A deep chuckle seemed to come from right behind her, and she spun around to face it, only to be greeted by darkness. "You believe in such a thing? A Happily Ever After? He scoffed, "With everything you've endured during your time as a mortal, you still believe in that?"

His humor was painful to her ears. She knew without even asking he had read her mind. For some reason, it did not surprise her. She turned in a slow circle, looking around blindly in the darkness as she answered. "Not like what you hear in stories, no, I don't." She stopped and looked up for a moment before simply sinking down to the ground. Her heart hurt as she exposed her pain. "Life is pain. In the mortal realm, there are no happy endings. Because, in most of mankind's way of thinking, the end is death." She didn't even try to stop the tears as they began to flow. "And everyone dies. Everyone leaves *someone* behind."

She took a shuddering breath, then released it. "But there are moments." A small smile graced her lips. "Moments that can be filled with such joy and love. Those moments are what make a mortal life worth living. It is those moments, that make for the happiness. Those moments are what make the elderly look back at all the happy times they had and think, *it was a good life.* So, in that way, yes. I do believe in happy endings. If I went back to the mortal realm, at the end of my mortal existence, I would look at the special moments I had lived and believe it was worth it."

Silence met her proclamation and she thought maybe he had grown tired of her speech and left. Even so, she addressed the faceless voice once more. "If you came to the end of your existence, what would you think of all your gathered memories?" She paused, listening. When he still gave no response, she ventured, "Would you believe your life had been worth it?"

She had almost given up on hearing a response from him, but suddenly she heard a finger snap. Immediately the room was illuminated, and she found him, seated before her, watching her intently as she simply sat on the ground before him.

He, on the other hand, was sitting on what she would have only described as a thrown. Made from the same marbled obsidian as the fortress itself, she noticed it looked to be carved from the same material.

He was terribly like Roerik and Doerin in the fact his skin was the same shade of shiny obsidian. His eyes were also much like theirs. However, that was where the similarities ended. Where she had noticed the day she met Roerik, his somewhat lengthened incisors, she felt a moment of serious fear at the length of his father's. The Drowmonger resembled a sabertoothed panther from simply the sheer length of his. They reached either side of his chin easily.

Too late, she realized she'd been staring and lowered her gaze to the floor. *Great job, Leanna.* She scolded herself inwardly. She could well imagine easily pissing him off by rudely staring at him.

She felt rather than saw him tilt his head and continue to contemplate her in silence before breaking the stillness with an unexpected roar of laughter. Taken aback, she couldn't stop herself from raising her eyes to again meet his. "He seemed to be laughing at the most amusing of jokes, and Leanna felt a little irritated that it seemed to be at her expense.

She wanted to demand exactly what he found so funny, but instead looked away from him again, taking in her surroundings. The entire place was as dark as the outside of the structure. She stood, her eyes roaming for any kind of doorway she could find to perhaps aid her in getting away from this dark creature whose very essence made her fear for her life.

"Oh, If I wanted to keep you, I could guarantee, you would not find any way to free yourself from me, Princess. I promise you, any escape mission you undertook would only serve to get you very lost." Turning, she saw he had leant down in his chair, and was observing, as well as seeming to enjoy her panic. He chuckled deeply again as he nodded, "Of course, I am. You have quite a loud mind." He offered

170

her a smile and she could almost consider him attractive... if it had not been for the way his teeth hung so far down.

Remembering how Roerik had explained how his race was known to drink blood, she tried to stifle the shudder that passed through her. He chuckled deeply again, and she threw an exasperated look in his direction, gaining enough anger to dim her fear enough she was able to curse him angrily, "Maybe there can be found a way to help those teeth of yours grow just a tad longer, and curve over your jaw, so your mouth could be kept shut!"

Unfortunately, her comment only made him laugh harder. "Oh, you are amusing, little human-raised princess. I am sorry for laughing so much." He looked her over from head to toe since she was still standing, rooted to the spot where she had stopped and sat once she had come in. "But I quite enjoy all the banter going on inside your brain."

Her jaw dropped. She had thought maybe he was laughing at her shock. She knew she had never been blessed with a poker face. Every emotion she had was always written clear as day in her expressions. But his words had proven he was privy to every single one of her thoughts.

For a moment, she simply held his gaze, not choosing to respond. She was not sure she had anything to say. He obviously had no need for her to put her thoughts into words.

No sooner than the thought crossed her mind, than he was laughing again. "Aye! You're a quick one. Dear girl. No need for your opinions to ever be given voice." His chuckle turned a little cold as his face lost all expression of friendliness. "Those who are mine never need utter a word."

Full panic hit her at his words, and she did speak then, "Yours? What do you mean, yours?" She shook her head even as she crossed her arms protectively over herself and backed away from him, even as he rose to approach her. "like a bride or something? I'm not marrying you!"

As he stalked toward her, she continued to backtrack, as swiftly as she dared without turning her back on this creature. He was huge, imposing. She felt he was very nearly a giant. Every three steps she took was one simple stride for him. When her back hit the wall, she stood against it, thankful for its support to continue standing, as well as terrified it prevented her from fleeing his advance.

When he stood before her, she made note her height barely reached his navel. Swallowing hard, she let her eyes travel up to see him staring down at her. The look on his face was cold and calculated.

"It will do you no good to run, Princess. I have already made up my mind. I had thought the best way to deal with the arrogance of the Light Elves would be to ensure this king was made to see." His hand moved, then, and he surprised her by tenderly brushing her hair from her face. "But I realize now it was not his downfall I needed to alter his people. It's you."

"Me?" She whispered the question so quietly because her voice would not rise any louder. "What threat could I possibly be to anyone's survival? I am only one person. They existed fine before I came. They will do as well, if not better, without me. I don't even have any real idea how to fit in with them."

No sooner than she had spoken, than he lowered himself, bringing his gaze level with hers. "It is because he has well and truly fallen in love with you. Now that he knows without any doubt that you exist, he will do everything he can to get you back. He will bring every single soldier he commands in his attempts to save you." He made a sad sigh, as he moved again, stroking her hair away from her face. "But when he finds you, you will not be as you once were. Then he will have to decide if he can still stand to accept you."

Sadness engulfed her at his words. She wasn't sure how, but she knew his threat was a valid one. He had something horrible planned. "Why?" she asked softly. "What are you going to do?"

His smile was actually kind as he continued to smooth her hair back from her face and neck. "My dear, you are such a sweet, kind and gentle person. You're filled with such light, it is no wonder the Light Elf fell for your charms." He leaned forward, placing a gentle kiss on her neck, where her pulse was frantically betraying how afraid she was. Without moving, he spoke clearly where she heard every word, "I wonder how much he'll love you, once I've given you some of my darkness."

Before she could even fathom what he had meant, she felt his bite. His fangs buried deep into her neck, and he

172

began sucking her life's-blood, moaning as if he was tasting the most decadent desert. She cried out at the pain of it, feeling her legs give out as he continued to feed on her.

Slowly, she began to sink, and his arms went around her, moving her gently to the ground, all the while holding her tenderly in his embrace. She stared out before her wondering if this was going to be the day she died. Even as the thought occurred to her, she felt no fear. She would miss Vlameir. But she would be reunited with her son and her husband. What was there to fear in that?

Retracting his fangs from her tender skin, the Drowmonger turned his attention to her face. "Oh no, beauty. I have no intention of taking your life. Instead, I've only drained away a bit of the light that fills your soul." His smile was delicate, and Leanna could almost believe he cherished her.

"I do cherish you, my beloved girl. All the time I spent spawning my seed to strengthen my race to match that of the surface walking Elves. All the wasted centuries I spent, biding my time, searching for ways to make them see. But they would not. They could not see what we can."

He kissed Leanna's lips gently. "And the secret to finding success, was in finding you." His voice made her eyes move to look at him. She saw raw emotion in their depths. "I do not mean you as a pawn in the battle against the Shades. WE only have so much time before they begin to infiltrate the other civilizations of the Fae Realm. They have no choice now. They must wake up and see the enemy, instead of blindly believing they have nothing but a happy, positive world." His eyes roamed over her face and he smiled at her. "I can easily see the reasons why Vlameir was lost to you so swiftly. You are exquisite.

"I do not want you to be afraid, Leanna. I know you are, but this will not change you to the darkness, my love. Your soul burns too brightly. But it will help you to find understanding for my children and a way to help the Light Elves to finally see our common enemy. Once everyone understands, peace will still not be easy. But it will come, with you to guide it. Now, you will be forever linked to me. Through that link, you will help find a way for my children to also flourish in the Light."

He pulled away from her slightly, and she watched as he brought his wrist to his mouth and bit into it. As the dark rich blood started to seep down his arm, he turned and pressed it to her mouth. Blood filled her mouth. She tried to resist but was helpless to do anything as her body felt so weak. "The power to prove is in the blood. My blood, which I now share with you. Once blended with yours, my blood will become part of you as well. My memories will be your memories and you can give a voice that will be heard, instead of shunned, or dismissed as insane."

After she had swallowed the dark bitter coppery liquid, the Drowmonger moved to kiss her again. This time, as a show of affection. She did not return the kiss, but the fight had gone out of her. In her weakened state, she could do nothing but let what was to take place, happen.

As she began to feel the burning sensation within herself, she moaned brokenly, "W-what h-have you d-done to me? Why do I feel like my insides are on fire?"

The Drowmonger relaxed back, rocking her gently in his arms. "Shh. Be still. Let this happen. You will soon see. There is beauty in my world, never seen by those who never venture out into the night." He smiled down at her when she relaxed. "I have searched for so many millennia for a way to make it so my children would not be made to suffer in the darkness. Believed to be monsters for so long, and beneath those who can be always in the light. But now it is not only my children suffering from the Shades. Light Elves are now falling victim to the Shades as well. Adrianna..."

He paused, closing his eyes and dragging in a ragged breath. "My sweet Adrianna took her own life because a Shadow found its way inside her head and made her believe something horrible of herself. Leanna, you must trust me. The Shades are something far more insidious than I could ever be.

"You are my masterpiece. You will truly be a being who is able to be a part of both worlds." He began humming to her as she felt her eyelids growing heavy. "There, there, my beautiful child. Sleep. Let your body make the necessary changes to become who you will be. Soon, you will see, there is also beauty in the dark. You will be able to help the others see. You will be their guide into a future where the Shades no longer exist," he whispered as she lost all consciousness.

Easily lifting her fully into his arms, he stood and began taking her deeper into his fortress. He would stay with her as she slept. He would watch over her as no other could in this time when she was weak.

A slight nagging of guilt hit him for what he had done to her, but he pushed it aside. For too long, he had allowed all at the surface to think him a monster. But not anymore. He had watched as his children had been tormented and persecuted.

Of course, there were a few who had been able to cross the boundaries between the world of night and the light. His son, for one. His heart beat heavy at his realization he had been so horrible to him. Roerik had braved many trials to prove he was trustworthy and even found his mate through it all. It had not been fair to judge him so harshly. He had done what his father could not—fit himself into the Light Elves' world.

Moving into the chambers, he spoke softly, "Give me candlelight." Immediately, the light of the candles, placed strategically through the chamber came to life, revealing a beautiful bedchamber, filled with vibrant colors of amethyst, rose quartz, emerald and tourmaline. The crystals sparkled throughout the room. If Leanna had been conscious, she would have marveled at the beauty before her.

Laying her on the bed, gently, he then grabbed a quilt and covered her with it before kneeling beside the bed. He felt horrid for scaring her, but he was beginning to become desperate. The races of the Fae Realm should no longer be divided. None of them should be shunned or looked down upon for who they were. Especially when there were worse enemies that needed to be dealt with.

He had tried so many ways to bring them all together. Long before resorting to underhanded and cruel tactics. At some point, he had begun to think it was the royal families who had poisoned their Clans so deeply. His determination to destroy the last of the royals was born from that poisoning. Too many of his sons and daughters had died from the unseen danger the kings themselves refused to acknowledge.

He believed the problem stemmed from the fact most Elves had begun not to use their magic abilities. Every Elf had some form of elemental abilities. The Light Elves had been the first to begin limiting the use of their natural magics. It seemed harmless enough, but after some time had passed, it became noticeable that an Elf who did not embrace his gifts, became not to be as sensitive to the hidden things around him.

The Dark Elves never really ceased to use their powers. They needed them because they thrived mostly in the dark, so it was not unusual for them to use magical means to light their way. This was why he believed his people could see the Shades, where the other Clans could not. By giving Leanna his blood, he helped to awaken the dormant abilities sleeping inside her. Soon, she would find herself able to use them, as if she had always done it.

Doerin entered the room quietly and moved to stand beside the Drowmonger. Watching her closely, he saw the bite marks on her neck and drew a deep breath before asking softly, "Are you sure this is what you needed to do? I have to say, I am not sure changing Vlameir's soulmate into one of us is the best way to gain his willingness to join in our fight.

The Drowmonger turned to look up into his son's eyes. "We are running out of time. I have spent most of my existence, trying to find a way to unite the Clans together. It is the only way we can defeat what is coming." He turned back to look at Leanna. "I once believed the only way to save us all was to overthrow the kings and take over, forcing the people to follow me. But now I know better. If Leanna's blood becomes even a third as ours, then she will begin to see what only we can see. She will also hear what we hear." He reached out again and ran a finger across her cheek gently. "Perhaps, with her kind and gentle soul, she can get through to them where I have failed.

Doerin crossed his arms over his chest and nodded in agreement. "Let us hope, Father, for the sake of all our Clans, you are right."

The Drowmonger nodded. "Yes. Let us hope. For she is our last chance." He closed his eyes to keep his son from seeing the desperation in them. "This is our last chance."

Twenty-Four

As they neared the cave system, Vlameir marveled at the change in the surrounding horizon. It was mid-day, and the sun was high in the sky. However, when they looked toward the Night Abyss Mountains, it was as if a wall stood between the sunlight and the land. There was no light. The sky above and surrounding the mountain was as dark as what would be expected at midnight.

Torlek shifted uncomfortably beneath him. His Dragon form sighed in frustration. "I do not like this place, Vlameir. It is unnatural."

Vlameir glanced around before acknowledging his friend's discomfort. "I do not know that it is unnatural, Torlek. It is merely not something that *we* are accustomed to seeing. What is unnatural to us, is a normal occurrence for them." Even as he spoke, he fought down the feeling of foreboding that went through him. He had witnessed the decimation of a few of the Clans whose territories were closer to the mountains when he was younger. In all those years, the Drowmonger had never been known to take prisoners. What if he had already killed Leanna?

"Stop!" Roerik's voice suddenly sounded in his head. "I am in your head, Vlameir. That means I am privy to all your thoughts." The Dark Elf said softly. "I realize the things my father has done over the centuries. But I will tell you, never in all that time was I ever witness to him killing a female who was not his equal as a warrior." His words echoed in the king's ears, giving a small semblance of hope.

Vlameir let his shoulders relax, forcing the tension out of his body before responding softly, "I hope you are right, Roerik. For I do not know how I will survive if she has been robbed of her life." He said the first out loud, then added silently, *"He didn't think twice about ordering the execution of a helpless infant."*

"You would feel it if she were gone, Brother." The Dark Elf answered in his mind.

When they at last reached the entrance to the caves, Vlameir turned and addressed his men. "I want a small group of you to follow me. I want the rest of you to separate. Half are to guard the entrance, and the others, to position yourselves sparingly along our path and stand ready for whatever may be lurking within these grounds to surprise us."

He wanted his men ready for a surprise attack. He dismounted Torlek and watched as his friend shifted back to his human form. Pulling the sword he'd been storing on his back, he handed it to the other man before drawing his own from his scabbard. "This actually isn't your fight, my friend. I would bear you no ill will if you were to stand down here."

Torlek laughed bitterly at Vlameir's words. "And let you have all the fun? Please. Do not flatter yourself."

Vlameir smiled ruefully. "If this does not end well, I cannot say I will not continue until my death. I just found her. I will not lose her now." He knew as he said it, he meant every single word. He would either rescue Leanna this day or die trying. She meant more to him than anything else.

Torlek lowered his sword and stared solemnly into his best friend's eyes. "I will die beside you, should it come to that. Leanna is an amazing creature and I count myself lucky to consider her a friend. I would have come alone should you have refused to ride to her rescue." Then he cracked a smile. "But do not hold your breath. No one dies today if I can keep us from it."

His guard, Drock chose that moment to step in. "Your Majesty, I would also die for Lady Leanna, if it helped to bring her back. She is a wonderful person and is well deserving of being part of your life." The guard had helped her find her way around the castle the first few days and had helped her come to terms with the fact time had moved so differently here than it did in the mortal realm.

Vlameir returned their smiles with one of his own. Knowing the others had developed their own attachments to her on their own only served to reinforce what he already believed. She was meant to be in their world. "Well, then... Let us go get her back."

With a shared nod between each other, the men began their descent into the long winding cave system. Using the mind link with Roerik, Vlameir stationed three guards to stay behind and keep watch in each major corridor upon the Dark Elf Roerik's advice. Traveling cautiously deeper and deeper into the caverns, it wasn't long before they came to the place Roerik had told them was the fortress.

Huge pillars of obsidian stood tall and proud in the illumination of their torches. Amethyst and Tourmaline seemed to be entwined with the obsidian walls, making for a marbling design. There was an energy about the area. It pulsed with a kind of consciousness which could not be ignored.

"This seems to be too easy." Vlameir directed his thoughts to Roerik. He was surprised they had made it so far without being confronted by the enemy.

He felt Roerik's agreement. "Yes, it would seem he wants you to come. I do not sense any traps inside, but I would still advice caution."

Taking his friend's advice, Vlameir shared his words to the remaining men with him. Torlek and Drock shared a look before moving closer to guard the king as he climbed the steps leading to the entrance of the fortress. The remaining guards split in half. One group stayed at the entrance, guarding it. The others fell in line with Vlameir, Torlek and Drock.

The throne was the first thing Vlameir saw as they entered. With a raised eyebrow, he dismissed the chair swiftly and began to pass it, searching for a hallway or doorway to lead them deeper into the castle-like labyrinth.

Frustration made him tighten his hold on his sword. Where was the bastard? Why would he take Leanna, then disappear when they came to take her back? Was she even here? What if this wasn't where she was being held?

Roerik's voice sounded in her head. *"She is here. The doorway is behind the throne. There! Do you see it?"*

Vlameir saw it immediately and swiftly passed through it, heading to the first room he could enter. Opening it, he released the breath he'd been holding when he saw her sleeping form on the bed. Crossing the threshold, he sat beside her and looked her over.

She looked pale. Why was she so pale? Gently he ran the back of his hand across her cheek. "Leanna? My love, wake up for me. I need to know you are okay." When she didn't respond, he fought down the panic that threatened to explode within him. "Why isn't she waking?" his voice echoed in the sparsely decorated room.

"She'll live." The unfamiliar voice came from the entryway. Vlameir gained his feet, swinging around, brandishing his sword, aiming at the newcomer, even as he noticed all his comrades had been frozen in place. Standing in the doorway was the Drowmonger, watching him closely as he took in his situation.

Realizing his friends were useless to him right now, he lowered his sword, speaking to his enemy. "Why did you let us get this far, only to stop us now?" He questioned softly. "I realize you are far more powerful than we are. Why not simply finish us off before we even reached you?"

The Drowmonger leaned against the doorframe, considering Vlameir for a moment, before answering. "I once was foolhardy and cruel like that. I admit it. But I have come to realize that what I want will not take place unless I can find a different approach to reaching the goal." He glanced beyond him to the beautiful woman lying on the bed, "She should awaken soon. She is unharmed, I assure you." He paused, "Somewhat changed now, I'd say. But she is still the woman you love."

Vlameir tilted his head inquiringly, "Changed? How exactly has she changed? What did you do to her?" He took a defensive stance, ready to fight.

The Drowmonger waved his hand, dismissively. "I am no threat to you or your kind anymore, Light Elf. I have realized now that the demons we must face must be faced together." He released Vlameir's men from his hold. They each shook off the weird rigor mortis and gave each other odd looks as they assimilated what was going on.

The Drowmonger smiled at the men who were so confused before saying. "I gave your lady a special gift. She will be a warrior equal to the best throughout our history. Together, you will raise children who will not fall prey to the demons that most of your kind cannot see."

As he began to vanish again, he directed his next words to Roerik, who was still there, through Vlameir. *"Forgive me,*

*my son. I treated you badly because you would not follow me
blindly as your brother would. Help your fellow Elves learn
about the things they cannot see. I know now it will take all
of us to rid ourselves of those things that lurk. Help Leanna
teach them. She cannot make them see all on her own."*

Then he was gone, leaving them alone, gawking at what
had just transpired. Vlameir returned to Leanna's side. She
was awake, and looking up at him with a small smile, "I
knew you'd come." She took his hand. "Can we go home?"

With a nod, he gathered her into his arms. "Of course,
we can." He rose, taking her with him. He held her close
enough he could feel her heartbeat.

She looked at him with wide eyes before looking down
to the ground and wiggling a little in his grasp. "I think I
can walk. Surely, you don't want to carry me all the way
through the tunnels back out of here."

He continued holding her for a moment longer. "I was
so afraid I had lost you forever. I don't think I'd ever tire of
carrying you."

She wrapped her arms around his neck and kissed
him. "I'm right here. You haven't lost me." He slowly let her
feet find the ground, even though he still held her in his
arms. Leaning down, he captured her lips again, sharing all
his love and passion in that kiss.

When he released her lips, his forehead touched hers
softly. "I would have been lost without you." In that moment, he let his guard down enough that all the fear he
felt was amplified to her heart. She knew immediately how
afraid he had been, and her arms tightened around him.

She felt her tears on her cheeks as she held him close.
"I'm never leaving you, Vlameir. "No force save the Creator
will ever take me from you again. I am right here, and I love
you."

When he pulled back this time, she saw his own eyes
shone with tears. Reaching up, she wiped them from his
cheeks. Softly, she whispered as she took his hand. "Let's
go home."

Vlameir squeezed her hand gently. "You have only to
tell me which Kingdom you wish to go to. I may be King,
but in this instance, I am merely your humble servant. I do
not care which castle we go to. I only want to be with you."

Leanna smiled at his words. "I like the castle my ancestors left me. Truly, I do. But I feel like yours is really home." She bit her bottom lip for a moment, before adding, "it always has been."

As she turned, he saw for the first time, the scabbard belted at her waist. "Where did that come from?" he wondered aloud.

Leanna followed his gaze. "Oh, this was a gift from him." She said wearily as she pulled the blade from its sheath. "There is so much you do not know. I only know now because of what he did." Her eyes went back to his as she handed him her sword. "He is no longer your people's enemy. He is asking for our help."

Vlameir scowled. "He has done so many horrible things. I don't know that we can ever trust him." Even as he said the words, he admired the blade. It was unlike any he had ever seen; made from obsidian and metal mix. The handle was silver with jade, amethyst and ruby encrusted throughout.

He handed it back to her and watched as she put it back in place. "I don't know what to tell you to make the trust come. All I know is he shared his blood with me, and I passed out. During that time, it was almost like I took a speed course on jousting and was made aware of what I can now see and recognize as physical and mental threats to our people." She shuddered, as if remembering something vile. "We have to find a way to train everyone's minds to see them. If you cannot see them, you cannot defend against them."

He was still unsure, but he wasn't against listening to her. "Then, when we get home, you must tell me more. Of course, I want to learn more." He worried a little that perhaps this was another of the Drowmonger's tricks. But something about it made him believe. He would proceed cautiously. He would watch Leanna closely to be certain there were no tricks here.

Twenty-Five

The trip home seemed to speed by for Leanna. She felt drained and exhausted after her ordeal and wondered if she was going to end up sleeping for a week to get over it. Sitting astride Torlek, with Vlameir sitting behind her, holding her close, she relaxed into his arms and rested her head against his shoulder. She felt safe and protected with him.

Closing her eyes, she willed all the visions that were bursting forth in her brain to stop. For now, she did not want to see any more. Her mind had been given a turbo charged history lesson on the battles the Dark Elves had been fighting for nigh on six centuries against a threat their brethren of the Light could not see.

Periodically, the Drow had attempted to ask for aid against the enemy, but every single leader of the other kingdoms had turned them down, most of them because they did not genuinely believe there was any kind of threat. Because simply put, if there was nothing to see, then the threat could not possibly be real.

The belief rose among the day dwelling Elves that the Dark Elves were looking to draw the leaders with their armies away from the common people, leaving them defenseless so the Darks could invade. It caused an almost permanent rift between the Clans. It was a discord which was only barely beginning to be mended between the Clans.

It was this disagreement which had separated the Dark Elves into two factions. Those who still lived above ground and had some interactions in the daylight. The others were the Drow. They stayed solely below ground. Most of them resided in the Caves, found in the mountain systems. Some were from the very same Night Abyss Mountains Leanna had just been rescued from.

As she rested against her beloved, she pondered how she would begin to work on trying to make the Elves of

Light understand the threat this unseen enemy posed. It was not going to be an easy task. As much as she loved Vlameir, she knew he had the same core beliefs as his ancestors. If it could not be seen, it was not there.

Almost as if he were in her mind, she heard the Drowmonger's words, "The power to prove is in the blood. My blood, which I now share with you. Once blended with yours, it will become part of you as well." His words resonated within her. She was a little hesitant, but she knew his words were true. To make him see, she would have to give him what the Drowmonger had given to her. She only hoped he would be open to it and willing to accept it. Otherwise, she would have to force the issue. The idea of her, at five foot five, forcing a six foot five Elf to bend to her will almost made her laugh.

When they arrived back at Vlameir's castle, the sun was sinking in the evening sky. Torlek flew straight to the tower above their bed chambers. After landing, Vlameir slid off of the Dragon's back and reached back up to help Leanna down. When her feet touched the ground, instead of pulling away from him, she stepped closer, wrapping her arms around his neck.

Vlameir rested his head against hers, letting the scent of her hair relax his nerves. She had the fragrance of lavender and lilies and he was so relieved that he was back in his arms, where she belonged. He smiled his thanks over her head to Torlek. "Thank you, my friend, for helping me go to get her back."

Torlek nodded his huge Dragon head. "I will leave you to get your rest." He turned his attention from Vlameir to Leanna, "I'm glad you are back with us, my Lady." Turning, he spread his wings and took to the air, leaving the two staring after him.

Vlameir was the first to speak. "Are you hungry? I can send down for some food if you like."

Leanna, shook her head, grasping his hand and leading him to the stairs that led down to his chambers. "What I am hungry for, only you can give me," she said softly, offering him a soft smile. "I need you. I need to feel you close and know you won't disappear."

Vlameir followed her down the stairway. His hand held tightly to hers. He yearned for her. His heart had already sped up at the prospect of holding her naked body against his. Her absence had affected him deeper than he would have thought possible.

Reaching his chambers, he stopped and pulled her to him. His lips found hers in a tender, gentle kiss. His tongue traced her lips. When he felt them part in response, he deepened it, tasting the sweetness of her mouth and reveling in the sound of her moan.

Her fingers threaded through his hair and she pressed herself fully against him. His hard chest pressed against her breasts filled her with longing. Within moments, she slid her hands from his hair, and down to his chest. There were too many clothes between them. She needed to feel his skin. It was an urgency which ruled her.

Pulling his tunic up, she broke the kiss, and watched, mesmerized when he lifted his arms for her to finish. His skin glistened in the low candlelight of his chambers and she caught herself staring.

When his hand tilted her head up her eyes met his, she couldn't stop herself from whispering, "You're so beautiful."

He smiled before shocking her by picking her up in his arms and striding swiftly toward the bed. When he sat her down, his hands moved to remove her scabbard first. He held it for a second, studying the blade before turning his gaze back to her. "So, he shared his blood with you?"

Leanna looked from him to the sword, answering honestly, "Yes. It gave me a first-hand view of many of his memories." She paused, debating how to best explain this enemy to him. "He isn't evil, Vlameir. He isn't the nicest person, but what he has done in the past was only his attempts to save the Dark Elves. He thinks of them as his children. I mean, I know Roerik and Doerin are his children, but the rest... they are all important to him."

Vlameir moved to sit beside her. His eyes searched her face and for a moment, she wondered if he was trying to see through any lie she might be telling. Offended, she moved to put a little bit of space between them. "Do you think I am lying? Do you think I would? What do I—" she stopped when he held up his hand and waited for him to respond.

She did not have to wait long. "I do not think you are lying. I am simply uncertain if he gave you completely true memories. I do not distrust you, Leanna. But I wonder what kind of game he could have involved you in that you simply cannot be privy to." When she opened her mouth to argue, he stopped her. "You must understand, he has been the enemy to my people for so long, I simply have an extremely hard time believing he has no ulterior motives. If you knew him as my people do, you would as well."

Leanna leaned back, supporting her weight with her arm, and considered his words. "The way he explained it to me, the memories shared through a blood bond cannot allow any falsehoods. It gives you the actual memories from the person you share the blood with. Is that correct?" He nodded and she continued. "He also said it is actually a practice that all Elves are capable of using. Not only the dark ones, right?"

When Vlameir nodded again, she took his hand. "So, since my blood has mingled with his, doesn't that mean if we shared blood, you would see his memories as well? Through the Blood bond you would be able to know the truth of it all?"

He shrugged and whispered, "The Blood bond can serve many different purposes. Among my people, it is an ancient practice shared between couples on their wedding nights. It was meant as a way to start off the new life to-gether with no secrets between them." He sighed, looking away from her as he continued. "It also can act as a track-ing guide. The Drowmonger will now always have a way to find you. I'm still not sure I like that new development." His face scrunched for a moment at the thought.

Leanna squeezed his hand to gain his attention. "So, I am going to be your wife, right?" at his nod, she continued. "Is there any reason we have to wait to do this ritual?"

Vlameir traced the lines in her palm absently with his finger as he answered, "It usually can take place at any time after they decide to wed. Although, young couples are usually urged to wait until their wedding night because in-timacies almost always inevitably follow."

Leanna could not stop the laugh that escaped her at his words. "Well, I suppose we are not in any danger of do-ing anything we have not already done, huh?"

He chuckled and pulled her back into his embrace. "Are you sure? About the Blood Bond? I won't force you to do it if you do not want to."

Her lips met his in a gentle kiss. "I have nothing to hide from you. Do you have something you don't really want me to know about?" Her eyes searched his, waiting for his response.

Without a word, Vlameir stood and moved to a table at the far corner of the room. He returned with a dagger held loosely in his hand. When he sat down beside her this time, he faced her with one hand clasping the dagger, the other, palm open and turned upward.

"Leanna, I give myself to you fully. I share with you my blood. It will open all my hidden doors. It will show you all of my secrets and it will guide you to me always. With this vow, I give you my transparency. You will know all of me."

No sooner had he spoken the words, than he pressed the blade into his palm and the blood began to pool. As if she knew her part without being told, she cradled his hand in both of hers and whispered, "Vlameir, I take your secrets, good and bad, as my own. I promise to love you, regardless of those secrets. I vow to know all your strengths, as well as your weaknesses. I vow to love you eternally despite them all."

Bending over his palm, she licked the blood from his hand, closing her eyes as she felt her soul flooded with all of his memories from childhood to adulthood. Her heart sped up as she witnessed his first duel. She felt her cheeks flush at his first sexual experience. His memories of his grandfather's death brought tears to her eyes. She watched him come to the decision that he would never find true love. So many memories found her, overwhelming her heart with even more love for this man she was taking as her own. His happy moments, his pain, every single part of what made him who he was flooded into her like a river.

Then she felt herself smiling when she saw his first memories of her and how deeply he had been moved by her beauty. She saw how he had lifted her from the floor of her son's room and carried her to bed, promising to give her a peace over the memories she had of her son. She felt her love for him multiply in that moment.

She witnessed the way his heart had sped up as they played the duet together, hearing the music they heard in their hearts truly completed for the first time. She felt his panic when he had been frozen in the Forest Castle and unable to come to her rescue. His mounting frustration and worry for her as he had been unable to move tore at her heart.

And then she saw through his eyes as he watched her drink his blood. Taking the ancient steps to tie them together eternally. The pride he felt at the knowledge she was his and loved him enough to join him in a world she did not completely trust was hers.

Then she was back to her own mind, staring up at him with unshed tears in her eyes. Without a word, she took the dagger from him, and pressed it to her palm. "Vlameir, I give myself to you fully. I share with you my blood. It will open all my hidden doors. It will show you all of my secrets and it will guide you to me always. With this vow, I give you my transparency. You will know all of me as well as the secrets bequeathed to me by one we once believed our enemy."

As the blood pooled in her palm, Vlameir looked down at it and took notice of the slight blue tint that seemed to act as an aura around the red of hers. He knew that aura was the Drowmonger. But he also knew knowing his true memories was not a bad thing. Not going forward.

Grasping her hand, he spoke, "Leanna, I take you, your secrets, good and bad, as my own. I promise to love you, regardless of those secrets. I vow to know all your strengths, as well as your weaknesses. I vow to love you eternally despite them all. I also promise to honor the secrets shared with you by the one we have considered an enemy. I will take this knowledge into myself and will consider it as I make any decisions as to how to deal with what he has shown you."

As Vlameir licked the blood from her palm, blinding light exploded behind his eyes and he knew a moment of earth-shattering panic as he began to see Shades stepping out from the darkness, moving on their own. He saw Dark Elves, attacked by these Shades when they were alone. He saw them driven mad by the things entering them. He saw the Drowmonger kneeling beside a beautiful Dark Elven woman, holding her hand, and begging her not to leave him, even though he could tell she was already dead. He then witnessed the Drowmonger, beseeching the rulers of the different races of Elves for help. He saw them make little of his requests. Dismissing his claims as unjustified and unfounded.

He felt shame at this. No one had ever told him anywhere in history that he had asked for help. He had never thought anyone would be so completely closed to another's plea for help.

But he knew they could not see. They could not see the Shades, jumping into people's minds and driving them crazy. They did not know the attack was the sort that made the victims take their own lives. The attacks were random enough in the beginning; most would think someone came down ill, then later took their life. But through the visions, he realized it was much more than that. The influence of the Shades filled its victim with unfounded, unreasonable fear, and made them do horrible, despicable things. They did not always simply take their own lives. One Elven woman drowned all her children in the river, then cooked them and fed their flesh to her husband, before taking her own life. He felt a rush of shock and disbelief at this, even as he witnessed the knowledge from the Drowmonger's memories. He felt the man's desperation as he had begged again for help, only to be turned down.

Then, he saw his aunt, becoming friends with him. She loved him. He cared for her as well, but told her they could never be together, as he would never be free to love another until he could sever the hold the Shades had over not only his, but what was beginning to be all of the Clans.

This was news to him. From her journals and everything else she had said before she had taken her life, he had believed this man to be evil incarnate. But even as he remembered, he saw the true plan of the abduction of the child who was the grandmother of his soulmate.

It had been nothing like his aunt had said. The taking of the princess was part of a spell to put him and the Shades he had found a way to magically control to sleep. It had been a sacrifice they had agreed to make to contain the evil before it could spread and poison any others besides those who had already been tricked into taking their own lives.

It was a desperate attempt as the Drowmonger had his Mages weave an intricate spell, trapping the Shades inside himself, then sending him into sleep. But the only way it would remain an unbroken spell was if her descendants never returned.

He saw his once believed enemy enveloped in sleep. He remembered the peace that had prospered over the land during his first century of life. They had nearly made it into a second century unscathed.

But then, he saw Leanna return. He saw the memories he shared with her so clearly. He saw the fear in his aunt's heart at her belief the Drowmonger would return. He recognized the spell a few of the Mages had worked over her to make her forget her love of the man, so she would not suffer so badly at the loss of her love.

But the false memory had cost her life. She was the first escaped Shadow's victim. It whispered in her ear how the Drowmonger would take revenge and use her against her nephew and his love. Thinking it was the only way to keep herself from being used against those she loved, she took her own life that night.

He also felt the pain in the Drowmonger's heart when he had physically felt his second love leave this Realm, slipping willingly into death's embrace. He had been closely enough linked to Vlameir's aunt, he had still felt her, even through his dreamlike repose.

Then the Drowmonger's memories slid away and Vlameir was filled with the memories of his love. He saw all her childhood years and took pleasure in knowing how well her parents had loved her. He witnessed her growing up with Max and found he had a healthy admiration for the young man.

He stood by and watched their wedding, a mixture of jealousy and happiness at their union. He saw their first years of newlywed bliss. He felt the emotion they felt at the news of the baby.

He found the memories of little Daniel overwhelmingly hard to take, because he could see where it was heading. The emotion of watching her lose first Max, then Daniel had very nearly killed him.

Then he saw her year of coping almost completely by herself. The friends she had once avoided her for lack of knowing what to say. He wished he could yell at them for leaving her so alone.

But he became aware of her one friend, who talked to her almost every day. A friend she had grown up with who had never abandoned her. Kinsley had called her often and she had been the reason Leanna had moved onto the property that had the portal.

Suddenly, he felt sad for taking her away so suddenly from that one friend. His brow furrowed as he considered if it would not suit to find this friend for her and offer to her to come here too. Would it be something Leanna wanted? He promised himself even as all the memories started to fade he would ask her if she wanted to find this Kinsley and invite her to come here.

Then he was sitting across from the woman he loved. He felt as if his heart were about to explode it was so full. Reaching out to her without a word, he dragged her into his arms and breathed in the scent of her hair. For several moments, they stayed just as they were. Then he whispered, "I had no idea bringing you here would unlock an enemies' prison. But now, even knowing, I cannot say I would change anything."

She pulled back and looked into his eyes before nodding. "But now we know. And now, we can see them. We may be the only ones who can, but we will make the others believe. And we will fight this enemy. And we will win!"

He agreed, softly saying. "Yes, we will." Then, he claimed her lips again, and before Leanna could even realize what he was about, she found herself devested of her clothing. Naked before him, she obeyed his silent communication to lay on her back before him.

Curious, she watched as he kneeled between her legs. She started to say something as his head dipped down, but all that came from her lips was a loud gasp as his lips closed around her clit, flicking it lightly with his tongue before beginning to suckle at it like a babe would a nipple.

Her hands wound into his hair and she cried out his name as he added his finger into her torture, sliding into her slick depths slowly at first, then beginning to find a rhythm, slowly drawing out a mewling sound from her lips as her hips lifted off the bed. She felt the first orgasm hit so swiftly it left her winded.

Before she could even come down, he stood, and swiftly removed his pants, before recentering himself. Positioned on his knees, he grabbed a pillow from the head of the bed and urged her to lift her hips. As she complied, he slid it beneath her, then moved to slide his shaft into her wet core. Slowly, he rubbed circles over her clit with his thumb as he pushed deeply into her. The two intrusions had her helpless in his arms as he took her any way he desired. Deeply, hard, soft, slow, and fast. He never stopped loving her that night. He never relinquished their intimacy together for sleep until the sun was beginning to peak above the horizon.

When at last he collapsed beside her, he pulled her to his side and she wrapped her arms around him. For a time, neither spoke, so moved were they by how much deeper their lovemaking had felt this time. It had been wonderful from the beginning. But now, with the memories shared between them, it suddenly felt so much more.

When Leanna finally spoke, it was in a voice filled with awe. "If people in the mortal realm could do that, there would be no such thing as divorce." She moaned, "That was amazing!"

Vlameir smiled at her words. "I know now the Drowmonger's history. We will find a way to bring all of the Clans together on this. But I do have a feeling, this is going to be a long battle." He paused, sliding his hand lightly over the skin of her belly, watching her closely. "So now, on a bit different subject, I have a question." When Leanna looked up to meet his gaze, "Do you want to invite Kinsley to our wedding?"

For a moment, Leanna looked stunned. Then a huge smile crested across her face. "Really? Could we? Would it be okay?" She held her breath waiting for his answer.

"Silly woman," he scoffed, pulling her tighter against him affectionately. "I wouldn't offer if we couldn't do it!" Her giggles warmed his heart, and he knew he would move heaven and earth to give this woman anything she wanted. "We will cross the Bridge back to the mortal realm tomorrow so you can ask her." He sighed, "I only hope she can get there quickly, because I want you as my wife before the month is out."

Twenty-Six

When they were ready to embark on their little journey, Leanna and Vlameir made their way from the castle to find Torlek waiting for them at the entrance in his human form. "Well, good morrow to you both." He smiled wryly at their joined hands. "I take it you had a good reunion?"

The mischievous look on his face made Leanna blush furiously. Vlameir, on the other hand only chuckled. "My friend, one of these days, you will find your soulmate." He quirked an eyebrow in his friend's direction. "When Leanna heckles you about your lover, you should remember this moment."

Laughing outright, Torlek slapped his chest. "Not me!" he reiterated. "I shall be a confirmed bachelor for the remainder of my existence." He winked at Leanna. "Not many women are willing to undergo the transformation which would be required in order to become what I am."

Leanna stopped short at his words. "What? I don't understand. Aren't female Dragons born?"

Torlek tilted his head and regarded her for a moment before answering. "Female Dragons are sometimes born. But they are an anomaly. More often than not, there are certain females within a race, who are born with a specific gene that makes it possible to be changed."

Vlameir nodded. "It's actually an interesting fact. Not very often can a woman with the right gene to become a Dragon be found. That's why there aren't very many Dragons around."

Torlek shrugged, moving out toward the field, to afford his shifting. "Can you imagine the overpopulation we would deal with if it was easy for a male Dragon to find his mate?" he paused before shifting to add, "Imagine if there were as many Dragons as there are people... It would not be a necessarily good thing."

Leanna watched as he shifted and felt a moment of sadness for their friend. Taking Vlameir's hand she resolved not to say anything more. She could well imagine it was actually a somewhat touchy subject for Torlek, even if he made light of it. She always sensed he was lonely, even if he never complained about it.

After Torlek shifted, Vlameir and she climbed easily onto his back, settling into place as he prepared to take off. She laid back against Vlameir's chest and laid her head on his shoulder. "Whoever thought I'd grow used to riding a Dragon? It's definitely better than any airplane."

Vlameir smiled at her, wrapping his arms around her, and pressed a kiss to her temple. He treasured this woman and how caring she was. She was truly a gift and he knew he was lucky to have her. He knew Torlek was content with how his life was, but he hoped one day, his friend would find a love like what he had with Leanna.

When they reached the bridge, Leanna slid down off Torlek's back and watched as Vlameir followed. She asked him softly, "It should be night there now, right?"

"Yes," Vlameir answered. "It is probably almost Midnight there right now. Will that be too late to call Kinsley?"

Leanna considered his question, then shook her head. "I don't think so. She probably is wide awake for a while yet." She groaned. "I hope my phone hasn't been turned off in my absence. I really don't know since I ended up being gone for so long." She gave him a pointed exasperated look, before turning to the bridge.

She felt Torlek shift, and both men joined her in crossing the bridge. It was just as it had been before. One minute, it was the middle of the afternoon with the sun high in the sky. Next, she was standing at the foot of the other side of the bridge, with a full moon and stars the only light, save the light in the window of the cabin.

Leanna stared at the light with an odd expression. "Hmm... That's odd."

Vlameir and Torlek both looked at her. "What's odd?" Torlek asked curiously.

She pointed toward the cabin. "I don't remember leaving any lights on." She sighed, shrugging. "Oh, well, I guess I could have. I just don't remember doing it."

They started approaching the cabin when the door swung open, stopping them in their tracks. At first, they stood stunned as the woman walked out onto the porch, staring at them with her arms crossed over her chest and looking well and truly pissed.

Both Vlameir and Torlek were immediately on guard as Leanna quickened her pace, moving swiftly toward her friend. When she got closer, her steps faltered, and she simply stared at the other woman.

Leanna spoke first. "Hiya Kins."

Kinsley glared at Leanna for a moment, without even sparing a glance at her companions. She drew a shaky breath before answering, "Hiya Leanna. Would have been nice if you could have let me know you were going to drop off the face of the planet for an unusual amount of time."

Leanna closed the distance between them, and they wrapped their arms around each other as Kinsley began crying. "You can't do that shit to me, okay? I thought you had killed yourself. I mean, I know it has been hard, Leanna. I do. But I am here. I was only a phone call away and I will listen at all hours of the night if need be." She sighed and pulled back, slapping Leanna's arm half-heartedly. "I should spank you for doing that to me! Do you have any idea how scared I was?"

Torlek and Vlameir shared a look between themselves before approaching the porch. They were not quite sure how to proceed but knew Leanna could probably handle this.

Leanna answered Kinsley with a small smile. "I know. And I am sorry. But I did not realize I was going to be gone that long. I swear. If I had known, I probably would have tried to get you to come with me." She frowned then. "Wait, what are you doing here, anyway? How long have you been here? What about your job?"

Kinsley huffed, tossing her hand in the air before resting it on her hip. "Oh, seriously? You've been vanished for like EVER, and you want to shoot questions at me about my job?" She half laughed, tossing her auburn hair over her shoulder. "This is the Internet age, girl. I can work remotely!"

Leanna laughed, raising her own hands in surrender. "Okay, okay. Fair enough." Then she straightened and bit her lip, glancing back at the two men, standing at the top of the steps of the porch. "Kins, I want to introduce you to Vlameir and Torlek."

Kinsley looked from Leanna to the men. Her face went slack, and she stood in silence for a moment, her green eyes taking in what she was seeing. "Uhm... hi." Her eyes turned back to her friend. "I'm going to guess you didn't go to Kansas."

Leanna burst out laughing at her words and wrapped an arm around Kinsley's shoulder, pulling her toward the two odd looking strangers. "Oh, girl... The Land of Oz has NOTHING to do with this."

Kinsley looked from the tall platinum blond man with the pointy ears, to the other whose hair was as dark as the night they were in. His eyes reminded her of amethysts, and she had to remind herself not to stare. Swallowing hard, she stepped out from under Leanna's arm and extended her hand in a show of manners. "Hello. My name is Kinsley. I've been best friends with Leanna since grade school."

Vlameir was the first to step forward and take her offered hand. "Hello, Kinsley. I know all about you. Leanna and I have actually come to invite you to our wedding. If you would be interested, that is?"

Kinsley dropped her jaw and looked from him, back to Leanna. "Wedding? But you," she looked back at Vlameir, "but he..." she closed her eyes, and shook her head. "All righty then. Why not?"

When she opened her eyes again, it was to find Torlek standing in front of her. Staring into his eyes, she did not even blink when he reached out and took her hand. "Uh... Hi." she said softly.

Torlek seemed to be under some kind of spell as well as he held her hand in both of his own and answered, "Hello, Kinsley." His voice was so soft, she imagined his voice was a hand, caressing her naked flesh. She almost purred at the visual it brought to mind before recovering herself.

Pulling away, she stammered, "Y-yes. Hello. N-nice to m-meet you." Leanna raised her eyebrows at their exchange, before saying, "Kinsley, this is Torlek. He is... uh... Vlameir's best friend."

Kinsley glanced at Leanna, before turning her eyes back to his purple ones. "I love your eyes," she sighed before catching herself. "I mean, your name. I-I didn't mean...

But your eyes are pretty too. You, uhm... are you staying long?" she backed up a step, scowling at her stupid nervousness. What the hell? "I mean, do you all have time for some tea? Or Coffee? Or, uh, water?"

Leanna covered her mouth to stop the giggle that threatened to break the silence. "Well, we do have a little time, don't we, honey?" she asked, looking at Vlameir, who also seemed to be taking notice of the connection between the two.

He nodded, smiling. "Of course, we have time for coffee before we head back. Don't you think, Torlek?" He was just as pleasantly surprised by Torlek's reaction to Kinsley as Leanna was.

Torlek nodded, never breaking his stare at Kinsley. "Yes. By all means, Coffee. I have always wanted to try it. Although, I've often been warned it could be a bit much on my system because I am already naturally hyper." He chuckled. "But I don't see how a small cup could hurt."

Nodding, Kinsley smiled brightly. "Well, then, why don't you all come inside, and I'll make us a pot." She looked at Leanna then. "And you can endeavor to explain to me where the hell you've been. I am really interested in knowing."

Nodding, Leanna took Vlameir's arm and together, the four moved inside the cabin. "Well, to break it all down simply," she began. "That bridge out there; it's a portal."

Kinsley stopped and looked at Leanna with humor in her eyes. "You weren't joking about this being bigger than Oz, huh?"

Twenty-Seven

Torlek was helping himself to his third cup of coffee as Kinsley was rushing around, trying to pack a few things to take with her. "Do you know if cell phones and computers might work in the Fae Realm?" she asked excitedly. "I mean, I could possibly stay for an extended amount of time, if I could still do my work there."

Vlameir considered her question before answering. "Well, that's not anything I've ever looked into before, but theoretically, I don't see why not. Bring your things. We can try."

Leanna stared at him, surprised. "You think so? I mean, it is a different Realm. I'm not sure things from this realm will work there."

Torlek piped up with a wide smile. "Why not? It is the same planet. Just basically a different dimension. And internet travels through the airwaves and bounces off those metal thing er-ma-hoochies your people put in space, right? Well, our people can still see them in space too, right along with the stars. So surely, there should be an easy enough way to tap into that little piece of mortal magic."

He downed the rest of the coffee in his cup and started to dance his way toward the coffee pot when Vlameir came up beside him and put his hand over the pot, shaking his head at his friend when he would have reached for it. With a dejected look, Torlek looked at his coffee cup, before shrugging and dancing happily over to set the cup in the sink.

When Vlameir looked back at Leanna, he said, "Why don't you take your cell phone as well? I'm sure you would at least like to try to stay in touch with your loved ones here." He smiled lovingly at her. "I'm sure we can find a way to make it all work."

Leanna smiled brightly at his suggestion. "Are you sure? It wouldn't be like some big breach of protocol, would it?" While she was fully prepared to walk away from the mortal realm, she had felt a little amount of sadness at the idea of not being able to keep in touch with her parents.

He nodded, crossing the room to her side, and enveloping her in a hug. With his back turned and preoccupied with his fiancé, Torlek, quickly grabbed his cup and snuck another cup of coffee. Kinsley watched him with a growing smile she could barely contain.

Covering her mouth, she turned and pretended to be taking stock of her belongings. "I don't know. Do we have far to travel? Maybe I need to leave a few things here."

Leanna moved to her side and checked that she had bags she could hang over her shoulder. "You really don't need to bring your clothes, Kins. The seamstresses there will have a whole wardrobe made up for you in no time. I swear!"

Kinsley glanced at her. "Well, okay. If you're sure it won't be any imposition. I don't want to put anyone out."

Torlek was suddenly beside her. "How could you be an imposition? I mean, If I were a tailor, I would beg to dress you." He smiled broadly before glancing over her bags. "Is this all? Oh, this will not be any issue. My saddle has a pouch as big as a person on it. I can carry it easily."

Kinsley gave him a once over before looking at Leanna again. "And he's a Dragon, you say?"

Leanna sat her own bags down beside Kinsley's and turned back to look the dark haired, somewhat human looking man over. "Believe it or not, yes. Although, as you can see; he takes other shapes as well." Leaning a little closer to her friend, she added softly. "First time he talked to me he was a cat. Imagine how crazy I felt."

Kinsley laughed. her eyes were wide and danced with humor. "Wow. I cannot fathom. Let me guess; black cat with purple eyes?"

Leanna nodded as she turned back to meet Vlameir's gaze. She was still staring at him when Kinsley asked, "You're really happy, aren't you, Leanna?"

The smile that lit up her friend's face was all Kinsley needed to tell her she was honestly happy. In fact, she believed Leanna might be the happiest she had ever been right now. "Okay, okay." She smiled. "Say no more. I believe you."

Leanna reached out and grabbed Kinsley's hands. "I can't wait for you to see this place. It is pretty spectacular. It's like what we might have imagined our world would have looked like back in the era of King Arthur." As she caught the odd look Vlameir gave her which made her smile as she added, "Except for modern toilets and magical baths!"

Kinsley responded with her own silly smirk. "I cannot tell you how happy I am to hear that last bit of information. I was picturing nasty chamber pots hidden under beds." As if to prove a point, she shuddered and stuck out her tongue.

Leanna laughed at Kinsley's expression. "No, but seriously. You will love this place. I promise."

When about an hour later, they were finally all packed up and locked up the house to ensure it would stay safe, they crossed the bridge. Vlameir and Leanna held hands, watching Kinsley and Torlek with amusement as he chatted with her happily, telling her all about the Realm she was about to see.

Vlameir glanced from the bag on Leanna's shoulder before looking at the teddy bear in her hand. He hesitated for a moment before asking, "Are you sure that's all you want to take? We can carry it all if that was your wish."

Leanna shook her head. "I don't need anything else. But knowing Daniel will sometimes be there... well, this was his favorite toy. I'd like to keep it close."

He looked from her to the bear and nodded. "Of course. If you decide you want to come back for anything else, we can do that." With a small smile she nodded before they both turned back to watch their two companions chat happily with each other.

Finally, Vlameir looked at Torlek with an odd expression. "Are you going to be okay to fly?" He was not sure the caffeine high had worn off yet and he did not want his friend to hurt himself or anyone else in a flying mishap.

The Dragon laughed. "Of course, I'm okay to fly! I did not imbibe alcohol, Vlameir. I only had some coffee. Who cannot drive when they have coffee? That is preposterous. I'm a tad excited and I feel like I could run a marathon around the solar system in an hour, but I'm not stupid." Torlek gave Kinsley a huge grin and waved. "Okay, so, as this is your very first time riding a Dragon, I'll make sure it's memorable.

No sooner had he spoken, before he shifted effortlessly before their eyes and Kinsley's mouth dropped open, taking him in. He was huge, with black scales that had an iridescent green and gold shimmer along them as he turned and moved.

When he saw how shocked she appeared, he dropped down on his belly. "It's okay, Kinsley. I am the same guy that was in that house only a bit ago chugging coffee and dancing around the room. I promise. I do not bite. I do not carry rabies." He tilted his huge head a little and beseeched her with his beautiful purple eyes. "I'm safer to ride than any car you've ever been in."

Leanna and Vlameir watched in fascination as Kinsley overcame her shock and stepped closer to him. Reaching out toward him, she asked, "May I touch your face?"

The Dragon chuckled happily. "You can touch me anywhere you want. I shan't complain."

She stroked his cheek and marveled, "It's kind of like snakeskin, but a bit coarser." She smiled up at him. "So," she turned back to look at her friend. "Where do I sit?"

Twenty-Eight

The Forest was green and fragrant and alive with the hum of excited Fae-folk, all gathered to witness the marriage of the long-lost Forest Elf Princess, to the Light Elf King. Elves from all the Clans were in attendance. It was more than a wedding. It was the joining of two of the strongest Clans.

The ceremony was done in the evening, with the setting of the sun, so Dark Elves were in attendance as well. Many of them had moved into the Forest Castle and the Light Castle, to begin training the Warriors and anyone else willing to learn how to detect and defeat the Shades.

The trouble they were causing was still brewing. Several Elves from the other Clans had already been attacked by them and some had already even moved into facilities to keep them from harming themselves or others as all Elves were finally beginning to take the threat seriously.

This wedding was special because it marked the beginning of a new era. Although there had never been a rule forbidding the intermingling of the Clans, it definitely did not happen that often. It had never happened between the royals. Faeries and sprites danced around the Elves, spreading baby's breath flowers amidst everyone's hair.

When the groom and his best man appeared to stand before the Ancient Forest Elf Mage, everyone knew it marked the beginning of the ceremony. As the guests formed a half-circle, the maid of honor made her way down the aisle. Her dress was dark emerald green and brought out the color of her auburn hair, as well as the green of her eyes. She carried a bouquet of white lilies in her hands, and she wore a smile so big there was not anyone there who would doubt she was happy.

Then the bride began her march. Her dress was silvery white, with silken seams of silver and gold, giving the dress an almost ethereal look. Her hair had been left down but was pinned back on one side with a single lily to match the ones in her hand. As she proceeded up the way toward the one to be her husband, she had eyes only for him.

When she was finally standing before him. She surrendered her flowers to a Faery, who kept the flowers floating off to the side while she held Vlameir's hands. They looked at each other as though no one else was around. Gwendolyn began the ceremony.

"It is not very often that a love story such as this one comes around. Even in the Fae Realm, such fairytales do not often exist, but the love which was believed to have been sabotaged before it had even had a chance to seed... still found a way to come to pass. That is a love deserving to go down in the history books. Ties that will never be broken were formed between these two long before today. Their love had already stood the test of time and I dare say, will burn brightly until the very end of it.

"The two of you have already made your private vows. I cannot add anything to them. So I will let you each profess the love you have gathered us all here to witness."

Vlameir's eyes never left Leanna's as he began to speak. "I had prepared myself never to have you. I had given up on you even existing. So, when you stumbled across that bridge and nearly had a heart attack seeing a Dragon, I had no choice but to cross that same bridge, just to assure myself you were all right.

"That night, I lost my heart to you. I knew in that night I would spend the rest of my existence trying to convince you to love me. I still plan to do exactly that. I promise to treasure every single day I am blessed to be with you. Every moment we have. From now, until Eternity. I love you." When he fell silent, he took a ring from Torlek, and turned to slide it onto her finger.

Leanna felt the tears running down her cheeks, but they were tears of such happiness, she could not contain them. "From the very beginning I felt so deeply for you, I was ashamed of myself. I thought I was being horrible, because it had only been a few years since my husband had passed. Some terrible side of my brain thought I was being unfaithful to his memory by loving you.' Her voice cracked on a sob. "But I couldn't stop. I could no more hold my feelings for you inside than I could have stopped the ocean's tides."

She took the ring Kinsley handed her and moved to slide it onto his finger. "You became an elemental force to me. For the first time in a long time, I did not feel alone. And you gave me so much. A reason to continue living. A life to love. And a place I finally feel is home. I love you, Vlameir. I've been yours from that first day."

The Festivities lasted long into the night and Kinsley and Torlek danced every dance. Somewhere in the midst of it all, the groom gathered up his bride, and the two of them escaped to their own private part of the palace.

As soon as the door shut, Vlameir's hands were on her, unlacing the stays that held the dress in place. "Vlameir, you have no patience." Leanna reprimanded with a giggle, only to be rewarded by his growl.

"Patience is for those who do not have an unquench-able thirst. It is for men who must bide their time to gain their prize." He claimed her lips in a passionate kiss, even as he continued divesting her of her clothes. "I am none of those things. I finally have you. I finally know you are mine. And I need you, like a starving man needs to be fed."

She pushed gently on his chest, until he released her. Slowly backing away from him, she let the shimmering dress fall to the ground, leaving her in a few really skimpy lace undergarments she had brought from home when they had made their trip to get Kinsley.

Vlameir's eyes widened at the beauty of his wife. Groan-ing, he moved to follow her as she backed farther into their chambers. "We may have to make trips to the mortal realm quite frequently, to keep you in ready supply of such wrap-pings." He smiled. "I feel as if I am about to open one of the very best of presents." His deep chuckle sounded through the room. "I quite like the idea of you having plenty of these kinds of treasures."

Her laughter joined his. "Well, then, my King, you should maybe divest yourself of some of your clothing. Surely you know you are entirely too overdressed for this party."

He raised an eyebrow at her words. "Well then, my Queen, your order is my command. Slowly, he began peeling away his fancy wedding attire, leaving a trail as he stalked her to the bed. When she would have sat down on it, he stopped her, taking her hand. "I have other ideas tonight."

Surprised, she looked into his eyes. "Yes, my Lord? What do you have in mind?"

He leant down and kissed her lips. Then whispered, "Let me show you." Taking her hand, he led her to the bathing chamber. Once inside, they finished stripping and stepped into the bathing pool of the oasis-like chamber. The water, which was deep enough to stand in was soothing to their muscles and easily relaxed away the tension which had built adding to their stress of the day.

Vlameir grabbed a burgundy flower from the side of the pool as Leanna dipped down and wet her hair before standing back up. She watched as he opened the petals of the flower and extracted the soapy center.

She moaned as he turned and began to lather the soap over her shoulders, then down her chest, taking the time to show attention to each breast, toying with the nipples to make them pucker. The abrasiveness of the soap added to her sensitivity and made her nether regions throb.

Taking some of the soap from him, she began to lather it over him as well. Biting her bottom lip, she slid her hand down, just below the surface of the water to grasp his staff. The soap only aided in the sensations as she rubbed her hand over him.

His hands traveled lower, pulling her flush against him as his head bowed to allow him to capture her lips with his own. When she thought her legs would give out from the sheer ecstasy she was feeling, he scooped her up and carried her to the side of the pool where the waterfall ran. Once they were under it, they rinsed each other clean, and he backed her up to the edge of the pool.

When her hands found purchase, he lifted her enough to step between her legs. As she wrapped them around his hips, his shaft had already gained entry and was sliding deep, making her cry out and tighten around him. Slowly at first, he worshipped her. His hands grasped her hips, setting the pace for their lovemaking.

It was exquisite torture and soon they were both building into a frenzy in each other's arms. As she crested, her walls tightened, squeezing him as he followed swiftly behind her. Wrapping his arms around her, he held her close as he emptied his seed into her waiting warmth.

For a while, they simply sank into the water, holding each other close and enjoying the heat and healing properties of the pool. Then he released her from his embrace, only to lead her to the steps and out of the water.

Grabbing the nearest towel, he turned and helped her dry off. Then she did the same for him. Once they donned their robes, they moved to their chamber, and relaxed luxuriously in the bed. She curled into his embrace and sighed contentedly. "I never believed I would ever be this happy again." She smiled as she looked up into his eyes. "Thank you for loving me."

His arms tightened around her. "Leanna, of everything I have had to endure in my lifetime and every decision I have had to make, loving you was most definitely the best one. I am complete. For the first time since I have been an adult, I face the future without fear of being alone." He kissed her forehead gently.

She hesitated to bring it up for a moment, because they had avoided the subject for the past week. But she needed to know what they were planning in readying themselves for facing their enemy. "Where are we at with fighting the Shades?"

Vlameir took a deep breath before answering. We have begun training with the other Clans. Most of both mine and your guards have successfully begun to recognize them. Once they complete their training on how to recognize and defeat them in case of attack, we will begin training the civilians." He smiled ruefully. "It is a slow process, but it has begun."

Leanna nodded, relaxing against his chest. "I want to help. The time I had with the Drowmonger's memories prepared me for the ways to battle them. It is not as easy as picking up a sword and hacking away at them. They are basically spirit. Normal swords will not touch them."

"Which is why we have the Druid priests blessing the steel and dipping each and every blade in the blessed fountain." He interrupted. "I know you want to help, Leanna. I want your new knowledge. I do. But I also want you kept away from any and all harm." He groaned loudly. "The very idea of any harm coming to you sends me into a panic."

She smiled sadly and nodded. "I know. I know what you say. I will try to stay out of the way." She was silent for a minute before adding, "But I will not cower in a corner, either. If it comes to dealing with an attack from them, I will not go hide merely to suit you. These are my people as well, now. I will fight for them standing beside you."

He pulled away from her then, and moved so he lay on his side, facing her. She retreated enough to afford him room. "Ah, and there it is," he whispered.

She quirked an eyebrow in his direction. "There what is?" she asked slowly.

He chuckled happily, "The whole reason I fell in love with you. That beautiful, brave soul. How did I ever get so lucky?"

She smiled at him then, moving back into his embrace. "I don't know. Maybe we should explore that a little deeper. Don't you think?"

His lips parted in a broad smile before he leaned down once again to capture her lips. His hands were already pulling at the ties of her robe. "I think maybe we have a lot of exploring to do. And what better time to start than right now?" Leanna surrendered to his desires. It was an easy thing to do. They were her desires too. She had found happiness again. It was with him.

On the far wall, left forgotten after she had unpacked it, was the little stuffed bear her son, Daniel, had loved so very much. As the lovers slumbered and embraced each other, the bear was lifted off the table, and wrapped lovingly in the little boy's arms. With a bright smile, he skipped out of the room, happy his mother had again found love, and thrilled to be reunited with his bear.

Also hanging on the far wall was the completed painting Vlameir had requested she create. However, instead of the simple portrait he had originally requested, it was a painting of the two of them facing one another, she, at the piano and he, with his harp. The love shining in their eyes would be there, eternalized for all future generations to see and find inspiration from.

About the Author

Shiloh first got bit by the desire to become a published author during a time when she had first found a way to transport herself from the everyday stress of real life, by either finding a good book to read, or taking time to write stories of her own. She loved the challenge of bringing characters to life in such a way that the reader would come to care for them almost as much as she did.

She works a full-time job in healthcare, caring for the elderly. She's been employed at the same place for nearly twenty-five years. She met her own Prince Charming there. While having such a demanding job has limited the time she actually gets to spend writing, it has never slowed down her imagination.

WEBSITE: http://www.shilohdarkefantasies.com
TWITTER: https://twitter.com/Shiloh_Darke1
FACEBOOK: http://www.facebook.com/shiloh.darke